LOVE WALKS IN

A BLISS COVE NOVEL #1

NINA LINDSEY

SNOW QUEEN
PUBLISHING

Love Walks In

A
BLISS COVE
NOVEL

NINA
LINDSEY

SNOW QUEEN

PUBLISHING

~

Welcome to Bliss Cove, a seaside town where love sweeps in on the ocean breeze.

Stay at the Outside Inn, have dinner at the Mousehole Tavern, take a walk on historic Mariposa Street, buy handmade lotions at Naked, and pick up a chocolate-loaded cookie from the Sugar Joy bakery. Don't forget to stop by Moonbeams for a tarot-card reading about your One True Love!

While you are here, enjoy the spicy-sweet Bliss Cove romances of powerful, compelling heroes and the women who capture their hearts forever.

Visit Bliss Cove by signing up for Nina Lindsey's newsletter. You'll receive the exclusive WE FOUND LOVE **free**:

www.ninalindsey.com

Please check your spam folder, if you don't receive the confirmation email.

Enjoy your stay!

PROLOGUE

"*B*liss Cove." Hunter Armstrong twisted his mouth around the town's name, which brought up sticky-sweet images of flower boxes, beach parties, and ice-cream cones. Things that had nothing to do with his life of glass office towers and retail complexes. "Never heard of it."

"Good." His boss gave a dry, humorless laugh.

Hunter folded his arms as he stood at the thirty-first-story window of the Imperial Properties conference room. An expansive view of the Manhattan cityscape, pierced by high-rises and skyscrapers, spread out toward the Hudson River.

"We intend to keep Bliss Cove a secret." Bruce Sinclair, founder and CEO of Imperial Properties, thrust his thick finger at the presentation screen displaying a picturesque photo of a downtown street. "It's useless little town right in the middle of a perfect stretch of California coastline waiting to be exploited—"

"*Explored*, Dad." Juliette Sinclair, president of Imperial's East Coast operations, arched a plucked eyebrow and met Hunter's gaze with a *"he'll never learn"* look of amusement. "Bliss Cove is a small town in a pristine location that's accessible to both southern and northern California residents."

She tapped a button on the computer. The photo on the screen changed to a map of the Pacific coastline. "It's a stroke of luck that no other developers have found it yet. That makes it an excellent place to start expanding Imperial's West Coast properties."

Hunter studied the map. Bliss Cove sat alongside the ocean midway between San Francisco and Los Angeles, with acres of redwood forests to the north and farmland farther east.

"What's the project?" he asked.

Juliette advanced the slide to a photo of a narrow cobblestone street lined with rundown buildings.

"This is Mariposa Street." Bruce gave a derisive huff. "It's the main street of a shithole district the town doesn't care about, but it's in a phenomenal location right near the beach. We're going to build the Oceanview Plaza here, an upscale multi-use complex of shopping, entertainment, restaurants, and commercial buildings intended to pump life into the whole town."

Juliette clicked forward to slides of modern steel-and-glass buildings—retail, condos, a megaplex movie theater. Despite the artistic renderings, it was still much smaller than Imperial's usual projects. Hell, it was minuscule compared to the ten-acre, five-billion-dollar complex of office space, hotels, retail, and apartments that Hunter had just completed in the Hudson Yards district.

He'd worked at Imperial Properties for twelve years, having started shortly after graduating from Harvard. One of the largest property development companies in the nation, Imperial had offices in seventeen cities and managed over three-hundred-million square feet of commercial space. A retail complex in a "useless little town" was hardly an impressive addition to the company's portfolio.

"What's the status of the project?" he asked.

"The former director fucked up the negotiations." Bruce shook his head in disgust. "He couldn't get the building owners to sell, and then he leaked the plans to the residents. I fired him, but by then, the damage was done."

"But the damage is not irreparable." Juliette crossed her arms over the front of her Gucci jacket. "The Mariposa Street buildings are owned by the shop owners, probably because they were able to buy them for peanuts. They haven't been cooperative about selling to Imperial. So we sweetened the pot and are ready to approach them again."

"That's where I come in," Hunter surmised.

"You've done an exceptional job finishing up Manhattan Row." Bruce clapped a heavy hand on Hunter's shoulder. "This may seem like a step down, but I need your negotiating skills and expertise to close the Mariposa deal."

"This is several *floors* down from Manhattan Row." Hunter edged out from under the other man's hand.

Juliette tilted her head, her sharp blue eyes gleaming. "Believe me when I tell you this project may *look* inconsequential compared to Manhattan Row, but it's a little jewel."

"I don't like *little* things."

"Yes, well..." Juliette slid her gaze over his chest and shoulders, her red mouth pursing. "You don't exactly *have* anything little, do you, Hunter?"

Ignoring the unsubtle remark, he studied his boss. "I want the Tokyo Cityview project."

"I need you in the US." Bruce pulled himself to full height, which was still several inches shorter than Hunter. "Juliette is the only other person I'd trust with this deal, and she's busy finishing our hotel in Atlanta. Close this deal for us, and I'll promote you to the president of Imperial's West Coast operations."

Hah. Well played, Bruce.

His boss knew Hunter had been gunning for that promotion. Reaching the company's highest executive level was another piece in the puzzle he'd designed back when he was a kid, planning a future that was the opposite of the shitty life he'd been living.

"Get this done." Bruce extended his hand. "The promotion will put you in a perfect position when the board of directors appoints a new CEO. Of course, you'll have Juliette to compete with…" he threw his daughter a smirk, "…and I'll need to retire first, but it never hurts to lay the groundwork early."

"No, it never hurts." Juliette gave Hunter a tight smile.

Smothering a rustle of guilt, Hunter shook Bruce's hand.

"You don't have a lot of time," Juliette said. "According to that hick town law, the Mariposa building owners have to vote collectively to sell their properties. Eighty percent majority wins. That's twelve out of fifteen votes. The association's next meeting is a month from now."

"They can't officially sign the contracts until the vote," Bruce added. "But you should have no trouble securing verbal agreements. We just need to keep them happy until they mark their ballots."

"Consider it done." Hunter started toward the door.

"Hunter." Bruce's bushy eyebrows pulled together. "Aren't you going to ask what will happen if you fail?"

"I never fail." He left the room.

Juliette laughed, a hard abrupt sound echoing behind him.

Returning to his office, Hunter stopped at his assistant's desk. "Margaret, get me a Monday flight into San Francisco, a car rental, and a hotel in a town called Bliss Cove, south of Santa Cruz."

"Certainly." She adjusted her glasses and peered at the computer.

Hunter glanced at his Rolex. Only four-thirty, but he was taking Victoria Davenport to the Rainbow Room tonight. She was potential marriage material, even if her father was a slumlord who illegally subdivided his properties to maximize profits.

"I'm taking off for a few hours." He strode past Margaret's desk. "I'll be back tonight around ten."

"I won't," she called after him.

Hunter went into his office and started packing up his briefcase. A light knock came at the door. Juliette entered, the epitome of cool poise.

"Congratulations." She stopped in front of his desk.

"I haven't closed the deal yet." He tossed a stack of folders into his briefcase.

"You will."

"Compared to Manhattan Row, this will be like playing with Legos." Hunter snapped his briefcase closed. "What else is Imperial planning for Bliss Cove?"

"That will be up to you, I suppose." Leaning forward, she rested her hands on his desk. "Why else would Dad insist you be the one to close the deal? It's clear he wants you to be CEO of Imperial when he retires."

"What about you?"

"Oh, I'm in the running. I'm just not the *front* runner." She rolled her eyes and straightened. "I'll spare you the garbage about both nepotism and glass ceilings. Since it looks like you'll be running Imperial soon, I wanted to assure you that you will also have *my* full support. I'd be happy to help you with the Mariposa deal in any way you'd like."

Hunter nodded his thanks and picked up his car keys. "Anything else?"

"Would you like to have dinner tonight?"

Wary, he lifted his head to look at her. She'd given off plenty of *interested* vibes over the years, but she'd never made a direct move.

She met his gaze. A hint of uncertainty gleamed in her eyes.

"You have a project you need to talk about?" he asked.

"No. God." She expelled a breath, her jaw tensing. "I'm asking you out socially. On a date. You do know what a date is, don't you?"

"Thank you for the offer, but I have plans tonight."

"Look, Hunter, it's not that complicated." Juliette huffed out a laugh and ran her hands over her hips. "We've been working together for a long time. We both hold top executive positions in a company my father started. Together, we can expand Imperial Properties and turn it into an international leader in property development."

She picked a nonexistent piece of lint off her sleeve. "And if we get to know each other outside of work and discover that we also get along personally, we have the potential to be a very powerful couple."

It wasn't a bad proposition. Juliette was intelligent and beautiful. She had an exceptional handle on real estate and property development. She checked all the boxes Hunter had when imagining a future wife. She'd lock in another piece of his puzzle.

"Think about it while you're in California." Juliette moved away from his desk. "Consider it a business proposition."

"What else would it be?"

She stared at him for a second before another laugh burst out of her. "Of course. What else would it be?"

Turning on her heel, she started for the door. "You know, Hunter, it's okay to actually *feel* something once in a while."

"What are you talking about?"

"Think about that, too."

She strode from the room just as Margaret entered.

"I've made all the arrangements." Margaret waved a photograph of a large white house at him. "One of the Oceanview investors had asked to meet with you, so I set up an appointment with him before you leave San Francisco for Bliss Cove. Which, by the way, looks really cute."

Hunter sighed. He didn't do *cute*. All the more reason to get this job done as fast as possible so he could return to his real life.

CHAPTER 1

*G*ood things came in large, thick envelopes. At least, that was what Aria Prescott had always believed. Wedding invitations, college acceptances, Christmas cards, love letters.

But this?

She sank onto a chair in her darkened café, crumpling the brown envelope in her fist. The formal letter was clipped to a stack of papers made heavier by the copious use of legalese —*clauses, conditions, title. Financial terms.*

Dropping the letter, she looked through the brick-and-glass partition separating the lounge from the front room of the café. Evening light illuminated the painted *Meow and Then* sign on the window. A chalkboard menu hung on the wall behind the counter. Wooden shelves held cat toys and cat-themed merchandise.

She'd created this. For the first time in her life, she'd gone the distance, gotten the job done, seen the plan through. She couldn't —*wouldn't*—let anything change that now.

Jumbo butted his fuzzy head against her arm.

"Sorry, sweetie." Stroking the tabby cat's ears, Aria got to her feet. "Thirteen orders of chicken bites in gravy coming right up."

Cats of all sizes stirred from various lounging positions around the room. Tails swishing and ears perked, they padded over to the row of food and water dishes.

Pushing the letter out of her mind, Aria retrieved cans of chicken from the storage cabinet and prepared dinner for her thirteen charges. A few of them meowed and slithered around her legs, while others sat waiting regally for their meal to be served.

A one-eyed cat with patchy fur, a torn left ear, and a sharp fanged tooth poking out of his mouth crouched under a table.

"Come on, Fang." Aria clicked her tongue at the old cat, who glared at her. "Yummy chicken."

She filled a separate dish and set it close to him. Only when she backed away did he edge forward to eat.

After refilling the water dishes, she tied the full trash bag and headed out the back door to put it in the garbage bin. A thick layer of ocean fog and encroaching rainclouds covered the sky, blocking the sunset. Though the April weather had been temperate, evenings were cool in the coastal California town of Bliss Cove.

It was Aria's favorite time of year—warm days bursting with color and new life followed by chilly nights of sweatshirts and bonfires. But this spring was more important than all previous ones because before summer arrived, Aria's mother and two older sisters would see that she could not only follow through with a plan, but make it a success. She'd finally prove that she was stronger and smarter than anyone—herself included—had believed.

The backdoor of the café creaked. A large calico peered at her from the crack in the open door, which she never forgot to close.

Until now. Not the greatest start to *smarter*.

"Hey, boy." Keeping her voice soft, she locked her gaze to his. "Go back inside. I'll...Porkchop!"

Faster than a blink, the cat shot into the alley and ran.

"Porkchop!" Aria slammed the door shut so the other cats wouldn't escape. She hurried around to the front of the café just as his swishing tail disappeared around the corner. "Who knew you could move so fast? Porkchop!"

Soon it would be dark and rainy. Breaking into a run, Aria followed the cat away from Mariposa Street. The rundown historic district was at least three miles from the center of downtown. Shops and restaurants lined the streets converging toward the popular and busy Starfish Avenue.

Annoyance flickered through her. In the two weeks she'd had Porkchop, he'd proven to be both wily and smug. He'd chewed rolls of paper towels, shoved other cats off the windowsill, and Aria swore he'd deliberately broken one of the cat figurines in the lounge.

There! A black-and-orange furball was just visible under a parked pick-up truck. She crept forward and extended her hand.

"Come on, Porkie Pie," she crooned. "Come back home and I'll give you some nice tuna fish...Porkchop!"

He darted away. Several passers-by paused to try and catch him. The overweight cat continued to move surprisingly fast, evading every grasp.

Aria's lungs started to burn. Skidding in her flat, strappy sandals, she caught sight of him crossing the street to the ramshackle Outside Inn. The old Queen Anne building sprawled over an expanse of tree-dotted lawn with a trail leading to Pelican Beach.

Heavy raindrops started to fall. Aria hurried up the pathway to the wrap-around porch. Thick shrubs and overgrown weeds lined the foundation of the inn underneath the multiple lighted windows. Porkchop shot behind a dense boxwood.

"You little..." She pushed through the shrubs, cursing as her flowy cotton skirt caught on a wet branch and tore. "You're lucky I took you on, you ungrateful little mouse catcher. If it weren't for me, you'd be…Porkchop!"

Tail swishing, he bounded to the corner of the inn. If he took off toward the beach trail…she'd never find him on the dark shoreline. But under the awning, he was protected from the rain. Maybe he'd opt for comfort over risk and adventure.

Comfort is a far better choice, my feline friend. Trust me on that.

The cat stopped. His whiskers twitched. His yellow eyes gleamed. Aria gritted her teeth.

"You come here right now." She clapped her hands sharply and raised her voice. "I work very hard to give you and your fellow feline brethren a nice place to live, and I do not appreciate being forced to race through the—"

A window slammed open right above her. "What the hell is going on out here?"

The deep male voice boomed like thunder. Aria's heart jumped into her throat. Forcing an apologetic smile onto her lips, she straightened and looked up. Right into the scowling face of a man whose glare burned right into her.

She opened and closed her mouth. No words came out. Her heart raced.

"Well?" His black eyebrows snapped together over his intense dark eyes. He was still holding the window sash up, and the lifted position of his arms stretched his white dress shirt over impressively bulging biceps.

"What are you doing out here?" he barked.

"I…there's a cat." Trying to gather her scattered wits, she ran shaking hands over her dress. "Uh, I was just—"

"You were annoying the crap out of me is what you were *just* doing."

Irritation stiffened Aria's spine.

"I'm sorry, I didn't *mean* to annoy you." She indicated Porkchop, who was still sitting at the corner of the inn, staring at the man as if he, too, were transfixed by his sheer potency. "I'm trying to save my cat."

His mouth twisted sardonically. "Your *cat*."

"My *felis catus*, if you want the Latin term."

He expelled an impatient breath, his scowl deepening. Letting go of the window sash, he raked a hand through his disheveled dark hair. His sleeves were rolled up to the elbows, revealing tanned forearms corded with muscle.

Good god. Who was he, this man whose glower ratcheted up his sexiness by about a thousand degrees?

And what was she doing *fixating* on him when she still had to catch Porkchop? The rain was coming down harder.

"I apologize." She drew her shoulders back and met his smoldering black eyes. "My cat escaped and made his way here, for some reason. I'm trying to catch him."

He shot a glare at the animal, who was still staring and twitching his tail. "Given his size, it doesn't look as if catching him should be that hard."

Aria frowned, stung by the dig about Porkchop's weight. "I'll thank you not to insult my cat."

"You named him Porkchop."

"I didn't name him. And he *is* on a metabolic feline weight management program."

"Maybe that's why he ran away."

"I know this doesn't *look* plausible, but he's led me on a wild goose chase...or maybe I should say a wild cat chase..." She chuckled at the joke. Glowering Stranger did not. "Anyway, my point is that despite his girth, Porkchop can run pretty darned fast."

He turned his scowl on to her. An oddly pleasurable shiver raced down her spine, which made no sense. Before she could move, or even think, he hefted himself over the window sill and landed onto the ground in front of her.

Aria's breath stopped. Like, stopped, right in the middle of her chest.

In addition to being dangerously sexy, he was also *big*—well over six feet with wide shoulders and a broad chest that was no doubt a landscape of hard muscles. With him standing right in front of her, she practically felt the power and energy coiling through every millimeter of his body.

The garden lights cast shadows over his strong features, emphasizing the cut-glass lines of his jaw and cheekbones, his thick-lashed eyes, and a beautifully shaped mouth that looked as if it were made to do dirty things to a woman.

Parting her lips, Aria forced air into her lungs before she started getting dizzy.

"If you'll step aside, I'll get my cat." She managed to sound both haughty and cool, even though her blood was hot and her heart pounding.

"Been real successful at that so far, haven't you?" Arching an eyebrow, he turned toward Porkchop.

After admiring the fact that his back was as appealing as his front, Aria edged away. If he approached the cat from this side, and she darted around behind Porkchop, they might be able to box him in.

He took a few steps toward the cat. Porkchop blinked at him. Glowering Stranger made a deep, rumbling noise that was obviously meant to soothe the animal, but that also had the strangest effect on Aria—like a hot wave rolling over her skin and settling right into her core.

Suppressing the ridiculous sensation, she prepared to move around and surround the cat as soon as the man got close enough.

"Good boy." Glowering Stranger bent and picked Porkchop up as if the cat were…well, a docile, pick-up-able creature who hadn't just fled through the streets of Bliss Cove like an escaped felon.

Aria gaped. Porkchop just...*curled* into the man's arms as if he didn't have the slightest interest in getting away. In fact, the little traitor even nuzzled his furry head against Glowering Stranger's chest.

Aria had the fleeting thought that she'd like to do the same thing.

"Well." Wiping the rain from her face, she extended her arms. "Clearly he was exhausted from all that running."

"Clearly." Though his voice was dry, faint amusement sparked in his eyes.

No, she was imagining that, or it was a trick of the light. No way did this man possess the slightest bit of humor.

Closing her arms around the damp Porkchop, she stepped away. The cat stiffened and squirmed. She tightened her hold.

"Thank you for your assistance," she said coolly. "I'll be going now."

"You're fortunate you ended up next to my room." Folding his arms, he pierced her with a disapproving glare. "Anyone else would have called the police if they heard someone prowling under their window."

"I'll just consider myself a lucky duck, then." She backed off through the bushes.

A ripping sound filled the air. Her heart sank. Gripping the cat with one hand, she pulled at her skirt and tried to dislodge it from another sharp branch.

Glowering Stranger walked toward her.

Great. Not only did he have to rescue Porkchop, he also had to rescue *her*.

Bending, he released the material from the branch with a deft flick of his fingers.

"Thank you." She lifted her chin, her face heating. Based on the feeling of cool air brushing against her leg, she'd ripped her dress almost up to her thigh. Not that she was about to look down and check, thereby drawing attention to her mishap.

Porkchop wiggled and clawed at her arm. *Troublemaker.*

"Good night." Mustering her dignity, she turned and walked away.

The cat squirmed again. His fur was getting wetter every second. She tightened her grip, praying she could manage to hold on to him for the walk back to Mariposa Street. Porkchop was not only big, he was strong and knew how to hold his own. He meowed and twisted wildly.

"Pork...oh, no."

With a hard pull, the cat jumped to the ground and took off into the backyard of the inn.

"Porkchop!" Panic flared.

The animal ran toward the trail leading to Pelican Beach. Aria started after him when a large hand clamped around her arm.

"He might be running because you're chasing him," the stranger said.

"I have to catch him!" She tried to yank her arm from his grip. She'd never forgive herself if she lost the cat. He'd been through enough in his life, and he deserved a good home. "He's heading for the beach, and I'll never be able to find him in the dark."

He bit out a sharp curse and released her, turning back to the open window. Aria flew after the cat, her flat-soled sandals skidding on the wet grass.

Just as she reached the trail, a pair of heavy male footsteps sounded behind her. The wide beam of a flashlight shone on the path. Glowering Stranger appeared at her side.

For an instant Aria wondered how in the heck he'd managed to procure a flashlight so fast. She caught sight of a tail swishing through the grass.

"There." She pointed.

He swung the flashlight toward the dunes and increased his pace, his much longer stride taking him past her in a blink. Aria rushed after him. The tall grass whipped against her legs as they emerged onto the open beach, where the waves lashed the shore and a wind pushed the rain side-ways. Tangled piles of seaweed and driftwood littered the sand. The multicolored carnival and Ferris wheel lights lining the boardwalk sparkled against the angry storm clouds.

Cold prickled Aria's skin. Glowering Stranger moved quickly, his body a large shadow skimming against the dark blue ocean and metal-gray sky.

He stopped and held up a hand. Aria came up behind him and peered around his shoulder. The cat was huddled beside a "No Lifeguard On Duty" post, licking his paw.

"He's playing with us," Aria whispered. "Do that rumble thing again."

He shot her a frown. His wet hair fell over his forehead and made him look even more menacing. "The what thing?"

"You know, that *noise* you made in your chest when you caught him before. It sounded like a cat purr. Well, a big cat purr, like from a tiger or something, if they even purr, which I don't know if they do. But that's probably why he let you pick him up. Do it again."

"I have no idea what you're talking about."

"Just *try*." She poked him in the arm. "Before he runs again. Give me the flashlight."

Somewhat to her surprise, he handed her the flashlight. Slowly he made his way toward the cat. Over the noise of the waves and wind, Aria couldn't tell if he was tiger-purring. Right before he got close to the cat, a clap of thunder boomed.

Porkchop freaked out. He bolted a foot into the air, flattened his ears, and ran.

Aria gasped. The stranger cursed. The cat let out a yowl and streaked toward the boardwalk. He careened through a tangle of seaweed and suddenly jerked to a halt.

Aria and the stranger ran toward him again. The icy tide splashed over her sandals.

"Porkchop!" She shone the light onto the cat, who pulled frantically to free his left hind leg from a rope of seaweed.

His defiance replaced by fear, Porkchop began to shake and mewl in little terrified bursts. He was soaked, his fur spiky with rainwater, and his frantic struggle to free himself seemed to be tightening the noose.

Glowering Stranger reached the frightened animal in a few long strides. He crouched and grabbed Porkchop by the scruff of the neck, then untangled the seaweed from his leg. Straightening, he hauled the frantic, dripping cat out of the trap.

Relief flooded Aria.

"Oh, *thank* you." She pulled in a heavy breath and held out her arms. "I'm really sorry about all the trouble and annoying the crap out of you and getting you all wet, and I swear I've never had a cat run away before, especially in the *rain*, but he's just so much faster than I expected him to be and—"

He walked past her, still holding the drenched cat. Porkchop twisted and protested, but there was no escaping the man's strong grip.

Since Aria didn't relish the idea of trying to wrestle a large, angry wet cat into submission, she hurried after the stranger as he started back to the Outside Inn. He lifted Porkchop into both arms and against his broad chest. The cat kept meowing, but stopped squirming.

No surprise this time. Likely the animal was absorbing a ton of the man's warmth. Even soaking wet, Glowering Stranger probably generated enough body heat to power the entire West Coast. Maybe even the whole country.

Shivers rippled over Aria's skin. Her teeth chattered. They emerged into the garden lights, and he strode back to his room. He hefted Porkchop through the open window and lowered him to the floor.

Aria stopped, stunned. She'd fully expected him to hand her the cat and walk away.

Oh, no. Was he going to call animal control now?

"Um." She rubbed her goose-bumpy arms and tried to stop her teeth from clacking together. "Can I have my cat back, please?"

"After you're both dry and warm." He frowned. "You can go in the front door, but there's a good chance you'll run into the innkeeper."

Aria opened and closed her mouth. Animals weren't allowed at the inn. As he'd clearly guessed, Mrs. Higgins was both chatty and gossipy. Aria had no desire to explain the current situation to her.

She also had no desire to enter a stranger's room, but she wasn't leaving without her cat. She'd already learned that she wouldn't be able to walk home carrying the hefty creature, especially in the storm. Another clap of thunder, and he'd bolt again.

Which meant she needed to figure out a way to get her van.

With a groan, she edged through the bushes, careful this time not to rip her already torn skirt. Her instincts told her that regardless of the stranger's glowers and frowns, she had nothing to fear from him. But in the event that her instincts were wrong —which had certainly happened before—his room was close enough to the lobby that there were likely other people close by.

He took the flashlight from her and tossed it through the window. She put her hands on the sill and tried to haul herself up over the ledge. His big hands settled around her waist. Aria's breath caught.

Despite the rain and the fact that he'd just been carrying a cold wet cat, his hands were shockingly warm, sending heat clear through her dress. As if she weighed no more than a cotton puff, he lifted her up so she could clamber awkwardly inside. As she swung her leg over the sill, a ripping noise announced that she was pretty much destroying her skirt.

She managed to get herself into the room—which was a kaleidoscope of floral rose wallpaper and chintz upholstery—before he climbed through the window after her.

Porkchop shook himself off, settled right in the middle of the rose-printed comforter, and licked his paw.

Scoundrel.

"You need to change." After closing the window, Glowering Stranger walked to the closet and removed a white terrycloth bathrobe that looked way too small for him. "Mrs. Higgins told me the robes are one size fits all."

Clearly a man like him wasn't included in the *all.*

He extended the robe and raked his gaze over her wet dress, which was plastered to her body and no doubt displayed details better left concealed. He lingered his attention on the length of her bare leg.

Her belly tensed, almost as if he'd stroked his hand over her skin. For a heart-stopping second, her mind flashed with an image of him trailing his fingers over her knee to her inner thigh, gliding upward until he found the—

She cut off the thought and pulled in a breath. How long had it been since she'd actually let a man touch her? Her recent tentative foray back into the dating world hadn't incited any great desire or passion, but she didn't want that.

Not yet, anyway. She needed to keep her focus on her business and on herself, not to get caught up in the whole sex-and-romance thing, especially spontaneously.

She'd done *spontaneous.* It hadn't worked out so well. Since returning to Bliss Cove six months ago, she was determined to do *planned* and *methodical.* This wacky night was throwing off her new game plan.

She took the robe. Much as she wanted to get home, she wanted to be warm and dry even more. She reasoned that Glowering Stranger was no longer exactly a stranger. He wasn't a friend or even an acquaintance, but he was a…cat-rescuing person. And she was a cat person. So they had that in common. Sort of.

"What's your name?" she asked.

"Hunter."

"I'm Aria."

"Get warmed up, Aria, before you start turning blue." He turned away.

She went into the bathroom, casting a glance back at Pork-chop. It was probably another trick of the light, but she could have sworn the cat winked at her.

CHAPTER 2

The second the bathroom door closed, Hunter pictured her naked. Okay, he'd pictured her naked when she was standing in front of him with that flimsy, wet dress clinging to every slender curve, and her smooth thigh peeking out from the rip in her skirt. In his mind, he'd taken off her clothes and imagined her bare breasts and perfect ass.

But in a futile attempt to be a gentleman, he'd cut the image short.

Unfortunately, now that Aria was actually stripping naked on the other side of the door, he couldn't stop his brain from conjuring up another fantasy of what she looked like. Tanned, silky skin, round breasts that would fit perfectly in his hands, little pink nipples...

Christ.

Rubbing his hands over his face, he smothered a surge of lust.

This series of events never would have happened to him in New York. Or anywhere else. Aside from day-to-day activities like driving and running errands, Hunter tended to live multiple stories above ground level. His office, his apartment, the conference rooms, the high-rise properties, even the gym where he worked out...everything was *elevated*. He rarely talked to people who didn't inhabit, or at least revolve around, the same world.

But in Bliss Cove, where the only places to stay were a motel on the interstate, B&Bs, or the Outside Inn, where Margaret had booked him...he'd ended up on the inn's ground floor because the rooms on the upper floor were either occupied or not ready for guests.

He wasn't happy about it. He'd worked damn hard to get off the ground floor—hell, *below* ground level—and he didn't like being back there for any reason.

If he hadn't been in this room, he wouldn't have heard the prowling outside his window or a woman's voice. He wouldn't have found himself jumping out the window to rescue an over-weight cat who looked at him like he was an idiot.

He wouldn't have run through a damned storm to rescue the same cat from a seaweed trap.

And he sure as hell wouldn't have encountered a stunning blonde who made his blood hot with one look. A woman whom he couldn't stop picturing naked.

He raked a hand through his wet hair and glowered at the cat, who was still sprawled in the middle of the bed, licking his paw and twitching his tail.

It was saying something that Hunter had rescued the infernal creature without even thinking about it.

What it was saying, he didn't want to know. One look at Aria —big blue eyes framed by thick lashes, that perfect mouth, a mass of shiny golden hair damp with rain—and the *urge* to help her had hit him like a lightning bolt. If Porkchop had gotten caught in an ocean riptide that carried him to Japan, Hunter would be swimming to Tokyo right now.

The idea alone defied all logic.

He opened the coffee-maker and filled the basket with coffee from one of the provided packets. He'd have to wait until Aria was out of the bathroom before filling the pot with water.

He slanted another glance at Porkchop, who was now pawing at the comforter. He couldn't fathom why the cat had wanted to escape his mistress. Why would anyone run away from a woman like that, especially in a storm? God knew she made *him* want to get as close to her as he could.

Yet another reason he disliked cats. They lacked both reason and good instincts.

"Excuse me?" Her musical voice drifted from behind the door. "Hunter?"

She said his name as if it were a cinnamon candy melting on her tongue.

He cleared his throat. "Yeah?"

"Do you mind if I use some of the complimentary lotion in here?"

The...?

"Not that I'm snooping, but Mrs. Higgins gets the lotions from Madeline Fox, who owns Naked, and—"

"What?"

"Oh, you're not from around here, are you?" She laughed. "Otherwise why would you be staying at the Outside Inn? Madeline sells handmade lotions and body scrubs at her store, which is called Naked, and for a couple of years, she's been providing Mrs. Higgins with the complimentary lotions and shampoos for the inn. She just launched a new line of oat milk lotion with lavender that I haven't tried yet, but I see it's here in the little toiletries basket, and I was wondering if you'd mind if I use it."

Hunter lowered his head and pinched the bridge of his nose. Tension laced his shoulders. Unless he got a lock on his fantasies, he'd be picturing Aria rubbing lotion into her smooth skin any minute now.

And...there it was.

With a grimace, he attempted to ignore the heat collecting in his groin. "Uh, no. I mean, go ahead. Use whatever you want."

"Great, thanks. I didn't want to use it in case you planned on saving it for your...um, wife or whomever. Or if you wanted to use it yourself. I try not to make assumptions."

Porkchop blinked and swished his tail. Maybe the cat was right in thinking Hunter was an idiot. Otherwise, why would he have urged an incredibly tempting young woman into his room and invited her to undress and wear a robe?

Well, it wasn't as if he'd had a choice. He couldn't have left her outside all wet and cold. And she couldn't hold on to that bruiser of a cat by herself, so...he *had* to ask her in.

The sound of a blow-dryer came from the bathroom. Based on his experience with women, between the hair and the lotion, Aria would be in there for a while.

In the meantime, his trousers and shirt were still drenched, clammy, and clinging heavily to his body.

Didn't douse your lust at all, though, did it?

He expelled his breath and grabbed some clothes from his open suitcase. After pulling off his socks, he unbuttoned his shirt and tossed it to the floor. He hitched his trousers and boxer briefs over his hips and added them to the pile. He could have used a shower, but that would have to wait until he'd dealt with this cat situation.

He pulled on clean briefs and reached for a pair of jeans.

"Okay, I'm..." Her voice faded the instant the bathroom door clicked open.

His heart crashed against his ribs. With the white robe loosely belted around her waist, her feet bare and her hair falling in a golden curtain around her shoulders, she was like a shot of concentrated sunlight.

He stepped into his jeans and hitched them over his hips before his arousal became any more obvious.

"...er, finished." Her eyes widened as she dragged her gaze

over his chest and shoulders. "Sorry. I didn't mean to take so long."

He yanked a shirt over his shoulders and fastened the buttons quickly—because if she looked at him with that heat brewing in her blue eyes for one second longer, he'd stride across the room and haul her right into his arms. Then he'd tilt her chin up and crush her mouth with his. She'd taste like bright summery things—peaches and...*what else was summery?* Ice cream. Lemonade. Treats he'd dreamed of as a child, but rarely had.

He grabbed the empty coffee-pot and walked past her to the bathroom.

Mistake.

Her flimsy little bra and panties—pink and flowered, no less, with lace around the edges—hung on the towel rack beside her torn dress.

No question. He was definitely an idiot. One who was about to lose his mind.

Forcing his attention away from her underwear, he filled the pot and returned to the room. She was sitting on the edge of the bed, scratching Porkchop behind the ears and crooning to him in a low voice. The cat smirked at Hunter.

He pulled in a breath and poured the water into the coffee-maker.

Focus. Discipline. Plan.

Those three words had gotten him to where he was now—on the brink of a major promotion and one step closer to being the CEO of Imperial Properties. He needed to use the same concepts to deal with the current situation.

He didn't want to risk running into Mrs. Higgins by taking Aria's clothes to the communal dryer down the hall. But he didn't want Aria to wear her wet clothes either. He didn't like the idea of her shivering and cold again.

After pushing the button to start the coffee, he crossed to

his suitcase and pulled out a T-shirt and a pair of running shorts. "Have some coffee, then put these on. I'll drive you home."

"You don't have to do that." She threaded her fingers into the cat's fur. "And Porkchop needs a crate when he's in a car. He hates riding."

Hunter rubbed the back of his neck. "So we'll get a crate from your house, and come back here and pick him up."

She shook her head. "He hates being alone too. He has anxiety issues. He might claw the furniture or yowl a lot, which means Mrs. Higgins might hear him. I don't want you to get in trouble because of me."

"What do you want to do, then?" He tossed the clothes onto the bed beside her.

She pursed her lips in thought. Rosebud mouth. He wanted to kiss her. He dug his fingers into his palms.

"I'll go home and get my van and a crate, then I'll come back to pick him up." She squinted at the window. "It's not raining quite as hard anymore. You stay here with Porkchop. It won't take me long, maybe fifteen minutes at most."

"What about Mrs. Higgins?"

"We'll have to go through the window again, but we're getting pretty good at that." She flashed him a smile. The area around his heart constricted.

The coffee-maker beeped. He poured her a cup and tried not to notice the way her lips closed around the rim as she took a sip. He didn't want to send her off into the dark alone, but he couldn't think of another option.

That had to be a first. He could *always* think of another option.

"This is good, thanks." Her slender throat worked as she swallowed more coffee. He'd always loved a woman's neck and shoulders, and he couldn't stop his gaze from traveling over her smooth, exposed skin. Her collarbones framed the hollow of her throat, and he suddenly wondered what it would feel like to kiss her there.

Heat rose up his spine.

"Let me put these on." Setting the cup on the nightstand, she grabbed his shorts and T-shirt and disappeared into the bathroom again. A few seconds later, she emerged looking as if she were drowning in the way-too-big clothes. The shirt fell to her knees, and she had to hold the shorts up around her waist.

Adorable.

Hunter frowned. Another first. He'd never thought the word *adorable* in his life. He'd sure as hell never said it aloud. He never would.

"This isn't quite going to work *as is*." She hitched the shorts up and wiggled her hips. "Hold on. I have an idea."

She went into the bathroom again and returned, fastening the robe belt around her waist. "This should get me home. Do you have an umbrella I can borrow?"

Though he pointed to the complimentary umbrellas provided by the inn, frustration tightened his chest. "If you won't let me take you, why don't you at least call an Uber or taxi? I don't want you to walk home alone."

Not until surprise flashed over her expression did he realize how possessive he sounded.

What the hell was going on with him? He always kept his emotions tightly controlled, especially around people he didn't know.

"The chances of me getting a driver I know are pretty high." She put on her sandals, grabbed an umbrella, and started toward the window. "Obviously that would lead to questions about my attire, not to mention there's the whole Mrs. Higgins issue. Plus, it's really not far. I'll be fine. I'll just take the side streets and be back in fifteen minutes."

Against his better judgement, Hunter lifted the window sash. The scent of her drifted to him—lavender and some earthy, sexy smell that seemed to belong to her alone. Her fingernails were painted light pink. A tiny stud glittered at the side of her nose.

"It's too dark out there." He picked up the flashlight that was still on the floor. "Take this with you."

"Where did you get this anyway?" She took the light from him and pushed the floral curtains aside. "Do you always have a flashlight handy?"

He jerked his thumb toward a wicker basket in the corner with a printed label reading *Emergency Supplies*. "Mrs. Higgins told me she stocks all the rooms with supplies in case of power outages, fires, earthquakes, or tsunamis. She didn't say anything about escaped cats."

"There's a first time for everything." She swung her leg over the window sash.

He stepped forward to hold the curtains, which put him close enough to her that he could not only smell her, he could *feel* her. Even lost in his overlarge clothes, warmth radiated from her like the heat of the sun. Hot enough to melt the ice inside him.

"I feel like a teenager sneaking out for the night." She paused and shot him a grin. "This is kind of fun."

He could think of another word. Like *insane*.

"What if your cat has a fit while you're gone?" he asked.

"Do the tiger rumble."

"I still don't know what that is."

"I told you, it's this noise you make way down here." She tapped his chest. Her eyes drifted from his face down to his torso. "It's deep and really...um, soothing."

"You're making that up." In the shadowy light, he could see the darker ring of indigo surrounding her irises.

"I would never make up a *rumble*." She lifted her eyes back to his.

God, she was pretty. Thick, sooty eyelashes, freckle-dusted nose, pale lips. He was so accustomed to refined, carefully polished women that looking at her was like a revelation. In almost thirty-five years, he'd never encountered a woman who seemed so...natural.

A flame flickered low in his body. His razor-sharp brain seemed incapable of forming a thought that made any sense beyond *I want to kiss you.*

Before he could counter that with *You're an idiot, Armstrong,* he lowered his head and brushed his mouth across hers.

CHAPTER 3

*I*nside Aria, a light clicked on. *Was he kissing her?*

He was kissing her. Or at least, his lips were gently touching hers. As her shock faded, bright sparks began to ignite in her blood, illuminating all her dark places. His lips were warm and firm, and the scent of him—rain and salt—filled her head.

He increased the pressure for an instant, and her heart jumped with anticipation at the idea of him *fully* kissing her. She imagined him cupping her face in his big hands, urging her mouth open, tilting her head to just the right angle so he could devour her.

Longing burst through her, almost as shocking as the fact that she was sitting on a windowsill being kissed by a man she'd met less than two hours ago. By *Glowering Stranger*, though he was no longer glowering and increasingly less a stranger.

But, *oh*, how long had it been since she'd been kissed with such gentleness, as if she were somehow precious? Lifting a tentative hand, she pressed it to his jaw. She rubbed her palm over his coarse whiskers. Tingles spread clear up her arm.

The light inside her burned brighter, hotter. He slid his hand to the back of her neck. Self-control laced his body. Aria curled her other hand into his shirtfront and parted her lips, but he kept the kiss gentle and restrained, almost as if he didn't want to scare her away.

She was anything but scared. Arousal coiled slowly through her lower body. Tightening her hand in his shirt, she slanted her mouth harder against his. A groan echoed in his chest.

What would it be like if he let go of his controlled self-restraint? If he pushed her against the windowsill, cupped her breasts, edged his body between her legs—

Breaking abruptly away, he lifted his head. Their eyes met with a jolt of hot urgency. Then he stepped back. A shutter came down over his hard features.

"Sorry." He shook his head, as if shaking himself out of a trance. "Didn't mean to do that."

She pressed a hand to her thumping heart, her pleasure evaporating. "What, your mouth just happened to *fall* onto mine?"

"I *shouldn't* have done that." He raked a hand through his still-damp hair, seemingly frustrated by his own impulses. "I don't make a habit of helping women rescue their cats and then kissing them. The women, not the cats."

"Well, I don't make a habit of kissing glowering strangers." Pulling in a breath, she gripped the edge of the windowsill. "Like I said, there's a first time for everything."

"Everything about this night is a first time." He shot a glance at Porkchop.

"Fifteen minutes." Aria hitched herself over the windowsill and landed on the ground. "Time me."

She opened the umbrella and hurried off into the night, feeling his gaze as he watched her leave. A hot sensation simmered in her belly, even as she told herself to calm down and not let her imagination run away with her. As a resident of the Outside Inn, Hunter was only in Bliss Cove for a short time, and she'd likely never see him again after tonight.

They were two passing ships, which was a good thing. She

was still just dipping her toe into the dating waters again—an hour or two, a casual dinner or drink, a bare minimum of physical contact and certainly no kissing.

Big, masculine Hunter with his sexy rumble, dark glower, and that incredible body that looked as if it were carved by a master sculptor...yeah, he was entirely too much for her right now. Or ever.

Even if just the brief caress of his lips had filled her with heat.

Trying to push the thought aside, she hurried home. She had to stop several times to tighten her belt so the shorts wouldn't fall down, but she managed to make it back to her Mariposa Street apartment, which was a one-room studio above the café.

After quickly changing into jeans and a T-shirt, she tossed a cat crate into the van and returned to the Outside Inn. The rain had let up even further, so she parked on the street to avoid Mrs. Higgins coming out to investigate her reasons for being there.

Hefting the crate, she hurried back to Hunter's window and tapped on the glass. The window shot up, and he grabbed her arm to help her back inside.

"Did you time me?"

"Twenty minutes and fifty-three seconds." He frowned and pointed at the clock on the nightstand.

"I had to stop a few times to hitch up the shorts." Aria set the crate on the floor beside the bed and handed him his folded clothes, which she'd stuffed into her oversized bag. She dug around some more and produced a can of tuna.

"His favorite." She tilted her head toward the cat. "I wish I'd thought to grab some before chasing after him in the first place. Then we wouldn't be in this predicament."

"That'd be a damned shame," he murmured.

Aria flicked him a glance, her breath catching at the heat lingering in his dark eyes.

Yes, it would.

Forcing her attention away from him, she tore the lid off the tuna and tossed it into the wastepaper basket beside the narrow desk. A sleek laptop computer and dozens of papers and folders cluttered the surface. A business trip, then.

Which begged the question...

She glanced surreptitiously at Hunter's left hand. No wedding ring, not that that meant much. Not that she should even care about his availability.

Porkchop side-eyed her, whiskers quivering and nose twitching. Aria set the open can in the crate. In a streak of orange-and-black, the cat leapt off the bed and into the crate. Gobbling sounds emerged.

"Gotcha." She closed and latched the door, throwing Hunter a relieved smile. "I made the mistake earlier of leaving the back door unlocked when I was taking out the trash. That's how he escaped. That definitely won't happen again."

He picked up the crate and carried it to the window. "I'll bring it to your car."

"No need. I can take it."

This time, however, he appeared determined to do things his way. After he'd hefted himself over the windowsill, Aria handed him the crate and climbed through. The rain had finally stopped, and they crossed the wet grass to her old, beat-up van.

"You can put him in here." She opened the passenger side door and indicated the seat. "I really couldn't have caught him without you."

"Not for lack of trying, though." Amusement shone in his eyes as he set the crate into the van and locked the seatbelt around it. He peered through the crate slats at the cat. "Don't cause any more trouble, okay? Your mistress isn't one you should run away from."

Though his tone was offhanded and casual, his remark lit a glow around Aria's heart.

Hunter closed the door and stepped onto the sidewalk.

Silence filled the space between them, threaded with a hint of tension.

"So." She tightened her fingers around her keys. "I'm sorry again for annoying the crap out of you and all."

"Actually, I take that comment back." The overhead streetlight made his dark hair gleam with strands of gold. "Thanks for annoying the crap out of me. You made my evening a hell of a lot more interesting than it otherwise would have been."

"Well, then. You're welcome." She took another reluctant step back and lifted her hand in a little wave. "See you."

"See you."

Aria dragged her gaze from him and started around the van to the driver's side. A sudden impulse seized her. She stopped. Her heartbeat ratcheted up.

Pushing aside all misgivings, all thoughts, she turned and ran back to him. In one movement, she leapt up and threw her arms around his neck. He startled, closing his arms around her tightly the second before she kissed him.

Hard. She pressed and rubbed her lips against his and flicked her tongue out to caress the seam of his lips. He stiffened in surprise. Then his restraint snapped like a rubber band. He lifted one hand to the back of her head and crushed his mouth to hers.

Desire sparked and flamed inside her. He'd lifted her clear off the ground, and her body was pressed fully against his. Tension laced his muscles. A throb pulsed in her veins. She opened her mouth and let him inside. As she'd suspected, as she'd *known*, he was as deliciously good at hot, greedy kisses as he'd been with a gentle one.

Better, even. He slid his tongue over hers, nibbled at her bottom lip, and licked the corners of her mouth. She squirmed against him, the friction of their bodies hardening her nipples against his chest. Her pleasure blossomed outward, filling her veins.

He drove one hand into her hair, threading his fingers

through the damp strands before moving to press his lips to her cheek. His stubble scraped her skin exquisitely, igniting little fires in her veins. She dug her fingers into his shoulders, forcing herself to lift her head.

Lust brewed in his eyes. Her heated breath puffed against his mouth. Slowly, he lowered her to the ground, sliding her body against his. Her heart hammered.

"Thanks for your help," she whispered.

Before he could speak, she broke away from him and ran back to the van.

"Aria—"

She shifted into gear and pulled onto the street. Every part of her felt warm and glowing. She'd thought the light inside her had gone out long ago.

How crazy and wonderful that *he* had made it burn so brightly—a captivating stranger she would never see again.

CHAPTER 4

"Honey, that was no coincidence." Destiny Storm lifted her coffee mug to her mouth. Her multiple silver rings winked in the morning sunlight. "The cat is your spirit animal. Spirit animals guide us to the places we need to be."

"I really didn't need to be on Pelican Beach in the middle of a storm." Aria sipped her takeout matcha tea and studied the front of Meow and Then, which sat across from Destiny's Moonbeams store on historic Mariposa Street.

"You came out of the storm, didn't you?" Destiny quirked an eyebrow. A voluptuous, stunning woman in her mid-thirties, she'd been the first person to hire Aria for a job when Aria was a high-school junior. They'd become fast friends and stayed close even during Aria's absences from Bliss Cove.

"I wouldn't be so quick to dismiss such a literal message, if I were you," Destiny added. "Especially one involving a man who sounds like a fantasy come to life."

Aria considered the idea that Porkchop's escapade last night had been motivated by spiritual guidance rather than feline defiance.

"It was a random encounter."

"No encounters are *random*." Destiny leaned against the doorway of her shop and flicked a lock of raven-black hair over her shoulder. "Though you might not know for a long time, if ever, *why* something happens, every single event in your life has led you to this moment."

On the surface, "this moment" wasn't much different than twenty-four hours ago, when Aria had also been having a morning cup of tea with Destiny before opening Meow and Then.

But beneath the surface? Deep down inside, in her heart of hearts? The place where she was still rebuilding what she'd lost and constructing the things she'd never had?

Maybe a small change had happened there. Like a seed breaking open or clouds parting. Creating a space for something new to happen.

Aria shook her head and took another sip of tea. She'd thought about Hunter all night. Not only *him* in all his glowering, cat-rescuing, gentle-kissing glory, but also about how she'd been prompted to throw herself at him. Though the kiss had been incredible, she'd learned her lesson about spontaneity a long time ago—primarily that it led nowhere good.

She'd told Destiny about the cat chase, but she hadn't confessed that she'd kissed Hunter. That would remain her own little secret. And his.

"Morning, *caras*." Nico, the owner of the pizza parlor, came out to sweep the cobblestones in front of his shop. "How are you lovely ladies today?"

"Better now that you're here." Destiny smiled.

Nico chuckled. "You both get the contract from that company? Imperial Properties?"

"Mine just came yesterday." Aria's shoulders tensed. "I put it right in the trash where it belongs."

"I hear the Howells are already planning to sign." Nico

nodded toward the large flower shop housed in a crumbling stucco building that had originally been used as a trading post.

"They've been wanting to retire for years." Destiny took a sip of coffee and shrugged. "Can't imagine anyone wanting to buy the old place. I'll bet they think Imperial is a godsend."

"They're a scourge." Aria frowned. "Have you responded yet, Nico?"

"No, *cara*." He tapped the side of his head. "Still thinking."

Aria shaded her eyes from the sun and swept her gaze over the old street. The long, narrow stretch of shops was anchored at one end by the Vitaphone movie theater and at the other by the boarded-up Hotel Casa Grande, a gray stucco hotel with half-a-dozen rooms that had once been the town's main lodging house. Now only the lobby remained open for the Mariposa Business Association meetings.

Mariposa Street had been the first area built by explorers and missionaries in the nineteenth century before a ship captain from Maine turned the town into a shipping port. Over the years Bliss Cove had transformed into a fishing community, then a college town, and then one of many places hit by economic hardship. Despite its struggles, the town retained its quaint seaside culture, with locally owned businesses, a community theater, and a historical museum that preserved Bliss Cove's colorful heritage.

As Bliss Cove's downtown grew over the years, the Mariposa neighborhood, unfortunately, had fallen by the wayside. Many of the shop windows were covered with splintered boards, and graffiti defaced the once-elegant building façades. But beneath layers of grime and peeling paint, the evidence of Mariposa's lively history and culture was clear in the painted clay tiles, intricate plaster ornamentation, and ironwork decorations.

Aria had a soft spot for the oldest part of Bliss Cove, which her historian father had always admired and appreciated. Though when she was younger, she hadn't really understood his dedication to history, she had distinct childhood memories of walking through Mariposa with him while he told her about the history of the area's indigenous people prior to the arrival of the Spanish missionaries and all the turmoil of the subsequent years.

Of course, she'd been more interested in getting an ice cream at the time, but when her father died unexpectedly in a car accident a year and a half ago, that memory resurfaced like a brilliant piece of sea glass. She'd clung to it, even after leaving Bliss Cove and plunging into a relationship with a man who had been anything but good for her.

Realizing Steve was capable of physical abuse—that it was only a matter of time before he turned his violent streak on to her—had finally given her the strength to leave him. When she'd returned to Bliss Cove, she'd wanted desperately to confide in her mother and sisters, but Eleanor Prescott's health scare had sent new shockwaves through their lives and prevented Aria from giving voice to her own mistakes. Even after her mother had been given the "all clear," Aria had been too ashamed to turn to her family or friends for comfort.

Well, not her human friends anyway. She'd spent countless hours with furry friends at the rescue shelter. Because of the animals—nonjudgmental, friendly, resilient, and loyal—the aftermath of the worst time in her life had become bearable and eventually even hopeful, giving her a purpose she'd never had before.

"I need to get over to Mom's to pick up my order." Aria clinked her cup against Destiny's and waved at Nico. "See you both later."

"Live in the light, honey," Destiny said.

Aria crossed the street to Meow and Then, a two-story terracotta building with a tile roof and wrought-iron balcony. In the early twentieth-century, it had been a rooming house owned by a Prescott ancestor, Christine Sterling, a writer, lecturer and suffragette who'd supported herself and her three children after her husband died.

Though Aria wasn't convinced her encounter with Glowering

Stranger was anything more than a random event, she had no doubt that she was meant to purchase the former Sterling House. Five months ago, she'd bought her ancestor's building with the money her father had left for her and made a plan to open the café.

Not that it had been easy.

Her mother and sisters believed the location was setting her up for failure, and her practical and brilliant older sister Callie, a Classics professor at Skyline College, had advised her to keep her money invested in mutual funds.

Though she understood their objections, Aria had been determined to see her plan through. Before her father died, she'd spent too many years flitting around like a bee, hovering around whatever flower looked the prettiest or smelled the sweetest, because she'd known her sisters and parents would always help her if she happened to choose wrong. But not until she broke up with Steve did she realize she'd never learned how to stand on her own.

Meow and Then was her chance. She had no intention of relying on someone else emotionally or financially ever again.

After picking up her keys, she drove to downtown Bliss Cove and parked in the back lot of the Sugar Joy Bakery. Her mother and older sister Rory were restocking the front counter following the morning rush.

"Hi, honey." Eleanor Prescott nodded toward three white boxes stacked on the counter. "Your order is just about ready to go. I haven't boxed the Chaos Cookies yet."

"I'll do it." Aria took the order form off the top box. "You still haven't invoiced me for last week's order."

"I'm happy to donate whatever you need." Eleanor placed a basket of muffins in the glass display case.

Aria smothered a prickle of exasperation mixed with affection. When they'd learned two months ago that Eleanor had a precancerous lump in her breast, they'd all feared not only the outcome but for her emotional state, which had been so fragile following their father's death. But Eleanor had proven both resilient and optimistic through the surgery. In fact, she'd been more focused on her daughters than herself, especially with regard to Aria's venture.

"Mom, you have to charge me. I'm running a business, not a charity."

"I know, dear." Though Eleanor smiled, a flicker of concern lit in her eyes.

Aria sighed. She did not want her mother to worry about her. "I need to pay my expenses."

"Are you using the bookkeeping software?" Rory, a software engineer with long black hair and a penchant for classic rock, took a tray off the baker's rack. "I can come over and show you how to get the most out of it."

"Thanks, but I'm figuring it out." Aria picked up a banana-nut muffin. Though she tried not to let their good intentions get to her, it was hard not to.

She'd grown up with two accomplished older sisters, a scholarly father, and a mother who'd run a successful bakery for years. She, on the other hand, had a personal history of either failing or giving up whatever she tried to start. It was hardly a wonder that her family was still struggling to believe that her café venture would be any different.

Aria was still struggling to believe that herself.

"Oh, good, I'm glad you're here." Callie's voice broke into Aria's thoughts. Poised and lovely in a beige suit and matching heels with her dark hair tied back in a neat chignon, Callie looked every inch the elegant, sophisticated professor.

Aria edged behind the cold case to hide the fact that she was wearing old skinny jeans with multiple holes. "No class this morning?"

"Not until ten. Rory, can you get me a coffee to go, please?" Callie waved a copy of *The Bliss Cove Times* at Aria. "Word on the street is that Imperial Properties has issued all the Mariposa owners a new offer. Why didn't you tell us?"

"Because I just got the letter."

"Does Imperial still want to build some sort of mixed-use complex there?" Rory grabbed a towel to wipe her hands. "I thought they'd backed off."

"Until yesterday, so did I." Aria scanned the front-page story.

Last year in their first takeover attempt—before she had even thought about opening a café, much less one in the district— Imperial Properties had lowballed the Mariposa shop owners. After failing to convince a majority to sell their buildings and land, the company had retreated. From what Aria had heard, everyone believed they were no longer interested.

Surprise.

"They've sent us all new buyout offers this past week." She folded the paper with a snap. Though she had no intention of accepting, her fellow Mariposa owners wouldn't be so quick to dismiss the deal this time around. "The offer expires at midnight on April thirtieth, which is the date of the next Mariposa Association meeting. That's when all of the building owners collectively vote on whether or not we want to sell."

If the majority voted no, Aria and Mariposa Street were safe.

But if the majority voted *yes*, she might not have a choice. She'd have to sell her property, and Imperial would bulldoze the entire district to make way for Oceanview Plaza.

Pushing the newspaper back toward her sister, Aria deflected a stab of fear. She had a month to convince her fellow business owners that their community and town history were far too important to sell to a company that would demolish everything to rubble.

"What are you going to do?" Rory asked.

"Say no." She took a white box from beneath the counter and started filling it with Chaos Cookies. "I'm not selling my home and business."

Callie clicked her tongue in exasperation. "You're kidding."

"No, I'm not *kidding*."

"Aria, your business is failing." Callie grabbed the paper, a frown carving lines around her mouth. "You don't even have a profit-and-loss forecast in place, much less any kind of estimated future revenue. Imperial is offering more than the fair-market value and no contingencies. How can you possibly turn that down?"

Aria's spine tensed. "Because it's my business, and I can do what I want. Thanks for reminding me I'm such a failure, though."

"I'm not..." Callie shook her head and pressed her lips together. "I'm just saying that you didn't take the most basic operations into account when you decided to open a business on Mariposa Street."

"And you didn't take into account the fact that I can choose to do what I want with my money," Aria snapped. "It still pisses you off that I actually did something big against your advice, doesn't it?"

"Don't you mean something *foolish*?"

"Girls, stop," Eleanor said sharply.

Lowering her voice, Aria glared at her sister. "I'm surprised you, of all people, would be in favor of a property company taking over the most historic part of town. You're a historian. Mariposa Street is where Bliss Cove started. We're related to the woman who owned the Sterling House. Why would you want it destroyed?"

"Mariposa Street has been a drain on the town's economy for years." Callie picked up the take-out coffee and tucked the paper under her arm. "Even if it weren't for Imperial's offer, I still don't think you realize that having a business and living on Mariposa is going to ruin you financially. You've already had to use the rest of your money on repairs, and—"

"How do you know I've used the rest of my money?" Not in a

million years would she have told Callie that. She shot Rory a suspicious look. "Did *you* tell her?"

Rory sighed and flicked her long ponytail over her shoulder. "I might have mentioned it after you refused my loan offer. We don't want you to end up in a money pit, and it sounds like that's what's happening."

"What's *happening* is that I won't let a property company kick me out of my own home." She taped the lid of the box, battling back old guilt over not being able to tell her mother and sisters all the reasons she needed so badly to make her café a success.

They didn't know anything about her relationship with Steve. They thought she'd moved to Colorado on a whim, not because she'd gone to live with a man who'd promised her security. Even though she'd extricated herself from Steve before things got worse, she was still too ashamed to tell her family. They'd all been through enough after Gordon Prescott's death without needing to know how vulnerable she'd been.

"Honey, don't be upset." Eleanor put her arm around Aria. "We want to support you, but surely you can see why we're concerned."

Aria smothered a bolt of anger toward both herself and them. Yes, she *saw*. That viewpoint was exactly what she was trying to change.

"I need to get going." She picked up the boxes and started toward the kitchen. "I'll see you all later. Mom, don't forget to invoice me."

Without giving them a chance to come after her, she hurried out to her car and drove back to Mariposa Street.

Pulling out her keys, she unlocked the door of Meow and Then. A chorus of howls and mews greeted her from the adjoining room. She opened the interior door separating the Cat Lounge from the food service area.

Over a dozen cats swarmed toward her, tails swishing and whiskers twitching. Porkchop was lolling on the sofa in a patch of sunlight. Hard to believe he'd masterminded a break-out just last night.

"Hello, my little sweeties." Aria knelt to croon and pet the cats, making sure to give each one equal attention before she rose to refill their food dishes and give them fresh water.

She cleaned out the litter boxes, vacuumed the Cat Lounge, and prepared the front counter for opening. The building's two rooms had clinched the deal for her—for health code reasons, the cats needed to be separated from the food service.

The Cat Lounge was the larger room, with big picture windows, round tables, and comfortable furniture. It was also a cat's paradise furnished with multiple cat trees, scratching posts, and toys. A brick wall perforated by a large window separated the lounge from the front counter, where she sold coffee, tea, drinks, and the baked goods from Sugar Joy.

After starting a pot of coffee, she flipped the Open sign and unlocked the door.

"Hey, Crazy Cat Lady." Her friend Brooke Castle, a slender brunette wearing a backwards baseball cap and a photographer's vest, bounded up the front steps.

"Hey, Dogged Newshound." Aria poured a cup of coffee and set it on the counter. "What are the Bliss Cove headlines today?"

"Apparently, Hal McGowan and Rodney Smith got into a fight at the Mousehole last night." Brooke hitched herself onto a stool at the counter. "Over which fry shape tastes the best—crinkle-cut, regular, wedge, or waffle."

"What about shoestring?" Aria took a kettle from the hot plate and poured boiling water into a mug.

Brooke shrugged. "Not part of the debate, I guess."

"Who won?"

"Neither. Grant broke up the fight before either one of them landed a punch. The chief was having dinner there too, so he took them both in." Brooke sipped the coffee. "You can read all the deets in tomorrow's paper."

Aria dropped a teabag into her mug. "Clearly the answer is regular fries."

Her friend lifted an eyebrow. "Excuse me? Clearly the answer is crinkle-cut."

"Crinkle-cut fries are way too machine-made."

"The crinkles make them perfect for dunking in ketchup."

Aria shook her head in mock despair. "After ten years, we can't be best friends anymore."

"You'd better be my best friend if you want this." Brooke pulled a thick, bound report with a red cover from her bag. The title read *Imperial Properties' Oceanview Plaza – A Vertical Mixed-Use Development Proposal.*

Aria's insides tightened. "Where did you get this?"

"From a contact, but it's not a secret. They revised the proposal a lot from the last one, hoping that the changes will get more people on board."

Aria flipped through the report. There were plans for retail and office space, luxury condos—*condos?*—and a multi-level parking structure. Architectural drawings showed pyramidal and square brick-and-glass buildings overlooking the beach and a concrete "plaza" lined with stone benches.

"What has the town council said?" she asked.

"As long as it fits all zoning and planning codes, they're leaving the decision to the Mariposa owners." Brooke picked up her coffee and stood. "That's the council's official statement, at least. Mayor Bowers told me privately she thinks the design is *ugly as sin.* But she's kind of stuck because the town council hasn't budgeted anything to fix up Mariposa for well over thirty years. Now it's almost too late."

Almost.

If there was one lesson that had stuck in Aria's mind over the past year, it was that *almost* didn't mean something was done.

Almost meant a narrow escape—but an escape nonetheless.

Almost meant being on the edge—but not over it.

Almost meant there was still a chance.

"I gotta get to the office." Brooke slung her bag over her shoulder. "You can keep that if you want. Mousehole Friday night?"

"I'll be there."

After her friend had gone, Aria glanced at the contact information on the Imperial Properties' report. She pulled up an email window on her old laptop and typed a message to Bruce Sinclair, CEO.

Dear Mr. Sinclair,

Prior to the forthcoming vote at the Mariposa Business Association meeting, I would like to inform you that I decline to sell my building to Imperial Properties.

Sincerely,
Ariadne Prescott, Owner
Meow and Then Cat Café

Send.

There. At least they'd know her decision was final.

Picking up several pieces of colored chalk, she climbed a stepladder to reach the chalkboard hanging on the brick wall behind the counter. She erased the list of yesterday's baked goods offerings and began writing down the treats she'd picked up from Sugar Joy that morning.

The cat-shaped wind chimes above the door jingled, signaling her first customer of the day. With a smile, she turned...and almost toppled off the stepstool in shock.

"Whoa." Hunter bolted around the counter at light-speed as she teetered precariously. He grabbed her. "Careful."

Aria clutched the edge of the chalkboard to steady herself.

Her heart raced. Sudden warmth bloomed through her veins, hot and hard.

He hadn't just grabbed her...he was *holding her*. One of his big hands was pressed to her hip, and the other was gripping her waist. And his strong arm was tucked right up against her rear end, which she didn't find disturbing in the least.

He also appeared to be in no hurry to let go.

Swallowing hard, Aria found her voice. "Thanks."

"My pleasure." He released her and stepped back.

Did he just slide his hand over her hip? Like he was *lingering*?

Aria put the chalk back into the tray and climbed down the ladder. A combination of excitement and wariness bubbled up inside her. She didn't quite know how to feel about the fact that Hunter was standing in her café. She'd thrown herself at him last night because she'd thought they'd never see each other again.

Okay, she'd also wanted desperately to kiss him properly, but still... She wasn't a spontaneous, leap-and-plant-one-on-an-almost-stranger kind of girl.

What was he doing here? Had he looked her up?

"Welcome to Meow and Then." Forcing her business persona back into place, she grabbed a dishcloth and wiped her hands before turning to face him.

Oh, mercy.

Last night at the inn, he'd first been a grumpy and strikingly gorgeous specimen of disheveled masculinity. Then, with his sculpted torso and bulging biceps on full display, he'd been a walking advertisement for any product or sport that needed to feature a seriously hot half-naked man.

And now? In a navy Armani suit, clearly tailored just for him, and a perfectly knotted silk tie, with his dark hair brushed back from his forehead and his clean-shaven face emphasizing his strong features, he was...

Wow.

"Hi." She rubbed her throat, unaccountably warm. "Again."

"Hi again." A smile tugged at his mouth. He picked up a brief-case and clipboard that he'd dropped and set them on the counter. "How's Porkchop?"

"Sleeping. I think he wore himself out last night. Though he's known for enjoying his bed quite a bit anyway."

"Hmm." His forehead furrowed. "I can relate."

"Me too."

A current of heat sizzled between them. Her breathing grew shallow. *Could Destiny have been right? About the cat spirits and no coincidences and all that?*

She ran her hands self-consciously over her apron. In the light of day, everything about Hunter—from his tailored designer suit to his expensive leather briefcase—clashed with her rolled-up, holey skinny jeans and loose tank-top. Even his dark hair was impeccably combed with not a strand out of place, while her messy mane was barely holding on to a bun.

"So you work here." He indicated the array of cat items and the little Japanese luck cat on the counter. "Looks like you can't get away from cats."

"I wouldn't want to." Aria pulled in a breath and tried to calm her jumping heartrate. "What are you doing here?"

"I stopped by to talk to the owner."

She blinked. "You are."

He went still. His attention sharpened and his shoulders tensed. "What?"

"You already are."

"I already am what?"

"Talking to the owner."

"No." He grabbed the clipboard and flipped a few pages. "I'm looking for an...oh, shit. You're *Ariadne* Prescott."

"Yes."

And you're Glowering Stranger who ended up being nice enough to rescue my mutinous cat, then insisted on making sure I was warm and dry while you made coffee. You're the tall, strong man with muscles that look carved from stone who kissed me so gently it felt like a leaf brushing across my lips.

He cursed again, his mouth compressing. He tossed the clipboard back onto the counter. An invisible shield slammed in front of him, dissolving their encounter last night and making him suddenly remote.

Unease twisted in Aria's gut. Why was he so shocked?

Abruptly, he turned away and narrowed his eyes on the glass door leading to the Cat Lounge, which was still covered by a window blind. His laser-sharp gaze took in the surroundings with one glance—the cat-themed mugs and greeting cards, the framed cat paintings, the cat-shaped cookies.

Was he judging her for owning a cat café? Obviously, he—

Her heart stuttered.

He rubbed the back of his neck. The movement caused his sleeve to ride up, revealing a silver cufflink attached to his crisp French cuff. A gold Rolex was wrapped around his wrist.

—was a successful corporate businessman.

Darkness encroached on her, like a thick layer of marine fog blocking out the sunlight. She grasped the edge of the counter.

"Why do you need to talk to me?" she asked. "The owner me, I mean. Ariadne Prescott."

He didn't respond. His back was to her, his spine stiff.

"Why do you need to talk to her?" Aria raised her voice, her unease deepening. "To *me*."

Hunter turned, his expression implacable, but his jaw tight. "I'm here on business."

The cloud darkened. "What kind of business?"

"You received a letter and contract from our company recently." He pinned her to the spot with the intensity of his gaze. "I'm Hunter Armstrong, Vice-President of Imperial Properties."

Shit wasn't a strong enough word.

Aria's breath escaped in one hard rush. Disappointment

stabbed her. She lowered her head and concentrated on wiping down the pristine counter so she wouldn't have to look at him.

Last night had been a roller-coaster unlike any she'd experienced before—from her huffiness with *Glowering Stranger* to her kisses with *Hunter*, who'd captured her against his chest so tightly that she'd felt his heart beating against hers. She'd experienced all the lovely, intense flutterings and shivers of physical attraction that she hadn't felt in longer than she could remember.

No, she hadn't expected to see him again. But she had expected to enjoy the memory of that crazy wonderful night for the rest of her life, like a chapter in a favorite book that she would re-read again and again.

And not in a million years would she have expected her hot cat-rescuer to be...

The enemy.

CHAPTER 5

ice one, universe, Aria thought. *I so appreciate being the butt of a cosmic joke. And by the way, those rainbows everyone oohs and ahhs about? Totally overrated.*

This was payback for leaping into Hunter's arms and kissing him like she was a starving woman and he was a big gooey piece of chocolate cake. Or like she was a woman who'd just eaten a substantial dinner, and he was still the cake.

Because…cake.

Steeling her spine, she lifted her head and looked him in the eye. He was watching her, his eyes dark and guarded.

"I need to ask you to leave, Mr. Armstrong." Somehow, she managed to keep her voice steady.

"Hunter." His mouth tightened. "I'd like to discuss our offer."

"I'm sure you would. I, however, want nothing to do with your *offer.*"

He folded his arms. With his wide stance and hard-set features, he looked like the epitome of a corporate tycoon who would stop at nothing to get what he wanted.

Who was she kidding? He *was* that corporate tycoon. Too bad for her and her hormones that she'd been so entranced by his hotness...okay, and the fact that he'd been good enough to chase after her cat in a storm...that she hadn't sensed the greed simmering in his blood. Or the fact that he was exactly the kind of man she needed to stay miles away from.

"Look." He held up one hand. "Last night was a...fluke. If we put it aside and approach this objectively, I'm sure we can come to an agreement."

Really?

"You want to *put aside* the fact that you kissed me." Her belly tensed as she fought back the visceral sensation of his arms locking around her.

"When discussing the contract, yes." His gaze slid to her lips, his eyes darkening. "It would complicate things."

Sharp disappointment stabbed her again. He was *that* kind of man. The kind who could shut down his emotions like turning off a faucet. The kind who compartmentalized his business and personal lives. The kind who approached things with rationality and cold objectivity.

"By all means, let's put the *fluke* of our encounter aside." Her tone grew icy. "In fact, let's pretend it didn't even happen. No need to mention it again. I still have no intention of discussing your offer."

"You didn't own this building when Imperial first offered a buyout a couple of years ago." He stepped closer. "But you should know that the current terms are infinitely more favorable and well over the fair market value of the property. You would easily be able to relocate somewhere with more foot traffic and a much better environment." He scanned the wall behind her and squinted at the shuttered door leading to the Cat Lounge. "A cat-themed café would go over well with the college crowd, I imagine. You could reopen over on Kensington Street."

"I've no intention of reopening anywhere else." Aria tightened her grip on the dishtowel. "I've worked very hard to establish the café right here."

His mouth twisted. "And how's business?"

"None of *your* business." She tossed her hair over her shoulder and folded her arms, matching his *I'm a tycoon* stance. "I said you need to leave."

"I heard what you said." He stepped closer, his broad shoulders blocking the view of the street. Suspicion gleamed in his eyes. "Where's the contract?"

She lifted her chin. "In the trash where it belongs."

"Did you read it?"

"Of course. My answer is still no."

He studied her for a long minute with that penetrating stare that made her want to squirm with discomfort.

"All of the other shop owners will vote to sell," Hunter said. "And if you don't, you'll be left on your own. When I have an eighty percent hold on this district, town law says I can force you to sell at less than the fair market value."

Aria's heart stuttered. She'd known she would be pushed into a corner, but could he legally make her sell?

"You can't *force* me to do anything, Mr. Armstrong. No one can."

He held up both hands, as if in surrender. She wasn't fooled. He didn't look as if he'd ever surrendered to anyone in his life.

"I've corresponded with most of the other owners on this street," he said. "They're more than ready to relocate or take an early retirement and say goodbye to the countless problems that come with owning an old property. Five have already agreed to sign the contract."

Ducking her head, Aria scrubbed at a spot on the counter. She hadn't known that several other owners had already committed.

Hunter must have intimidated or coerced them into agreeing. His good looks weren't that intoxicating. Okay, maybe they were, but most of her fellow store owners were well beyond the hormonal whiplash she was currently experiencing.

"They can't officially sign until the vote at the Mariposa Business Association meeting," he continued. "But I'm confident that they will."

Aria bit her lip. This was why he was in Bliss Cove—to sweet-talk people into selling or bulldoze them if they resisted. Either way, he hadn't come here to lose.

She didn't intend to lose either. Not anymore.

"Aria." Flattening his hands on the counter, he leaned in toward her. "Any property lawyer will tell you this is an excellent offer."

"I don't care what property lawyers will tell me."

"This street is dying," Hunter said. "Hell, it's already dead... and though you might have some success, I guarantee you it won't last. Especially when the other businesses start shutting down."

A knot of anxiety formed in her stomach. Much as she wanted to believe in herself and her decision, she knew he was right. It was all well and good to root for the underdog and to believe that heart and community would prevail over corporate greed, but money talked. Power was power. And men like Hunter Armstrong didn't give up.

However, she had the home field advantage. She owned this building and land. She'd known most of the other shop owners for years. She considered them friends. Her family had deep roots in Bliss Cove. She'd finally found something she was good at. So if anyone could go head-to-head with Imperial Properties and win, it was Aria Prescott.

At least, that was what the uplifting movie trailer playing in her head was saying.

"Mr. Armstrong—"

"Hunter."

"You need to leave. Now." Turning on her heel, she opened the door of the Cat Lounge to make a swift exit.

"I'll go," he said. "But we're not done here."

"Yes, we are."

"If you—" He stopped.

A plaintive meow echoed through the open door from the adjoining room. Aria started to close the door so the cats wouldn't escape. Hunter's gaze shot to the gray tabby poking his head out of the lounge.

"What's that?" he demanded.

"A cow." Aria bent to pick up the cat. She strode into the Cat Lounge, closing the door behind her, and pulled up the blinds on the glass door and the window separating the lounge from the front room.

Hunter stared into the lounge, where thirteen cats sashayed, jumped, lolled, and licked various body parts. He opened the door, his eyes narrowing.

"What are all these cats doing in here?"

Aria blinked, momentarily confused by the idiotic question. "This is a *cat* café."

She gestured to the logo above the register and all the feline decorations in the storefront. Had he not even bothered to look into what businesses he was trying to demolish?

"I thought that meant it was a cat-themed café. Not that you have actual live animals here." A deep V formed between his eyes. "How many are in here?"

"I usually have between twelve and fifteen total, depending on adoptions. Porkchop is one of them. Could you close the door, please?"

He stepped into the room and shut the door. "Adoptions?"

"All of the cats are available for adoption." Aria scratched Jumbo's ears and nuzzled the tabby's head. "That's one of the reasons I started the café. I was doing a lot of pet care and dog-walking, and my friend Sue over at the Rescue House shelter mentioned that they were getting overcrowded with cats. I'd heard of cat cafés in Japan, and I've worked for years at my mother's bakery over on Dandelion Street, so I looked into the logistics of opening a cat café here." She spread her arm out to indicate the lounge. "This building and this street turned out to be the perfect place for one."

Still frowning, he regarded the old, one-eyed cat crouched under a table. The cat glared at him through his single, slitted yellow eye, his torn ear quivering.

"That's Fang." Aria experienced a rush of defensiveness, in case Hunter was internally judging the cat's unfortunate appearance. "He's had a rough life."

"Having animals in a café has got to be a health code violation."

"Not when the cats are separated from the food service area. Guests can take food into the Cat Lounge, but they're two distinct areas."

"Why would anyone want to eat with a bunch of cats running around?"

Aria tried to hold on to her temper. She'd gotten the sense last night that he wasn't a fan of cats, but she'd also attributed that to the circumstances—cold rain, being "annoyed the crap out of," a defiant Porkchop—rather than a life philosophy.

But given the disapproval and faint disgust etching his strong features at the moment...Hunter was no friend of felines.

"This may be a foreign concept to you, but a lot of people love cats." She set Jumbo down and planted her hands on her hips. "Playing with them and just being around them can be very soothing and relaxing. And if a guest finds a cat they connect with, then I help facilitate the adoption process."

He peered at another cat who'd leapt onto a table. "There is no way this is sanitary."

"It's entirely sanitary. All of the cats have regular check-ups and vaccinations, and I keep the café in spotless condition. Guests are required to take off their shoes before entering the lounge...you are violating that policy, by the way...and are not allowed to share food and drinks with the cats."

"So Porkchop isn't actually your cat."

"He's an orphan who needs a forever home."

"A what?"

"A home with a loving, caring family where he can live happily for the rest of his life." She knelt to try and coax Fang out from under the sofa. The cat hissed at her. "All of the cats are looking for forever homes, and they'll stay here until they're adopted. I assure you I've done my due diligence and have my business license for this establishment. Everything is up to code."

"From what I hear, the building codes on Mariposa Street are a mess because no one knows how to handle modernizing old structures. And no thanks to small-town politics, half the shops on this block look like they haven't been inspected in decades."

"Small town doesn't equal stupid," Aria snapped. "But I'm starting to believe big city *does* equal arrogant asshole."

A humorless laugh escaped him. "Take the offer, Aria."

"No."

"You won't win." His eyes narrowed, twin flames of irritation rising in their green depths. "And if you end up selling at a loss, you won't have the money to reopen somewhere else."

"I don't intend to reopen somewhere else. I'm staying right here."

"You're making a mistake."

"Trust me." She lifted her chin in defiance. "I've already made my mistakes. Meow and Then is absolutely not one of them."

When he still didn't move, Aria ducked past him and strode to the door. Yanking it open, she gestured sharply to the porch. "Please go."

For an instant, he didn't move. She had the sense that he'd stand there forever until he got what he wanted. His hands fisted. A sharp, angry current arced between them.

He strode to the door and stopped in front of her, so close she could smell his aftershave, something deliciously masculine and rich, like bergamot and cloves. The opposite of his wind-and-rain scent from last night, but equally enticing. Her blood warmed, his proximity eliciting a pulse deep inside her.

Tightening her hand on the doorknob, Aria steeled herself against his potent effect. Everything had just changed drastically. Now she had to remind her body that being attracted to the man trying to rip her livelihood away was entirely *against the rules*.

"I believe I've made my position clear, Mr. Armstrong." She opened the door wider. "And once I make up my mind, nothing can change it."

"As you said," he slipped his gaze to her mouth, heat brewing in the depths of his dark eyes, "there's a first time for everything."

He strode past her in a rush of good-smelling air before stalking down Mariposa Street. No doubt to continue his invasion to conquer the rest of the shop owners.

Aria closed the door and pressed a hand to her chest. Her heart thumped heavily. Disappointment still seethed inside her, bitter and hot.

Well. That was that. She could still keep *The Escape of Porkchop* chapter in her heart, leafing through it whenever she needed a reminder of a cosmic joke.

Or a night that had left her warm and fuzzy in more ways than one.

With a sigh, she returned to writing the menu on the chalkboard. It was her own damned fault for not remembering that spontaneity was a bitch.

CHAPTER 6

A hundred curses blistered Hunter's brain. He pulled into a parking spot on Starfish Avenue near the Bliss Cove town hall. A three-person band was playing in the gazebo on the square, and the cheerful strains of a folk song drifted in the air.

It was a direct contrast to the heaviness in his chest. The anvil-like feeling had started the instant he realized honey-and-sunlight Aria was the Mariposa shop owner most opposed to Imperial's terms.

Of all the—

Shaking his head, he crossed the flagstone path of the square. The April sun burned through his suit jacket. It shouldn't matter who Aria was. It wasn't as if he'd thought he'd see her again. Last night had been a random encounter, one that had no bearing on his reasons for being in Bliss Cove in the first place.

He just had to stop thinking about her with her wet dress plastered to her body and the little stud in her nose glittering in the light. He had to banish the memory of how soft her lips had felt, how she'd tasted like cherries, and how perfectly her curves had fit right up against his chest. He had to ignore the fact that he'd dreamt about her last night.

All of that would only interfere in the negotiation he intended to win.

He needed twelve votes from the fifteen Mariposa owners. He'd already made the mistake of letting Aria get to him. When he was talking to her at the café, he'd forgotten every one of his long-ingrained business tactics. *Strategy, timing, planning, a level-headed approach.*

Instead, he'd struggled not to be distracted by the fire in her blue eyes and his intense urge to kiss her again. He'd let his frustration get the better of him. That never happened.

Not until now. Not until *her*.

Pushing an image of her out of his head, he walked into the town hall. The tile-floored front room had a curved reception/visitor's desk laden with brochures and flyers of local events. An older woman sat behind the desk, her attention on a novel displaying a half-naked couple on the cover.

Hunter stopped and cleared his throat.

"Hello. Can I help you?" She rose to her feet and adjusted her glasses. "I don't think I've seen you here before. I'd remember. Are you new to town?"

"I'm here on business. I need to look into the city health codes. Is there someone I can talk to?"

"Fred's not going to be in until ten. Dentist appointment." She shuffled out from behind the desk. "You're welcome to look through the code books if you'd like, though. Come with me."

He followed her to a small room where shelves overflowed with books, binders, and rolled-up plans and maps. He sighed. If this was the town's filing system, there was no chance they'd digitize their records any time soon.

After the woman pointed out the ordinances and regulations shelf, Hunter spent a frustrating hour looking for evidence of a violation. Not a single rule mentioned cats. Nothing forbade keeping animals in an eating establishment. As long as the food service area remained animal-free, the town didn't seem to care that Aria was serving sandwiches and coffee amidst hairballs and cat fur.

Grabbing his briefcase, he strode back into the main hall and headed for the doors.

"Don't forget to join us for the Artichoke Festival this weekend!" The receptionist waved a flyer at him. "Food, music, games, all sorts of things. The mayor is going to judge the pie contest."

Though Hunter had no interest in either artichokes or festivals, he skimmed the flyer. On the back was a list of participating local vendors.

Including the *Meow and Then Cat Café.*

He thanked the receptionist and stepped back outside. As he returned to his car, he recalled one of his most important business tactics.

Know your enemy.

And who was the enemy? Anyone who was an opposing force. Especially at a negotiating table.

In all of his property dealings, he made it a point to understand his competitors' strengths, weaknesses, and especially their motivations. He needed to know why they wanted what they wanted so he could formulate an effective attack strategy. He needed to understand as much as he could about them.

He tucked the flyer into his breast pocket. Every small town had at least *one person* who was an encyclopedia of town gossip. And if his instincts were right…

∼

"Mr. Armstrong, how lovely to see you!" Mrs. Higgins, innkeeper of the Outside Inn, hurried across the dining room to greet him.

A spry, white-haired older lady with twinkling blue eyes, she'd informed Hunter when he first arrived that she'd lived in Bliss Cove for forty years, had twice won the town's Best Tulip competition, considered NSYNC far superior to the Backstreet Boys, and would forever be #teampeeta.

"You're just in time for tea. I serve it every afternoon at four." She spread her hand out to indicate the round tables, all of which were empty aside from dingy chintz tablecloths and a variety of ceramic teapots. "I have a chocolate fudge cake and sugar cookies, and I'm serving a special oolong blend tea. I do hope you'll join us."

Suspecting that by "us," she meant, "me," Hunter nodded. "I would love to."

Thirty seconds later, he was seated at a table while Mrs. Higgins poured the tea and loaded a plate with a huge slice of cake and five cookies.

"Would you join me?" He indicated the empty seat across from him. "I hate to eat alone."

"Of course." Smoothing down her floral apron, she sat across from him. "I'm delighted you're staying for so long. Oh, I meant to tell you I have a room upstairs available, if you'd like to move. The Zinnia Room, overlooking the back garden. My dear Hank, God rest his soul, came up with the idea of calling it the Zinnia Room because zinnias are my favorite flower. He always used to line the front walk with zinnias for me in the summer."

She rested her chin in her hand, a wistful look crossing her face.

"Thank you, but the Rosebud Room is fine." He took a sip of the overly sweet tea and tried not to wince.

"Oh, but the TV." She shook her head, as if reminding herself that the TV in his room didn't work. "I'll have Jim bring you the TV from the Zinnia Room, at least."

"That's not necessary. I don't watch TV."

"Too busy working, hmm?"

"Something like that."

"Well, you just let me know if you change your mind." She

reached over to pat his arm. "I hope you don't work so much that you have no time to enjoy our little town."

"I plan to look around." He ate a few bites of a cookie. "I've heard a lot about the Spanish mission. Is that near the Mariposa district?"

"It's a couple of miles away, but it's a lovely walk." She picked up the teapot and filled his already full cup to the brim. "If you're in that part of town, be sure to stop at Ruby's Kitchen. Hank and I used to have a regular date night there every Friday. He had steak, and I always had their chicken pot pie. Then we'd go over to a movie at the Vitaphone, then when we'd treat ourselves to hot fudge sundaes at—"

Hunter cleared his throat. "Isn't the Vitaphone on Mariposa Street?"

"Yes." She pushed the plate of cookies closer to him. "Unfortunately, there's not much to see on Mariposa Street anymore, but some of the old architecture is lovely."

"Do you know anything about the cat café there?"

"Oh, of course. If you're a cat lover, you must visit Meow and Then. It's actually one of the few cat cafés in the entire United States. Aria has a great passion for helping animals."

Of course she does. That's why she was chasing an overweight cat through a storm.

"Aria?" He lifted his eyebrows inquiringly.

"Aria Prescott, the owner," Mrs. Higgins explained. "Lovely girl. Her family has lived here for years. I even remember when Eleanor and Gordon first moved to Bliss Cove."

Jackpot.

Hunter took a bite of cake. "This is delicious. Doesn't Eleanor own a bakery in town?"

"Sugar Joy, yes. I'm not surprised you've heard of it." She gave a little laugh. "Eleanor supplies all the baked goods for most town events. It's not a Bliss Cove party if Sugar Joy isn't involved."

"It sounds like a town institution."

"Oh, it is. It's hard to believe Eleanor ever considered closing it down, but she did." A frown curved her mouth. "She and her girls had a rough time after Gordon Prescott passed away. She came close to shutting down Sugar Joy, but they pulled through and have been doing very well this past year."

Hunter's shoulders tensed. "What happened to Gordon Prescott?"

"Car accident." Mrs. Higgins clicked her tongue and shook her head sadly. "Terrible, and so unexpected. Over a year and a half now. He was a professor at UC Santa Cruz for years...Greek and Latin languages or something like that...but he'd retired. Eleanor and the girls were devastated, of course. Callie...she's the oldest...was a rock in the aftermath, taking care of all the details and plans. Thankfully they had help at the bakery, a lovely young woman named Kate, and Rory moved back from San Jose to help out. She's one of those high-tech computer programmers or whatever, and her coming back was huge. Bit of a surprise that she's still here after all this time."

"What about Aria?"

"I'm not sure." Her forehead creased. "She moved away for a while after her father passed. We were so glad when she came back. She was always such a ray of sunshine. I was delighted when she opened the cat café. It's so *her*, you know?"

Yeah, he knew. Aria radiated an overall pleasure for life, so surrounding herself with people and animals would come naturally.

He struggled to deflect a pang of guilt. He had a job to do, both for himself and for the company. No way would he let Aria distract him, even if he couldn't stop himself from thinking about her in her tank top and torn jeans. She was so damned sexy that if he wasn't careful, she could make him forget they were adversaries.

"I've been thinking about changing the inn's *no animals* policy and adopting a cat from Aria." Mrs. Higgins pursed her lips in consideration. "Every inn should have a cat, don't you think? I'd have gotten one years ago, but poor Hank had allergies. Such a shame too because he was the most kind-hearted person and he would have just doted on a cat or a—"

"Mrs. Higgins, this was delicious." Hunter set his napkin down and pushed away from the table. "Thank you."

"My pleasure, Mr. Armstrong." She beamed at him. "I keep cookies on the sideboard all the time, so you just come help yourself whenever you'd like. I want guests to feel at home here."

Though the words *feel at home* failed to resonate with him, Hunter nodded his agreement. After thanking her again, he returned to the Rosebud room and pulled up a document on his laptop. He typed what he knew about Aria so far—parents, sisters, history.

He knew other things about her, too. Things no one else needed to tell him.

She has a laugh like a silver bell.

She likes "oat milk" lotion scented with lavender.

Her lips taste like cherries. Her body has curves in all the right places and her skin is smooth as honey.

Her kiss starts an inferno inside you. One that you have no idea how to put out.

Letting out his breath, he tossed the laptop onto the bed and stared out the window at the trail leading to Pelican Beach. All the sappy stuff had to go. He'd had some unexpected fun last night, but in the cold light of day, there was no time for *fun*.

He had a job to do, and he never failed. Especially when he had so much at stake.

By the time he was finished *getting to know* his opponent, he'd be able to write a damned book about her.

CHAPTER 7

*A*ria wove her way around the crowded tables of the rustic Mousehole Tavern, where she and her friends got together for drinks and gabbing most Friday nights. Lanterns decorated all the wooden tables, and a long bar curved through one side of the room.

Brooke, Destiny and Rory had already secured a booth near the massive stone fireplace dominating the wall opposite the bar.

"Is he kidding me with this?" Aria plunked herself next to Destiny and slammed her hand on the table.

"Is who kidding you with what?" Rory glanced at her, one eye still on the screen of her phone. "I cannot believe Grant still doesn't have this place wired for Wi-Fi."

"Hunter *Armstrong*. He's the Imperial VP trying to strong-arm all the Mariposa owners." Aria huffed out a breath, secretly pleased by her word play. "He thinks he can bribe us into selling our property to him. Well, I will not be bribed."

"Atta girl." Grant, the chestnut-haired, stubble-faced owner of the Mousehole, set Aria's usual mojito in front of her and extended his fist. "That complex will lead to a bunch of problems we don't want."

"Are you coming to the Mariposa Business Association meeting?" After bumping his fist with hers, Aria pulled the drink toward her. "Even though you're not officially in the district, I could use the support when the owners all vote."

"I'll be there." Grant set his hands on his hips and frowned. "I saw the plans for Oceanview. Automatic fountains and a skywalk? What the hell does a place like this need that for?"

"Grant, you're my hero." Aria smiled. Though Grant had only moved to Bliss Cove a few years ago, he'd established a large degree of influence and respect among the locals. If word spread that he was opposed to Oceanview, then people would pay attention. "Too bad you can't actually vote."

"If Grant were voting, he'd send up a smoke signal." Rory pushed a lock of long black hair over her shoulder and glanced at Grant, amusement flickering in her navy-blue eyes.

He folded his arms over his chest. "Last I heard, it's an old-fashioned paper and pencil ballot. Maybe you've heard of paper and pencil?"

"Maybe you've heard of Wi-Fi?" Rory slouched farther in her seat, her thumbs working swiftly over her phone. "Some customers would prefer bandwidth over your stupid singing fish."

She jutted her chin toward the mounted, robotic fish hanging behind the bar that sang "Love Me Tender" with the push of a button.

"By *some customers*, you mean *you*," Grant replied.

"I *mean* anyone who lives in the twenty-first century."

"Excuse me for interrupting, but we're hungry," Brooke announced with a roll of her eyes.

His gaze still on Rory, Grant took out his order pad. After they ordered, and he returned to the kitchen, Destiny patted Aria's arm.

"I'm certain Hunter is not as bad as you think," she said. "He doesn't have a negative aura."

"He hates cats," Aria said. "He thinks I'm violating a health code. He'll probably file a complaint. He's going to try and hard-ball me."

Oh, lord. She took another swallow of her drink as a flush heated her face. If she were a woman with a dirty mind—which sometimes she was—she could interpret that remark in all sorts of ways. Not the least of which involved Hunter hardballing her naked.

Yikes. Screeching, halting full stop.

"Regardless of what you think of Hunter personally, the contract is straightforward and solid." Destiny sipped her wine. "It's been reviewed by five different property lawyers."

Aria sniffed in derision. "Are they on Imperial's bankroll?"

"I can find out." Rory tapped the screen of her phone. "Or I can do a deep search on this Armstrong guy. See if he has any dirt you can use against him."

"Aurora." Destiny clicked her tongue. "Bad karma."

"Please. I've dealt with a lot of male crap in the tech industry." Rory set her phone aside. "I guarantee a man like Hunter Armstrong didn't get to where he is by playing nice."

Aria didn't doubt it, even if Hunter had been...well, sort of nice on the night of Porkchop's escape.

"I've done five different readings about this situation." Destiny sipped her wine. "They all point to a favorable future regardless of the outcome. Everything will work out."

"Thank you, Pollyanna." Aria set her glass down unnecessarily hard. While she usually appreciated Destiny's *mystical* approach to life, with the knowledge of what she was up against, she was in no mood to believe that the storm clouds gathering on the horizon were about to give way to a rainbow.

Not wanting the shadow of Hunter Armstrong to ruin their evening, she changed the topic of conversation to the upcoming Artichoke Festival. Grant arrived with their food, and they all began eating with murmurs of appreciation.

When Rory left the booth to get a refill of her drink, Aria slipped out of her seat and followed her sister to the bar.

"Hey, Rory, can you really do some digging on Hunter Armstrong?"

"Sure." Rory leaned her elbows on the bar as Grant set a glass in front of her. "There's a crap ton of stuff out there that's not indexed on regular search engines."

Aria bit her lip, deflecting a stab of guilt. "It's not illegal, is it?"

"No." Her sister took a sip of her drink. "Are you sure you want me to, though? Blackmailing isn't your style."

Aria frowned. "Why, because I'm so sweet and nice?"

"Well, yeah."

Smothering a groan, Aria poked her sister in the arm. "For your information, I can be ruthless. And in this case, maybe blackmailing is exactly my style."

Raising an eyebrow, Rory slanted her a glance. "You're *sure*."

"Why wouldn't I be?"

"Because you have a rather strong interest in him already."

A flush heated Aria's cheeks. She'd always been closer to Rory than Callie, whom she saw as another maternal figure—albeit one she could argue with more readily. As a teenager, she'd often confided in Rory about her loves and losses.

Though Rory was hardly an expert on relationships—always having preferred data over dating—Aria appreciated her sister's logical input.

But there was nothing logical about her twisty feelings for Hunter, which ran the spectrum from intense dislike to a throbbing attraction she couldn't escape. Their kisses were imprinted in her mind with indelible ink. She'd *dreamt* about him last night.

There was no way she could tell Rory about all that.

"Do the deep search," she told her sister. "And tell me everything you find out about him."

"Okay, then." Rory picked up her glass and headed back to the booth. "But be warned. Once you know something, you can't *unknow* it."

~

After dinner, Aria and Destiny walked back to Mariposa Street. As always, Aria's spirits rose at the sight of her café. In the window, Jumbo was peering out into the evening dusk, his tail twitching.

"I have something for you." Destiny dug around in her large beaded purse. She took out a hemp-cord necklace holding a red amethyst pendant. The streetlight glimmered on the rough, jagged edges of the raw crystal.

"Red amethyst bolsters your courage and heals your self-worth." Destiny fastened the necklace around Aria's neck. "You need a little extra help now."

"It's beautiful." Aria touched the crystal. "Thank you so much."

"You know I haven't made my decision about the contract yet." A shadow crossed Destiny's features. "I don't love the idea of a modern retail complex here, but at the same time, the money they're offering would allow me to relocate. I could never afford to do that right now. But whatever happens, I don't want it to come between us."

"Neither do I." Aria swallowed her fear that it very well could.

After hugging her friend goodbye, she entered the café. She fed the cats and picked up Jumbo before heading up the narrow staircase to her room.

Jumbo bounded onto the sofa and curled up on his favorite pillow. He was the only cat Aria would never give up for adoption. When she'd walked out on Steve, she'd had her suitcase in one hand and Jumbo in the other.

The cat had given her the courage to finally take the step she'd been too scared to take before. Jumbo had been at her side the entire time she was building her new life.

A life she had to protect.

She sat beside Jumbo and opened her old laptop. She typed *Hunter Armstrong* into a search engine and perused the results.

Her heart sank a little lower with every word she read. Of course, she'd known he was successful, but the *level* of his accomplishments surpassed what she had imagined. He'd earned his MBA at Harvard, then worked for several commercial real estate companies before landing an assistant position at Imperial Properties.

He'd skyrocketed up the Imperial Properties ladder by expanding the company's New York and Chicago holdings and spearheading billion-dollar complexes. He'd won countless awards and appeared on magazine lists of the "Top 25 Property Developers," "30 Under 30," and "Best Young Entrepreneurs."

In addition to numerous publicity photos, there were pictures of him—movie-star handsome in a designer tuxedo—at New York charity galas, theater openings, high-end parties hosted by editors and celebrities.

She opened a new browser window and searched social media sites. Compared to the public information available about him, he appeared to have no social media presence. There was also no mention in his official biographies or anywhere else about his family.

Against her better judgement, Aria typed *Steve Redmond* into the search box. His work profile as an investment banker showed up first, followed by numerous social media accounts.

She let out her breath. Not even Destiny knew what had gone down with the wealthy financial consultant who'd found her at her lowest point following her father's death.

The shock of the tragedy and a terrible argument with Callie over the money her father had set aside for her had caused all of Aria's past failures to crash around her. When she'd distanced herself from her mother and sisters, Steve had swept into the empty space in front of her.

After only a few weeks of knowing him, she'd *spontaneously* moved halfway across the country to live with him under the mistaken notion that she'd found security. Instead she'd started to lose whatever she had left of herself.

Aria quit the browser and closed her laptop. Jumbo pawed at her thigh. She set the computer aside and scratched his ears. He stretched out on her lap, his warm furry body vibrating with a purr.

She leaned her head against the back of the sofa, trying to suppress a rising sense of hopelessness. She'd needed to use everything she had to walk away from Steve.

And for all her determination, just standing her ground against a man like Hunter Armstrong wouldn't be enough. Not to mention, she had no idea how to counter Imperial's billions and their experience with properties all over the—

Manhattan. Tokyo. Chicago. Atlanta. Miami.

With that kind of portfolio, why was Hunter focusing on Bliss Cove?

CHAPTER 8

*W*hat was he supposed to do with her underwear?

As Hunter got ready for his jog the next morning, he caught sight of Aria's flimsy bra and torn dress still hanging in the bathroom. Yesterday, he'd figured he'd throw them away later, but now that he knew who she was...

Feeling both a little creepy and a lot clumsy, he folded her cotton dress and lacy lingerie and put them on a chair in a corner of the room. Returning them to her would be awkward, not to mention an unwelcome reminder of the other night.

A knock came at the door. He pulled it open to find Mrs. Higgins holding a plate of sugar-drenched French toast and a mug of something that unfortunately wasn't black coffee.

"Hot cocoa and special marshmallow-chocolate stuffed French toast with raspberry maple syrup." She pushed past him into the room. "I saw your light on, so I thought I'd bring you a complimentary breakfast since you missed it yesterday. A good breakfast is such an important start to the day."

Hunter sighed. He should've stayed at the motel out on the interstate, where eggs and black coffee took precedence over a sugar overload.

At the motel, he wouldn't have encountered a sexy firecracker chasing her cat through the rain, much less helped her out. He didn't need the distraction of her in his thoughts.

"Thank you, Mrs. Higgins." He held the door open in the hopes that she'd leave quickly.

"I see you're working." She placed the plate and mug on a table. "Do you need extra towels? Pillows? Blankets?"

"Everything is fine, thanks."

She lifted her eyebrows expectantly. He realized she was waiting for him to try the cocoa. He lifted the mug and took a swallow, barely managing to smile instead of grimace.

"Delicious."

Mrs. Higgins beamed. "I make it from scratch and add a dash of cinnamon. It was Hank's absolute favorite. We started serving it to guests over the holidays, but people loved it so much that we decided to serve it year-round with breakfast. Hank would always—"

"It's really delicious." Hunter forced himself to take another sip and indicated the door. "If you'll excuse me, I was heading out for a jog."

"Oh, of course." With a little wave, she started into the hall. "Dinner is at seven in the dining room. The chef is making her famous apple-baked ham. When Hank and I were—"

"Thank you, Mrs. Higgins." Hunter closed and locked the door.

He couldn't get out of this town fast enough.

As he was attaching his fitness tracker to his arm, his phone buzzed. Juliette Sinclair's name appeared on the screen. After a brief hesitation, he answered.

"I figured you'd be up already," she said. "Have you visited the district yet?"

"Yes, and I'm going over there again today." He tightened his grip on the phone, aware of a shift in the air between them. They'd always had a good professional relationship, and he considered her a friend, but he didn't know what to do with her implication last week that they should be *more*.

He'd played the field in his younger years and enjoyed the company of a lot of women, but the plan had always been to get married by the time he was thirty-five. Though the deadline was fast approaching, he hadn't yet found anyone he could imagine spending his life with.

But Juliette...she had all the qualities he was looking for, and she didn't seem to care that they wouldn't have any hearts and flowers. The issue was their business relationship.

On the one hand, she was right—they could be a powerful couple.

On the other hand, if it didn't work out, they'd have to navigate a minefield.

Hunter shook his head to dislodge the thoughts. He had more important things to focus on right now.

"I just emailed you the inspection reports for the Mariposa buildings," Juliette continued. "And new revisions on the Ocean-view drawings."

"I'll take a look later today."

"So what's it like there?" Amusement threaded her voice. "Have you gotten a shave at the barber shop? Bought penny candy at the general store? Chatted with Boss Hogg or that funny little deputy sheriff from the show with Andy Griffith?"

"The Andy Griffith Show."

"Barney Fife, right? Have you run into him?"

"Not yet." He wasn't about to tell her *who* he'd run into. He couldn't imagine two more opposite women than Juliette and Aria. "I gotta go, Juliette. I'll get back to you later today about the drawings."

Leaving his phone on the desk, he headed outside into the early morning air. After jogging the length of Starfish Avenue, he turned left and approached Mariposa Street. The district was an unfortunate blight in a perfect location. Every building would have to go. The plan was to construct the multi-level parking structure and build the complex out west toward the ocean.

Juliette had been right. It was a jewel—even if it was still a relatively small addition to the company portfolio. It was standard operating procedure for Imperial to keep plans under wraps until finances and contracts were secured, but there had to be a bigger picture for the Pacific Coast. Hunter made a mental note to ask Bruce again the next time they spoke.

He passed Meow and Then. The café was shuttered and dark, but a light glowed in a window on the second story.

Against his better judgement, Hunter stopped. A woman's silhouette passed in front of the window. Though he'd seen her in person exactly twice, he'd have known Aria's figure anywhere.

His heart was beating as if he'd just finished a five-mile run. That made no sense. His recovery heartrate was exceptional. It should have normalized within seconds of his slowing to a walk.

She sat down at a table in another window and lifted a coffee cup to her mouth.

Did she live here?

Unease twisted in his gut. Whatever old "charm" the district had, the state of disrepair combined with the surrounding vacant lots and forest...it couldn't be safe. Especially for a young woman living alone.

All the more reason she should sell. With the money Imperial was offering, she'd be able to afford moving to a nicer neighborhood. She could even have her own place in an apartment building instead of living above her café.

An overhead light shone on her face. Even from a distance, he saw the elegant lines of her profile. She tucked a lock of hair behind her ear.

What the hell was wrong with his heartbeat?

"Honey, you define the word *longing.*"

Hunter turned. Destiny, the new-age shop owner whom he'd

met briefly yesterday, was approaching her store with a takeout coffee.

"Excuse me?" Hunter said.

"Longing." Tossing the dangling end of a multicolored scarf over her shoulder, she stopped at the door of Moonbeams. "It's a yearning or a hunger for something or someone."

"I know what *longing* means." He'd gotten the sense that Destiny was something of a wingnut with her "energy crystals" and "intuitive readings," but she hadn't been opposed to the Imperial proposal. So he intended to stay on her good side.

"Every so often, I can read a person's energy, especially when it's as intense as yours." Destiny pulled a large keyring out of her flowered bag. "Usually that indicates a supreme imbalance in your psyche or a search for your One True Love."

Hunter managed not to roll his eyes. "Good to know."

"She told me you helped her rescue Porkchop." Destiny's lips curved. "It was no coincidence that you happened to be there right when she needed you."

Aria had told her friend about their cat chase? Interesting.

Destiny glanced at Aria's window. "She know you're watching her?"

"I'm not watching her. I was out for a run—" he indicated his fitness tracker, "—and I saw her light on. How long have you known her?"

"Since she was a teenager." Destiny pushed open her shop door. "She opened the café and turned the second floor into her living space about three months ago, after she moved back to Bliss Cove."

"Where was she before that?"

"Not my story to tell, honey."

"What is your story to tell?"

"About Aria?" She eyed him speculatively. "She puts her whole heart into everything she does. She has more backbone than she knows. And I'll tell you two extremely important things about her."

Every part of him went on alert. "What?"

"Her astrological sign is Cancer. And her spirit animal is the cat." She pursed her lips, nodded sagely and stepped into her store. "Live in the light, honey."

The door closed. Hunter shook his head, a humorless laugh erupting from his throat.

Astrology and spirit animals. *No coincidences.*

As if new-age crap would give him any further insight into Aria. He'd bet the cat spirits didn't know she wore pink flowered underwear.

~

After returning to the inn to shower, Hunter pulled on jeans and a T-shirt. Taking his laptop and car keys, he headed out again to the Sugar Joy Bakery on Dandelion Street.

"Morning. What can I get for you?" The young woman behind the counter straightened from sliding a basket of cookies into the glass display case.

One look at her face clinched Hunter's belief that this was still a family-run bakery. The woman was wearing a Grateful Dead T-shirt and bright red lipstick, and with her pale skin and long dark hair, she was the opposite of honey-like, summery Aria. However, her fine-boned features and thick-lashed eyes left no doubt that they were related.

"Chocolate-chip cookies are fresh out of the oven," she added.

"No, thanks." Hunter scanned the baked goods. "I'll have a blueberry muffin and a black coffee, please."

He dug into his pocket for his wallet and paid for the food.

"Have a seat, and I'll bring your food out to you." Aria's sister nodded toward the round tables.

He took a table by the window. If he were the kind of man

who liked cafés that served coffee in oversized earthenware mugs and had a shelf full of board games for customers, he'd have appreciated the homey atmosphere. Green plants flourished in colorful pots, people sat reading or talking in comfortable chairs, and bright paintings decorated the walls.

Nice for a small-town bakery, but he'd never understood how people could spend hours at a place like this. Didn't they get bored?

He opened a browser on his laptop. Though it was stupid, he typed "Astrological sign Cancer" into a search engine and studied the results.

Strongly connected to family and home. Ruled by the moon. Led by her emotions and heart. Guarded at first, but if you earn her trust, she'll be a lifelong loyal companion. Deeply erotic. Bonds passionately with one person.

Strengths: tenacious, imaginative, loyal, emotional.

Weaknesses: Moody, suspicious, insecure.

Yeah, well, he could have figured all that out on his own. Not to mention, most people exhibited those traits at one point or another. They weren't exclusive to Aria.

Deeply erotic.

Based on her responsiveness to his kiss, he already knew that.

"Here you go." The counter girl's voice sliced through his thoughts.

Hunter moved his laptop aside. She placed the muffin and coffee in front of him.

"Thanks." He took a swallow of the coffee. "I understand this place is a town institution."

"We've been here for twenty-five years, at least." She tucked her hands into her apron pockets. "My mother opened it when my sisters and I were kids."

"Hey, Rory, can you pack up two dozen cupcakes for me?" A woman in her early thirties dressed in a beige skirt and white blouse hurried through the front doors. "Some of my students are getting together for a study group, and I want to bring them a treat."

"Careful. You don't want to get a reputation for actually being nice." The dark-haired woman—Rory—returned to the counter and took a box from a shelf.

"I'm only doing it because they took the initiative to plan it on their own." The other woman, whom Hunter guessed was Aria's other sister Callie, started toward the wooden doors leading to the kitchen. "Is Mom here? I need to ask her about the roofing estimates she was supposed to get."

"She's doing payroll in the office." Rory began placing cupcakes in the box. "I'm sure she can handle the roofing estimates on her own."

"I just want to look them over." Callie disappeared into the kitchen, not catching Rory's eye-roll and heavy sigh.

Hunter pulled up Aria's document on his laptop and added information about the bakery and her sisters.

Okay. He could work with this. Aria had roots and family here. That would partially explain her attachment to the old district. Most of the other Mariposa building owners also had a history here, but they'd been around for a lot longer and were ready to move on. They also recognized that he was offering them something much better than what they had.

"Oh my god." The incredulous voice spilled into his veins like cherry syrup.

His heart kicked against his ribs. Slowly, he turned to find Aria standing at the wooden doors leading to the kitchen, her hands planted on her hips and her face darkened by a scowl that was a direct contrast to her flowy, rose-colored sundress.

"Are you stalking me?" she snapped.

Rory whipped her gaze toward Hunter, her features hardening. A few other customers glanced his way warily.

"Just having a coffee."

Aria's eyes flashed. She started toward him. Rory grabbed her arm and hissed something in a low tone. Aria whispered back, pulled her arm away, and strode to Hunter's table.

He remained seated so he'd appear less physically intimidating, but the closer she got, the heavier his heart pounded. By the time she was standing in front of him, his pulse was racing.

Even though he'd just seen her close-up yesterday, her beauty hit him with renewed force. Again, she wore no makeup aside from a lip gloss that made her mouth even more kissable. Her hair was pulled back into a messy knot, leaving little strands dangling over her bare shoulders that looked as if they tasted like cream.

He shifted, trying to ignore the heat pooling in his groin.

"Not for one second do I think it's a coincidence that you showed up at my mother's bakery the day after trying to bully me into selling my café." Aria folded her arms. The movement caused the bracelets on her wrists to clink together. "I heard you were looking into health code ordinances to see if I was violating any rules. Whatever other tactic you're planning to use to try and get to me, it won't work. In case you need me to repeat myself…"

She placed both hands on the table and leaned in close to him. His head filled with the scent of her, a thousand tropical summer aromas—coconuts, salt, oranges, sunshine.

"I. Am. Not. Selling. My. Café." Aria spoke through gritted teeth.

For the life of him, Hunter couldn't think of a retort. All he could do was think about how badly he wanted to slide his hand around her warm nape, pull her closer, and crush her pretty mouth with his again.

Hard, this time. More of the hot, open-mouthed kiss they'd shared on the sidewalk. He wanted to devour her, inhale her, eat her right up. Everything about her was so damned tempting.

"What's going on here?" Callie marched up behind her sister, her spine ramrod straight and her glare sharp enough to cut through an iceberg.

"None of your business." Aria whirled to frown at her sister. "I can handle it."

"Is that why I heard you all the way in the kitchen?"

"Would you please go away and let me take care of this?" Aria snapped.

Hunter shot his gaze to Rory, who was tapping her fingers impatiently on the glass counter as if she were poised to leap over it and enter the fray.

"I'm Callie Prescott." Callie stepped in front of Aria and extended her hand to him. "You appear to know my sister."

Somehow, he found his voice. "We've met."

"Mr. Armstrong is from Imperial Properties." Aria moved into her sister's space, her mouth compressing. "And Callie is a bossy professor who can't stand not being in control of everyone else's lives."

"Someone has to try and stop you from making colossal mistakes." Callie smiled thinly at Hunter. "I assume you're here to discuss the contract."

"Mr. Armstrong stopped by Meow and Then yesterday and attempted to intimidate...excuse me, *convince* me to sell my building to him." Aria grabbed Callie's arm and dragged her a few feet away. They started arguing in low voices.

"All right, break it up." Rory approached, pushing between her sparring sisters. "Back to your corners, both of you."

Callie and Aria stepped away from each other, their eyes shooting sparks.

"Look." Hunter rose to his feet. He loved a challenge, and he appreciated Aria's fire—hell, he liked it a lot—but he also wanted...*needed* her to understand the facts. "In three weeks, I'll have the votes of at least eighty, if not over ninety percent of the Mariposa Business Association owners. If you're the only hold-out, I'll then be legally allowed to make you an offer as low as thirty percent of what you paid for the building. Do you really want to be forced to sell at that kind of a loss? Especially while knowing what kind of profit you refused?"

Callie started to speak. Rory pinched her arm.

"Of course not." Wariness darkened Aria's expression before she lifted her chin in defiance. "But I won't find myself in that position because despite your arrogance, I'm here to tell you that you *won't* convince my fellow business owners to sell. I've known those people much longer than you have, and I sure as hell know them *better*. They believe in Mariposa Street as much as I do, and they're not going to see it torn down to make way for a bunch of stupid high-rise condos and offices."

"What do they want done in that district, then?" Hunter crossed his arms, his shoulders tensing. "What do *you* want? The numbers speak for themselves. Mariposa Street has been in a steady decline for years. The vacancy rate is at an all-time high. You're the first person to have opened a new business there in well over two years. The thread is about to snap, sooner rather than later, and then what? What's your plan for turning things around?"

"Do you seriously think I'd tell you the first thing about my plan?" she replied crisply. "Everyone knows you don't show your hand to your opponent. You may think I'm a naïve small-town girl who doesn't know the first thing about property development, but I've done my research. You've built multi-billion-dollar centers in cities like New York and Tokyo. The Oceanview Plaza would be Bliss Cove's first and *only* high-rise complex, but it's easily one of Imperial's smallest developments. So why did our little town catch your eye, Mr. Armstrong?"

Great question.

When he opened his mouth to respond, she shot her hand out, palm up.

"On second thought, don't answer that. I'm not interested in a bunch of bullshit about economic growth and increased revenue. The fact is that your *plaza* will destroy an integral part of this

town's history and create an industrial blight leading to pollu-
tion, gridlock, congestion, and a terrible environmental impact
on the redwood forest and beaches. Would you like to ask me
again why I will never sell my building to you?"

"Go, girl!" shouted a gray-haired man wearing a bandana and
torn T-shirt. He rose to his feet and applauded along with several
other customers.

"What's the alternative?" called a woman standing near the
counter. "I'm sick of paying taxes for that part of town. It's
brought us nothing but trouble for over thirty years. I say it's
about time we get rid of it and do something useful there."

"Hear hear!" Another man clapped in support.

"What in the world is all this noise?" A woman in her sixties
flew out from the kitchen, wiping her hands on a dishrag. With
short blond hair and elegant features, she was an older version
of Aria.

Callie hurried forward. "Mom, don't get upset."

"It's just a minor debate." Rory shot Aria a warning look.

"The town hall is a far better place for debates." Mrs.
Prescott's glare swept over both Aria and Hunter. "Rory, grab
that tray of fresh croissants from the back. Complimentary
coffee and a croissant for everyone. I apologize for the
disturbance."

Murmurs of surprised pleasure rose from the customers as
they settled back down at their tables. Callie and Rory began
quickly distributing the coffee and pastries.

Mrs. Prescott approached Aria, concern darkening her eyes.
"Are you all right?"

"Yes." Aria sighed and indicated Hunter with a grudging
thrust of her chin. "Mom, this is Hunter Armstrong from Imperial Properties. Mr. Armstrong, my mother Eleanor Prescott."

"Hunter, please." He extended a hand, somewhat relieved
when Eleanor chose to shake his hand rather than slap him.

"Mr. Armstrong and I are on opposing sides of an issue," Aria added, tossing him a scowl that was the visual equivalent of a slap.

"So I see." Eleanor flung the dishtowel over her shoulder and flicked her gaze from Hunter back to her daughter. "I'm entirely in favor of healthy debate, but not when it disrupts my bakery."

Aria looked at the floor, a shadow passing over her face. Hunter picked up his laptop and tucked it under his arm.

"It's my fault, Mrs. Prescott. I apologize. I won't bother you or Aria here again."

"Everyone is welcome at Sugar Joy, Mr. Armstrong. We don't discriminate." Eleanor lifted her chin in a way that was so like her daughter's that he was mildly startled. "I just ask that you keep your visits civil and respectful."

She looked pointedly at Aria, encompassing her in that statement. Aria spun on her heel and stalked back to the kitchen, her back stiff.

Hunter muttered another apology and left the café, certain he'd just hurt his cause with that exchange. Arguing with the town sweetheart in public wasn't going to win him any points with the locals.

He strode back to his car. Time to lock this down. The other Mariposa owners were all so close to capitulating that it wouldn't take much to push them over the edge. When Aria was the only one left standing, she'd have to surrender.

No, he didn't like the idea of forcing her hand, but she left him no choice. And he'd do well to remember another important credo of business.

Keep emotions out of it.

Especially his feelings about a woman who was making his heart beat again.

CHAPTER 9

*P*lan. What was her *plan?*

Hunter's question rang in Aria's ears for the rest of the day. Truth be told, aside from a vague notion of drumming up community support, she didn't have anything remotely resembling a plan. All she had was indignation and an uplifting movie trailer in her head.

Based on the papers and reports she'd seen on Hunter's desk at the Outside Inn—he had a dozen *plans*, all backed up with measurements and data. He'd probably been born with a plan in mind. He'd be eating solid food at six months, walking by nine months, enter an accelerated kindergarten program to prepare himself for Harvard...

With a snort of amusement, she closed up the café and drove to her mother's house. She'd struggled with plans her entire life. And though she didn't like the idea of taking a page out of Hunter's book, she couldn't just huff and puff about the negative impact of Oceanview Plaza. She also had to *do* something practical.

She steeled her spine as she entered her childhood home. Though she'd considered begging off their weekly dinner, she also had to stand her ground against her family. Her mother and sisters were in the kitchen, which smelled deliciously of chili and cornbread.

After greeting them, Aria settled on a stool at the kitchen counter as her mother scolded her for how she'd handled Hunter's appearance at Sugar Joy that morning.

"Mom, he's trying to push me out of a building I own." Aria gratefully accepted a full glass of wine from Rory. "I'm sure as heck not going to be polite to him."

Callie vigorously stirred the pot of chili on the stove. "Your confrontational approach is no way to get him to see your point of view."

"Thanks, professor." Aria eyed her oldest sister. Callie would have been a fantastic pioneer woman, all straight-backed, hard-working, butter-churning forcefulness. "You've made it clear you're on Hunter Armstrong's side."

"It's not a question of *sides*." Impatience edged Callie's tone. She set the wooden spoon down and grabbed a towel. "Given the state of Mariposa Street *and* your café, you should consider his offer. Getting angry with him won't make him back down."

"Just the opposite." Rory arched an eyebrow. "A man like him will fight fire with an inferno."

Aria clucked in irritation and took a healthy swallow of wine so she wouldn't have to admit that her sisters were right. Like they'd been her entire life.

But what was her alternative with Hunter? Despite what had happened between them, she couldn't befriend him. She certainly wouldn't try and use the *Rescue of Porkchop* night in an attempt to sweet-talk him into agreeing with her—and they weren't going to bring it up anyway. All she had was her hope of rallying the Mariposa owners to her cause.

What's your plan for turning things around?

His question poked at her again.

"Has the town ever allocated funds to renovate Mariposa

Street?" Rory picked up an oven mitt and took a batch of cornbread muffins out of the oven.

"A long time ago," Eleanor said. "But after the fishing company shut down and the economy went downhill, the town council rightly diverted funds to schools and downtown initiatives. They had to close the Historical Preservation Society. Businesses started moving away from Mariposa, so there was less and less reason to preserve it."

"Now it would cost a fortune to renovate." Callie stepped aside so Rory could set the muffins on the counter. "To stay alive, a historic neighborhood needs financial and community support."

"That's what I need to do for Mariposa." Aria lifted her head, a faint spark of hope lighting inside her. "I can drum up support with a petition to present to the town council and to the Mariposa Business Association. If the other owners know how many residents are against the construction, they'll be a lot more likely to vote no on signing their contracts. I can start a fundraiser too."

There. A plan.

She glanced at Callie, but her sister was at the sink, her back turned.

"I'll donate to the fund," Rory said. "And sign the petition."

Aria shot her a grateful smile.

"I will too, of course." Eleanor took the chili pot into the dining room. "Rory, bring the wine in, please."

Rory grabbed the bottle of wine and followed her.

"You think I'm being foolish." Aria looked at Callie, unable to keep the hurt note from her voice. "Like I always am."

"I just don't see why you think this will be any different from all your previous ventures." Callie tossed the spoon into the sink, her mouth tightening. "A fundraiser is fine and good, but you're going up against a company that puts billions of dollars into their projects."

"I *know*." Frustration gripped Aria. "But I have to start somewhere, don't I? I have to do *something*. Or Hunter Armstrong is just going to railroad over the whole district."

"I really don't think he's trying to railroad over anything." Callie rubbed her temple and sighed. "Have you even *thought* about what he told you this morning? He made some excellent points. Your café would get a lot more traffic if you were in another location."

"You think I don't know that?"

"Then why are you fighting him so hard?" Callie threw her hands up in exasperation. "Why are you being so stubborn? Even if you win the vote, you'll still have to struggle to keep your business going. It's not as if winning means Mariposa will suddenly have a bounty of revenue and support."

"That's why I need to convince the town council to make renovation a priority." Aria pushed herself off the stool and faced her sister. "And before you start telling me how amazing the Imperial deal is, I've crunched the numbers. If I relocate, I'd have to pay commercial rent, and the Imperial money won't last long. Plus I'd need to find a place with a very specific configuration so I wouldn't be violating any health codes. The chances of there being *the* rental space available in a high-traffic area right now are pretty slim."

She spread her arms out. "If I couldn't find something turnkey, I'd have to use the money to refurbish a space, possibly even involving construction, and I have no idea how long it would take for me to open again. Not to mention, I'd need to rent an apartment, which means another drain on my so-called profit. So don't tell me that taking his offer will suddenly prevent me from *struggling* because it won't."

Callie opened her mouth, but Aria held up a hand to stop her sister's words. Which she knew Rory and her mother would echo.

"I know you'd help me out." Her chest constricted. She'd lost track of the number of times her sister had bailed her out of one bad decision or another. "You've done it my whole life. I've never deserved it, and I've always been grateful. And you've made it abundantly clear that you think my café was a bad idea from the start, but I'm doing this on my own. If I fail and get forced out of my building, then it's all on me. You can say *I told you so*, but you won't lose anything."

Callie stared at her. A shadow darkened her expression.

"Aria, don't you..." She paused, her throat working with a swallow. "Don't you know by now that when you lose, *I* lose?"

Tension stretched the air. Breaking her gaze, Callie turned and strode into the dining room.

Aria lowered her head. Tears stung her eyes.

Brilliant overachiever Callie always won. Scholarships, awards, tenure-track position at the college. *Losing* was Aria's domain. And if she lost the Mariposa Street battle, she'd not only disappoint herself, she would again be her sister's only failure.

CHAPTER 10

"I'm sorry, Aria." Lois Howell took off her glasses and let them dangle on the gold chain around her neck. The florist shop was redolent with the fragrance of fresh-cut spring flowers, though only a few bouquets decorated the shelves. "I appreciate everything you're doing, but Ray and I have been running this place for thirty years."

"Exactly!" Aria reached across the counter and grasped the older woman's hand.

Though she'd only been petitioning since yesterday afternoon, eight of the ten signatures she'd collected had all come from Meow and Then customers. Plus, herself and Grant from the Mousehole Tavern. She hadn't been able to convince a single Mariposa owner to sign.

"Thirty years," she told Lois. "The Bloom Room is your legacy. How can you stand the idea of selling it to a corporation that will bring out the wrecking ball the instant you sign on the dotted line?"

"Your dedication is admirable." Lois smiled and patted Aria on the cheek. "However, times change. As much as I love this old building, it's become an albatross we're ready to turn over to someone else. And it would cost a fortune to renovate the whole street."

"That's why I've started the Mariposa Renovation Fund." Aria extended a flyer on which she'd written the details of her fundraising plan. "All proceeds will go toward renovation and revitalization."

"How much have you raised so far?"

"Two hundred and six dollars and forty-three cents." Aria tightened her grip when Lois shook her head affectionately. "I've just gotten started. We *can* raise enough money to save Mariposa, but only if we stand together."

"I love your passion, but our minds are made up." Lois released Aria's hand and picked up a pair of shears. "Ray and I don't want to be forced to close The Bloom Room, so this is a great opportunity for us. Did I tell you we're going on a Caribbean cruise? Our first one."

Aria stepped away from the counter in defeat. "That sounds great."

"Don't be disappointed about this, dear." Lois turned to head into the backroom. "It's time to move forward. This is just part of the town's evolution."

To what? Aria thought bitterly. An overdeveloped city with high-rise buildings blocking the expansive views of the rocky Pacific coastline and the redwood forests?

She knew about moving forward—they'd all had to do that after Dad died—but that didn't mean forgetting all the things you cherished about the past. Just the opposite. People, places, photos, songs, memories...everything was woven into your being. You took the past with you when you moved forward.

Clutching her clipboard to her chest, she continued down Mariposa. The bright morning sun shone on the cracked cobblestones and old windows. A Metalworks Hardware truck was the only vehicle parked on the street. Across from the café, Destiny stood in the doorway of Moonbeams with a cup of coffee.

"Morning, honey." She lifted the cup. "Have time to join me?"

"No, but thanks. I noticed yesterday that Porkchop has been limping, and Max is coming over to check on him." Aria approached her friend. "Sounds like Lois and Ray are planning to sell."

"That's what I heard too." Destiny's lipsticked mouth twisted as she glanced a few doors down, where Hunter had stopped to talk to Gary, the Corner Store owner.

Ignoring the awareness bolting through her, Aria narrowed her gaze on the two men as they paused to speak. Hunter had forgone his tailored suit today, opting instead for dark khakis and a navy button-down that fit beautifully over his broad shoulders. He held a tablet out for Gary to see and spread his hand toward the street, likely telling the other man how they were going to tear everything down.

The men shook hands. Aria's chest tightened. Hunter crossed the street to the florist shop and disappeared inside.

"Morning, Joe!" Destiny waved toward the tall man wearing jeans, a T-shirt, and a tool belt who exited one of the closed shops halfway down the street.

He gave a short nod in her direction before disappearing behind the Metalworks Hardware truck.

Destiny let out a gusty sigh. "Am I coming on too strong?"

"Saying hello to someone is hardly coming on strong." Aria smiled sympathetically. "He still hasn't asked you out?"

"Honey, aside from saying hello, he barely glances my way." Destiny took a sip of coffee, pursing her lips. "I don't get it. You remember when he fixed my leaky roof last winter? I happened to have a pot of soup on the stove, so I invited him to stay for dinner. The man gobbled down two bowls full, but when I casually said, 'We should do this again sometime,' he looked as if I'd suggested we get naked and dance the tango."

"Are you sure you didn't actually suggest that?" Aria nudged her friend in the side.

Destiny *tsked*, even as a gleam appeared in her eyes. "Maybe I need to go to those lengths to get his attention." She fiddled with one of her dangly earrings. "You think I'm too much for him? Maybe he's scared of me."

"Then he's not the man for you."

"I wish he'd give me the chance to figure that out for myself." Destiny nodded toward an approaching van, the sides emblazoned with *All Critters Pet Clinic and Hospital*. "Looks like hot doc is here. Hey, have you ever considered going out with him? You've known each other long enough."

"That's kind of the problem." Aria watched as the driver parked the van a few stores down from Meow and Then. "We went on a couple of dates years ago, but it ended up being just two old friends hanging out. Besides, it's tough to feel romantic about a man who ate paste in kindergarten and who knows that you once considered getting a Justin Bieber tattoo."

"Yeah, don't lead with that." Destiny grinned and turned back to her shop. "I'll do an Oracle card reading on him and figure out who would be a good match. A man like that is just oozing One True Love energy."

Amused, Aria headed across the street, where Max Weatherford was taking his bag out of the passenger seat. With thick blond hair and striking green eyes, the tall, handsome veterinarian had operated Bliss Cove's only animal clinic for the past ten years.

"Hey, Aria." He closed the door and extended his arm to give her a quick squeeze. "Sorry I couldn't get over here yesterday. How's your patient?"

"He's been limping since yesterday, but he's been eating well… of course…and doesn't seem to be in much pain." Aria unlocked the café door. "I was able to check his paw and couldn't see a visible injury, but I'm worried about the limp. I didn't notice it when I brought him back home after his little escapade, so I can't tell if it happened that night or since."

"Hmm. Might have gotten more inflamed over the past few days."

After tossing his hoodie onto the coat rack, Max followed her into the lounge. Several cats swarmed toward him as if he were a magnet. He crouched, extending his hand and murmuring to them in a low voice.

Aria coaxed Porkchop out from underneath a chair and brought him over to Max. He sat on the sofa to check the cat's paw and sore leg.

"It's a little swollen, but not too bad." He pressed the cat's joint, and Porkchop tensed and squirmed. "I'll take him in for an X-ray. I doubt he'll need a splint, just some rest. You said in your text that he escaped?"

"Monday night." Aria flushed and scratched Porkchop's ears. "I feel terrible. I was taking out the trash, and I didn't close the door all the way. He just darted right out. Thankfully he was the only one who did."

"Where did he go?" Max stood, holding the hefty cat in his arms.

"All the way to Pelican Beach." Aria brought Porkchop's crate from the storage room. "It was raining, and a clap of thunder scared him. He got his leg stuck in a pile of seaweed. That was the only way we were able to catch him."

"Who's *we*?"

Aria's heart stuttered. "Uh, a guy who ended up helping me."

Max touched the cat's leg again. "Is this the leg that got stuck?"

"I think so, but I'm not entirely sure. It was dark and pouring rain, so I couldn't see very well. Hold on, let me get some tuna or Porkchop will fight you."

After putting the tuna into the crate, Max slipped the more docile cat in and closed the door. "How's Fang?"

"The same." Aria bent to look at the old cat who was huddled under a chair. A scar crossed his closed left eyelid, which concealed his empty eye socket.

Of all the cats she'd fostered, Fang was the one who made her heart ache the most. Two months after she'd taken him in, he was still wary and defensive, prone to cowering when people got too close. He never let anyone pick him up and spent most of his time crouched in hideaways or under the sofa.

"He hasn't had issues with the other cats." She clicked her fingers at Fang, but the cat only glared at her. "But he's been scared of the few customers I've had. I'm not sure I can keep him much longer, especially if he starts getting hostile."

"I'll ask around some more, see if any of my clients would be willing to take him." Max carried the crate into the front room. "I'll bring Porkchop back tomorrow."

"I can pick him up, so you don't have to make the trip."

"I have some house-calls to make anyway, so it's not a problem. Should be some time in the afternoon."

"I'll be here." Aria closed the lounge door behind her. "Do you have time for a coffee and one of Mom's cookies?"

"I wish I did." Max pulled on his hoodie. "Unfortunately, I have a full schedule this morning."

"Thank you so much for stopping by." She stepped closer to embrace him. As she closed her arms around him, she saw a large male figure coming up the steps of the café.

Her heart crashed against her ribs. Over Max's shoulder, Hunter's gaze collided with hers. His expression darkened.

Shit.

She backed away from Max, all of her defenses slamming into place. His forehead creased quizzically at her sudden withdrawal. Hunter opened the door, his broad frame almost blocking the doorway.

Though just the sight of him shot heat down her spine, Aria forced a cold note into her voice. "What do you want?"

"To talk to you." He glanced from her to Max, his jaw tight.

"Funny. I don't want to talk to you."

Hunter held up a folder. "Just some revised plans, that's all."

"Not interested."

"I'll leave them here." He set the folder on the counter, moving almost deliberately closer to her.

Aria's insides tightened. She could practically feel his body heat, even though a good three feet still separated them.

The cat began mewling in little bursts. Hunter's gaze went to the enclosed crate. "Is that Porkchop?"

Max lifted his eyebrows. "You know him?"

"We met the other night." Hunter bent to peer through the grated door. "Where's he going?"

"He hurt his leg," Aria admitted grudgingly. "Max is a vet, and he's taking Porkchop to his clinic for an X-ray." Aware of Max's growing curiosity, she added, "Max, this is Hunter Armstrong of Imperial Properties. He helped me rescue Porkchop."

The two men exchanged abrupt nods of acknowledgement.

Hunter straightened. "Did his injury happen the other night?"

"I think so," Aria said. "He might have sprained his leg, but he didn't start limping until yesterday."

"I don't think it's anything serious," Max added, "but I'll give him a full exam at the clinic. Good of you to have helped Aria out."

Hunter nodded. His phone buzzed. Pulling it from his pocket, he settled his gaze on Aria. "We'll talk later."

"We have nothing to talk about."

"Then I'll talk. You can be quiet and listen."

Before she could respond, he left the café. The door shut behind him.

"Damn." Max whistled into the sudden silence. "Territorial bastard."

Aria swung her gaze to him. "What?"

"The vibe he was throwing off." Max picked up Porkchop's

crate and started toward the door. "Threatening and territorial. Staking his claim on you."

"What the...I am not a *parcel of land*."

He shrugged. "Men stake claims on women, whether they like it or not."

"What are you talking about?" Aria followed him outside, her skin heating at the idea of Hunter *claiming* her. "The only claim he wants to stake is on Mariposa. Not me."

"He wants both." Max set the crate into the van and closed the door.

"And you know this how?" Aria stopped on the sidewalk, fisting her hands on her hips. "Through some macho male telepathy?"

"A guy acts like that around a girl, no telepathy needed. Situation understood." Max walked to the driver's side and pulled out his keys. "The problem is that women are never as transparent. That's why you always keep us guessing."

"You're being ridiculous." She couldn't help glancing in the direction Hunter had gone.

Territorial? No way.

"I'll text you before I drop Porkchop off tomorrow." Max climbed into the driver's seat. "Good luck keeping that dude away from you. As far as he's concerned, he's NASA, and you're the moon."

He winked and drove off.

CHAPTER 11

For the rest of the week, Aria couldn't get Max's remarks out of her head, even as she realized that, of course, she wouldn't be able to keep Hunter away from her. How else would he try and intimidate her, if not with his decidedly *physical* presence?

Not that she would be intimidated.

In-between running the café, she spent her time going door-to-door with her petition and donation requests. On Saturday morning, she woke early to get ready and load up the cats for their day at the Artichoke Festival. After showering and slipping into a cream-colored sundress and cardigan, she went into the tiny kitchen to have coffee and cereal.

As she rolled up the window shade, she caught sight of a man jogging toward Mariposa Street. Her breath caught.

Not *a* man. Big strong Hunter Armstrong who'd supposedly looked at her as if he intended to plant his flag right inside her.

On her. Right *on* her.

Heat prickled her skin. She couldn't take her eyes off him. His performance T-shirt clung to his chest, and even from the distance, she saw the exertion lacing his body. He ran with an easy, masculine grace, thumping his feet hard on every cobble-stone as if he were securing them in place.

Or *claiming* them.

As he passed her building, he glanced up at her in the window. A sharp current of electricity crackled between them. She ducked back against the wall, her heart pounding. Did he know she lived here? Had he jogged around the area before now?

Despite her attraction to him, Aria knew Hunter had *tactics* and *strategies*. He was a crazy successful developer who had all kinds of tricks up his sleeve. She couldn't let his hotness or his territorialism or anything else get past her guard.

She waited to ensure he was gone before she went downstairs to corral the cats into their crates. By the time she got to Wild-wood Park, the festival had already started. People wandered around the food booths, played games, and listened to the ten-piece band on the main stage. Along with the strains of "Love Me Do," the smells of fried artichokes, burgers, and tacos drifted through the air.

Aria set up her booth and the cat enclosure before letting the cats out onto the grass. They quickly started prowling around, enjoying the sunshine and attention from all the passers-by.

She eased Jumbo out of his crate and fastened a little sign around his collar reading *I'm Taken, Sorry!* before setting him in the enclosure. He bumped his head against her hand, insisting on an ear-scratch before he went off to join the others.

After ensuring that the cats had enough food and water, she went to the folding table where she'd set up signs for both the cat adoptions and the petition against Imperial's proposed develop-ment. She spent the next couple of hours chatting with people who stopped at her booth.

"Here you go." Brooke bounded up, her camera slung over one shoulder. She extended a smoothie and paper-wrapped straw toward Aria. "Mango-peach."

"Thanks so much." Aria unwrapped the straw and stuck it in the cup.

Brooke pulled the lens cap off her camera and stepped back to take a photo of Aria's booth. "Any adoptions yet?"

"One application, and several other interested parties. They liked the donation idea too." Aria indicated the poster board advertising that fifty percent of the adoption fee would be donated to the Mariposa Renovation Fund.

"How's the fundraising going so far?"

Aria peered into the jar where she was collecting donations. "Looks like a good fifty bucks. If I add that to the money I've already raised, I might be over four hundred."

"Not bad considering you just started this week." Brooke scrolled on her phone. "When's the Mariposa Business Association meeting? Gramps wants me to cover it. He says the vote will be historic."

"April thirtieth."

"Will Hunter Armstrong be there?"

"That meeting is the only reason he's in town. He probably has a whole speech planned."

"But remember you have a personal stake in Mariposa, and you're friends with the people who live there. No matter how much money Armstrong has, he can't buy loyalty."

Though Aria's heart filled with gratitude toward her friend, Brooke's pep talk wasn't enough. Hunter didn't need to buy loyalty. He just wanted to buy up the entire Mariposa district. For most people, all that might take was the right price.

"Is that Sam?" Brooke squinted at a tall, scruffy man wearing jeans and a plaid shirt, who was ambling down the midway with a paper tray of fried artichokes. "I thought he turned to ash in direct sunlight."

Aria chuckled and waved at the reclusive bookstore owner. "Hey, Sam! Interested in a feline companion? Half the adoption fee goes to the Mariposa Renovation Fund. Or you can just make a donation."

Setting down his food, Sam dug into his pocket for his wallet. "How much do you need to raise?"

"A lot." Aria twisted her mouth ruefully. "Bliss Cove used to have a Historical Preservation Society, but it was dismantled years back because of budget cuts. We can use all the support we can get."

Sam emptied his wallet of bills and stuffed them into the donation jar, then scrawled his name on the petition. "I'll take some flyers to put up at the bookstore."

Tucking the flyers under his arm, he slouched off toward another food booth. Aria nudged Brooke, who was watching him go.

"Enjoying the view?" she teased.

"Are you kidding me?" Color rose to Brooke's cheeks. "Sam? I mean, I guess if I were forced to admit it, I'd say he would be kind of hot if he tried, but not only does he not try *at all*, he's the most anti-social person I've ever met. Why does he own a bookstore? He doesn't even keep regular hours there. And what does he do in his off-hours? I never see him around town. He could be living a double life, like a vampire or a serial killer."

Aria grinned. "Not that you've given him much thought."

"Right." Brooke adjusted her baseball cap and straightened her shoulders. "I've got far better things to do, like write an opinion piece about creamed versus steamed artichokes. You want me to bring you anything else?"

"No, I'm good. Dinner tomorrow night?"

"Sure. Text me." With a wave, Brooke headed off, her camera at the ready.

Aria went to the cat enclosure, which was protected from the sun by a grove of leafy trees. She checked the food and water dishes, chatted with people who stopped by to play with the cats, and handed out adoption applications.

By the time the festival started winding down around five, she was tired and sunburned, but thrilled to have applications for five of her feline orphans. The crowd began drifting away from Wildwood Park as vendors dismantled their booths.

Aria boxed up the remaining flyers and the table signs. Her folding table was unfortunately old and warped, the metal underside coated with sticky rust. With a grunt, she shoved the whole table upside down and struggled to push the legs into the slots.

"You need help."

The deep male voice skimmed over her arms, eliciting a little shiver. She'd expected Hunter to show up at the festival—he wouldn't miss the chance to ingratiate himself with other residents—but she'd figured he would have left by now.

She straightened and turned to face him. Her insides fluttered and tensed. How did he manage to be so strikingly gorgeous *every time* she saw him, whether he was wearing an Armani suit or jeans? At the moment, he was in cargo shorts and a forest-green T-shirt that clung to his broad shoulders and made his thick-lashed eyes even more brilliant.

As if his threats weren't bad enough, he had to have a *presence* that made her body react in totally inappropriate ways.

"I do not need help." Pulling her gaze from him, she shoved at the table leg again. It didn't budge, which only intensified her bitchiness. "Are you talking about your grandiose Oceanview plans to anyone who will listen?"

"Actually, I came here to sample the artichoke ice cream, which I didn't know was a thing until now." His mouth twisted. "Can't say I was happy to discover it."

"Bet it wasn't happy to discover you either." Aria gave the table leg another futile push. "Who knew I had so much in common with artichoke ice cream?"

"If you keep trying to force that, you're going to get hurt." He stalked toward her and bent to push one of the steel rings farther away from the bracket. "You need to put pressure on the hinge first."

"I know how to fold my own table, thank you." Aria barely resisted the urge to shove him out of the way.

"Do you store this thing in the rain?" He pushed the table hinge and folded a leg into place with one tug. "Or is it rusty from age?"

"It's perfectly serviceable." She clenched her jaw, not wanting to tell him she'd bought the table at a thrift store. "It's just a little temperamental."

"Like its owner," he muttered, moving to unlock and fold the other table leg.

"Oh, look who's talking." Aria attempted not to stare at the flex and pull of his muscular forearms. "In addition to bullying, you have a terrible tendency to railroad over people. I *told you* I didn't need help."

"Too bad." He slammed the table shut and locked it. "You've got it."

Grabbing the handle, he hefted the table with one hand. Before she could stop him, he strode to the van and pushed the table inside.

Aria huffed out a breath and rolled up the plastic sign advertising Meow and Then. Hunter returned and picked up the cardboard box filled with leftover flyers and the donation jar. Glancing at the sign on the jar, he raised an eyebrow.

"The Mariposa Renovation Fund?"

"Yes." She tilted her chin defiantly, feeling like a kid selling candy bars for a school field trip. "I'm raising money for a fund to fix up the whole district."

"This is your plan?"

"Well, making you *disappear* wouldn't go over well with the town council, so I had to go with option two."

Amusement glinted in his eyes.

"Don't you dare laugh at me," Aria ordered.

"I wasn't going to." He shrugged. "Plenty of towns raise money to save old buildings. It's an admirable goal."

She stared after him as he returned to the van. He was probably being decent about it because he knew she didn't stand a chance against Imperial Properties' millions. Or *billions*, as Callie had so helpfully reminded her.

Aria snapped a rubber band around the rolled-up sign. She could easily imagine what Hunter was thinking.

Sure, little girl, have fun with your homemade donation jar while I have a conference call with my property investors. No doubt he'd tell all his partners about the Crazy Cat Lady when he went back to New York.

She walked to the van, where he was fitting the box alongside the table. Aria reached around him to grab two empty crates.

"You bring the cats with you for adoption?" He picked up two more crates and followed her back to the enclosure.

"Yes." Aria climbed over the plastic fence. Three of the cats swarmed around her feet, mewling. "I got five applications today. Sue has to process them and follow-up with a screening to make sure the cat and owner are a good match before they can be officially adopted. Then if the shelter is full, she brings me another one who doesn't yet have a home. Now if you'll excuse me, I have to get them back into the van."

Aria knelt to coax Libby into the open crate and locked it shut. Before she could stop him, Hunter grabbed the crate by the handle and strode back to the van.

"Come on, Jumbo." She cornered the tabby and guided him into the crate. The second she locked the door, Hunter appeared to take the crate to the van.

Maybe he thought being helpful would soften her up. Hah. Once upon a time, she'd have fallen for such a trick, but not anymore.

She reached for Fang. The cat bared his teeth at her, his eye glinting with suspicion. Aria backed away and corralled Pork-chop and Buster before Hunter carried them back to the van.

"How's Porkchop's leg?" he asked.

"It'll be fine. Thankfully it was just a mild sprain." Aria extended a hand to the old one-eyed cat. "Come on, Fang."

"Is he the last one?" Hunter set the crate next to her.

"Yes. He has a lot of anxiety, but Max suggested bringing him today to help with socialization." Aria eased closer to the cat and gentled her tone. "Come on, sweetie."

"You want me to try?"

"Fang doesn't like *nice* people." She threw him a derisive look. "He sure as heck isn't going to like you."

A smile twitched his mouth. "Well, I don't like cats. So since old Fang and I share a mutual dislike, we already have something in common."

He stepped forward and crouched on the balls of his heels beside Fang. The cat glowered at him. Aria bit back a laugh. Both the man and the cat also had the art form of *glowering* in common.

A deep rumble came from Hunter's chest.

Aria almost gasped, swinging her gaze to him in shock. "That's *it.*"

"What?"

"The purr. The noise you made when you caught Porkchop. The *tiger rumble,*" she added, when he continued to look bemused.

Too late, she realized she'd done the unforgiveable by mentioning that night. The one they weren't supposed to talk about. The one that "had never happened."

"You mean this?" He rumbled again.

The sound rolled through Aria in a hot, slow wave and settled right in her core. *Pulsing.*

"Well, it...uh, it might have been something like that." She clicked her fingers at Fang, trying to stop the inevitable flush from heating her face. "Not that I can remember exactly. Not that I *care*."

She didn't dare look at him, but his amusement was tangible. Her lips twitched. A warning sign flashed in her head. She'd been forced to sever whatever connection they'd made that night, but nothing—not even his tiger rumble or her visceral memory of his kiss—would change her mind about selling Meow and Then.

She was no longer the girl who didn't know how to stand her ground. To fight back.

A lock clicked into place inside her. No matter what Hunter said or did to try and convince her to sign the contract, she would refuse. And she wasn't the one who needed a majority. All she needed was enough votes to prevent him from reaching his goal. She could still win. God knew she'd try her hardest.

Hunter eased closer to Fang. As much as Aria enjoyed his rumble, there was no way it would have an impact on the old defensive cat.

If it did, she'd have to give up her Cat Lady card.

Hunter stepped closer. Fang suddenly hissed and lunged, sinking his claws into the man's leg before flying across the enclosure.

Told you.

Aria swallowed the snarky comment and instead asked, "Are you all right? That's the first time I've seen him attack someone."

"Yeah." He glanced at the scratch marring the side of his leg. "Even Porkchop was easier to catch."

"Two of the applications today were for Porkchop." Aria walked toward Fang again. "No one has ever asked about adopting Fang, and I've had him for a while. He needs a special home situation too because of his socialization issues. If you go stand on the other side, I'll put the crate in front of him. He might go in on his own."

Hunter moved to stand beside the plastic fencing near Fang.

Aria opened the crate door and set it near the cat. Fang's whiskers twitched. He blinked.

"Get in there, man," Hunter urged. "I'm sure when you get home, Aria will feed you."

The sound of him speaking her name stirred her with warmth. The way he wrapped his deep voice around *Aria* was the aural equivalent of how it had felt when he'd folded her into his arms.

"Close it!" He darted toward her.

Aria jerked out of her reverie just in time to see Fang's tail disappear into the crate. She hurried to close and latch the door.

"Nice work. You and I should start a cat-capturing service." He flashed her a quick smile, his eyes crinkling at the corners.

God. He was sexy with a glower. He was devastating with a smile. She didn't dare imagine what effect he'd have on her if he actually laughed.

Picking up Fang's crate, he started for the van. Aria rolled up the plastic fencing and followed him. They got everything stored in the back, and he closed the doors.

"Do you want a ride to your car?" Aria pulled her keys from her pocket.

"No need. I walked from the inn."

She lifted an eyebrow. "That's clear across town."

"Yeah. Good exercise."

"Get in." Against her better judgement, she indicated the passenger side door. "I'll give you a ride back, but I need to drop the cats off at home first. Most of them hate being in the car, and they won't tolerate a ride to and from the inn."

"You don't need to give me a ride." He jerked a thumb over his shoulder. "I'll walk."

Aria let out her breath in an exasperated sigh. "Look, I appreciate your help with the cats, but I don't want to owe you anything."

Darkness flashed over his expression. "I didn't help you

because I expected payment. But if I did, I'd want a lot more than a ride in your old van."

She looked up sharply, caught by the hard note in his voice. He closed the distance between them, his broad shoulders blocking the view of the park. Sunset light glowed on his hair. Awareness skated down her spine.

She lowered her gaze to his mouth, remembering with exquisite clarity how beautifully his lips had pressed against hers. How something inside her had come to life again.

Smothering the memory, she turned away. With their opposing positions, there was no way on earth she and Hunter would ever find middle ground. They were Batman and the Joker, Sylvester and Tweety, Frodo and Gollum.

It was just too damned bad that she was still so powerfully attracted to him. It was even worse to think that if he hadn't been her arch-nemesis—if he'd just been cat-rescuing Glowering Stranger—she would have liked him. A lot.

Maybe deep down inside, she still did.

"Look." He dragged a hand through his hair, the lines of his body tensing as if he were fighting an internal battle. "I'll stop pushing you to sign the contract."

"What dirty negotiation tactic is this?" Suspicion lanced through her. "A sucker punch? A *Game of Thrones* twist? You pretend like you're walking away before you turn around and hit me with a battle-ax?"

"I don't play dirty." His jaw tightened. "Do I want and need your signature? Yes. Have you made it crystal clear that nothing I say can convince you to sell? Yes. Am I going to cut my losses and leave? No."

"What are you going to do then?"

"Let the contracts speak for themselves and be available to answer any questions, both before and during the Mariposa Business Association meeting." He reached past her to open the driver's side door. His bare arm brushed against hers, sending a jolt of heat straight into her blood.

Aria flinched. Their eyes collided with a sudden crackle of electricity.

"You..." She paused, rubbing her hand over the spot on her arm that he'd touched. *Focus.* "According to council guidelines, any association member is allowed to request a topic for debate at the meeting."

He lifted an eyebrow. "A debate?"

"Yes." She folded her arms and gave a short nod. "I challenge you to a debate about Oceanview Plaza before the vote. We can put all the issues and controversies on the table. You state your case. I'll state mine. No moderator and no preassigned questions. Just you, me, and the crowd at the Hotel Casa Grande."

"Why the Hotel Casa Grande?"

"We hold the association meetings in the lobby."

"The meetings aren't at the city hall?"

"The Mariposa Business Association meetings are *on* Mariposa Street. I'll ask Nico to put our debate on the agenda. But until then, we agree that any fighting about the contract or Oceanview is off-limits." She arched an eyebrow and slid her gaze over his T-shirt. "You in?"

He studied her. She could almost see the assessments and considerations snapping together in his mind.

"I'm in." A husky note edged his voice.

"Truce?" She extended her hand.

He hesitated for a second, then closed his fingers around hers, almost engulfing her hand in his big grip. Her nerves jumped to full alert at the scrape of his warm palm against hers. She tightened her hold as they shook hands firmly.

Then a moment passed, as if they were each waiting to see who would pull away first. She loosened her fingers slightly and their hands slid apart. His fingertips brushed her palm. The light touch sent heat clear up her arm.

Her pulse accelerated. She'd never known a handshake could be so sexy.

"I'll take that ride, if you're still offering," he said. "As an olive branch."

Aria nodded. As she started toward the driver's side door, the tightness in her shoulders eased. Though she would stand her ground and fight if she needed to, she disliked actually sparring with Hunter. Or with anyone.

Her arguments with her sister Callie had always left her prickly and raw, and any conflict with Steve had been downright frightening. That was why she'd turned to animals after she'd come back to Bliss Cove. They never made her feel bad.

She pulled herself into the driver's seat as Hunter got in beside her. Sexy stuff aside, she liked the idea of them returning to a degree of cooperation. She'd enjoyed their unexpected teamwork the night of Porkchop's escape far more than she'd even been willing to admit.

While she was under no illusions that they could ever work together again, maybe they could coexist with some degree of accord. Though that wouldn't resolve their situation, it might make it easier to deal with.

She hoped.

$\mathcal{A}$s Aria coaxed the old engine to life, she tried to think of a topic of conversation that might keep her and Hunter on peaceful grounds. She shifted into gear and started out of Wildwood Park.

"How's everything at the Outside Inn?" she asked.

"Sugary and chatty."

She smiled. "Mrs. Higgins is very social. Her husband Hank used to be that way too, so together they were a force to be reckoned with. They just loved running the inn and having guests over. They also used to host a big town Christmas party every year."

"I'm guessing hot chocolate was involved."

"A hot chocolate fountain, in fact." She shot him an amused look, only to find him watching her with an intent gaze. The last time he'd looked at her like that had been the night of Porkchop's rescue.

Warmth swirled through her. "So...you're from New York?"

"No. I just live in Manhattan." A sudden tension radiated from him, and he looked out the side window. "I was born and raised near Chicago."

"Does your family still live there?"

"No."

"Where do they live?"

"I don't know."

A strange pressure constricted her heart. "You don't *know* where your family lives?"

"That's correct."

"But…" How was that possible?

Even when she'd distanced herself from her mother and sisters after her father's death, she'd always known exactly where they were. She'd sent them her contact information in Denver. And *knowing* her family was in Bliss Cove—that home was still a possibility, a destination, a refuge—had been one of the few things that kept Aria's faint hope alive during months of fear and despair.

"How can you not know?" she asked.

"It's not important." Hunter's broad shoulders moved in a shrug. "I left Chicago years ago anyway."

Aria stopped at a red light, suppressing the urge to ask more. Did he have any family at all? It was none of her business, even though the idea of him being alone in the world elicited a pang of sorrow.

"How long have you lived in Manhattan?" Pressing the accelerator, she turned toward Dandelion Street.

"Ten years. I moved to the East Coast for college."

"My sister Callie went to Harvard too."

"How do you know I went to Harvard?"

Heat flushed her cheeks, though she had nothing to lose by telling him the truth.

"I looked you up. You're pretty fancy with all your accomplishments and awards." She shot him a glance. "Not to mention your status as one of New York's *Most Eligible Bachelors Under Thirty-Five.*"

He gave a self-deprecating chuckle and shook his head. "The firm likes that kind of thing. Good publicity."

"They must also like all the photos of you out on the town with various beautiful women."

He slanted her a glance. "You sound jealous."

"I have nothing to be jealous of." Aria shifted, her chest tightening with discomfort. "I wanted to find out more about you so I'd know what I was up against."

"Good strategy. I looked you up too."

Her heart jumped. "What did you find out?"

"Not much aside from the café website. You don't have any social media accounts, from what I could tell."

"Neither do you."

"I prefer to keep my private life private."

"So do I."

"Destiny told me you moved back to Bliss Cove six months ago," Hunter said. "Was that when you decided to open the café?"

Aria flexed her hands on the wheel. Though she was a bit wary of his motivations for probing into her life, it might be easier to learn more about him—and refine her strategy—if he knew about her.

"I'd had the idea for a while." She turned the van toward Mariposa. "I spent a few years working at the Rescue House while helping my mother at Sugar Joy. Doing both of those things made me think of opening a cat café, but I didn't get around to actually doing it until last year."

She didn't want to imagine what he'd think of her scattered job history, her constant stops-and-starts, and then losing herself in a bad relationship before she'd even figured out who she was or what she wanted to be.

Despite his vagueness about his family, she suspected Hunter was the kind of man who'd always had a direct, clear path to follow. Who knew what he wanted and how to get it. He hadn't reached the pinnacle of the Imperial executive team without driven ambition.

Well, good for him. Some people built multi-billion-dollar complexes. Other people took care of stray cats and hosted Saturday game nights. Who could say one was more important than the other? The world needed both. A lot of people would probably rather have hot cocoa and Monopoly than Rolex watches and expensive cars.

She certainly would. And she would much rather have her family than all of Hunter's wealth and success.

She pulled up behind the café and turned off the engine. "If you want to wait here, I'll get the cats squared away."

"I'll help."

She unlocked the backdoor while he grabbed two crates from the van and hauled the meowing cats into the lounge. Within a few minutes, they had all the crates inside.

He helped her unlatch the doors and release the cats. Aria started filling the food and water bowls.

Hunter picked up a copy of *The Bliss Cove Times* lying on one of the tables. "Is your friend Brooke a reporter for the paper?"

"Yes, her grandfather owns it." She scratched Libby's ears as the cat twined around her legs. "How did you know?"

"I read the article." He tapped the headline about Mariposa and Imperial. "It's good."

"You don't mind an article about Imperial's takeover attempt?"

"Why would I?" He shrugged. "It's the truth. The article was relatively unbiased, except for the somewhat lengthy list of potential problems."

"Also the truth."

He studied her over the top of the paper, his expression giving nothing away. "The Imperial proposal addresses environmental impacts and green initiatives. We don't intend to wreck every-thing and leave town. The company will have a presence here, and as such, we want what's best for the town. I get that it's easy to think of me as the bad guy wanting to bulldoze everything and build skyscrapers, but that's not the case."

Aria filled another bowl, ignoring a prickle of guilt. "Hunter, even if you were building a bunch of yurts on the land, it wouldn't matter. You'd still want to destroy every building on Mariposa Street with no consideration for the fact that they all mean something."

She waved a hand to encompass the café. "*This* building was once owned by a woman named Christine Sterling, whom I'm actually related to on my father's side. She was a writer and a journalist who covered stories about suffrage and immigration. After her husband died, she started a rooming house here to support her three children. Until the Hotel Casa Grande was built, this was the only hotel on Mariposa Street."

"Aria, I know this neighborhood has a rich and complex history." Hunter began helping her fill the cats' water bowls. "But Bliss Cove hasn't deemed any of these buildings worthy of being saved. Towns and cities are living, evolving entities that need to change. I'm in favor of preserving historic buildings if they're important, but not just because they're old."

"That's exactly why I've started the Mariposa Restoration Fund," Aria said. "The district can be so many things, but it needs money and people who care about saving it. I'm just sorry it took a threat from Imperial for us to realize that."

She turned away from him and let out a breath. "I thought our truce meant we're not supposed to fight about this."

"We're not fighting." He set a bowl in front of Fang, who was crouched by the window. "We're talking."

She huffed out a laugh. It was kind of amazing to think two people could disagree about something and *talk* instead of fight.

She put the cat food in the cupboard. Yes, it was too damned bad that Hunter was who he was, but it was also for the better. Better for *her* anyway.

She'd made a vow to focus on herself and her business, with just a couple of casual dates intended to prevent her from being a total hermit.

But if circumstances were different and she and Hunter were both free to pursue their attraction, she doubted a casual date or two would be enough. With him, she'd want more. Too much more.

"So, we should probably get going." She glanced at the wall clock. "Does Mrs. Higgins have a curfew?"

"Not that I know of." Jumbo twined around Hunter's legs. He squinted at the *I'm Taken* sign around the cat's neck. "Did someone adopt him?"

"No." Aria went to the sink to wash her hands. "Jumbo's not available for adoption. He's mine."

"How'd you pick one cat out of all the others?"

"I didn't. He picked me."

She half-expected him to scoff. Instead, he lifted an eyebrow in inquiry.

"He'd been left behind when a family moved away, and he ended up at the Rescue House shelter." She dried her hands on a dishtowel. "Some cats and dogs get adopted right away, but others have a harder time finding a home. If it takes a while, the animals end up in the Lonely Hearts Club, which means that their adoption fee is reduced. That's what happened with Jumbo."

Hunter eyed the cat. "Why wasn't he adopted?"

"I don't know. Sometimes it's obvious, like with Fang, but we couldn't figure out why no one wanted Jumbo. He was only two years old at the time, he's good-tempered, and he's obviously handsome. I guess he just didn't make a connection with anyone."

"So you brought him home?"

"Not right away. A while ago, I was helping Sue out at the shelter, and one of my jobs was to take care of the cats. Within a few days, Jumbo started waiting for me by the door of his enclosure. He'd stay close to me the whole time I was feeding the cats and cleaning the litter boxes, and if I sat down, he'd curl in my lap. It was like he was asking me to adopt him. Then my..."

Old sorrow formed a lump in her throat. She didn't want to get too personal with Hunter—despite their uneasy truce, he was still her opponent—but she also wanted him to understand that the café was more than just a cute little place for people to drink coffee and play with cats.

"My father died in a car accident." She folded the dishtowel into a neat square and set it on the counter. "I stopped working at the shelter because I was trying to help my mother and sister—"

Even though Callie hadn't wanted or needed her help.

She took a breath, her chest knotting. "Then Sue called to tell me that Jumbo was showing symptoms of anxiety...fearful, meowing a lot, not eating. I offered to foster him at my apartment until he found a forever home. After a week, it was pretty clear he'd decided that his forever home was with me."

A faint smile tugged at Hunter's mouth. "And you saved him from being a lifelong member of the Lonely Hearts Club."

"Actually, he saved me."

The confession was out before Aria realized it was far too personal. His attention sharpened on her in that penetrating way he had, as if he were sensing there was much more to that particular story.

Not that she would ever tell him.

"We should get going." She turned to pick up her keys. Hunter stood with his hands flat on the counter. The position made his shoulder muscles bunch up beneath his shirt.

"Did you buy this building only because of the ancestral connection?" The question was slightly puzzled, as if he couldn't fathom another reason for opening a café in such a location. "I get that it would be affordable to open a business in the Mariposa district but..."

His voice trailed off.

"But it's a stupid business decision," Aria finished. "My sister Callie has told me that many times."

"I wasn't going to say that." He shook his head, his jaw tensing. "Keeping your overhead low is always a good idea. I'm just wondering about your other reasons."

Aria studied him, trying to see past Hunter Armstrong, VP of Imperial Properties, and back to the man who'd rescued Porkchop and insisted that she change into dry clothes. Though she didn't think she'd ever be able to reconcile two such different sides of him, she could—grudgingly—accept the fact that he had a right to do his job. Just as she had a right to stand her ground.

"My father loved this district, too." She started for the door. "And after we lost him, I…made some bad decisions and left Bliss Cove for longer than I should have. I wasn't really in touch with my mother or sisters either. When I came back, I had a lot to prove to myself and to other people. As Destiny would say, it was no coincidence that this exact building went up for sale less than three weeks after I came home. Or that I could afford to buy it and open the café with the money my father left for me."

She turned to find him watching her, his arms folded over his chest. Though his expression was shuttered, an emotion gleamed in his eyes that she'd never seen before.

Envy? No. What reason did Hunter have to envy her?

"Come on." She tilted her head toward the door. "I'll bet you didn't know there's a secret to Mariposa Street."

"I didn't." Hunter followed her outside to the van. "What is it?"

"I'm not going to tell you." She shot him a sideways glance and pulled open the driver's side door. "It's something only the property owners know."

"So, what if I ask Lois or Gary?" He climbed into the passenger seat.

"They won't tell you either." She pushed the key into the ignition. "Destiny won't tell you even if you flirt with her. I guarantee it."

"You sound smug."

"It might be nice to have something over you for a change."

"Does the secret involve a curse or a wicked spell?"

"I wish."

She caught his glance. Heat simmered underneath a twinkle of amusement before he turned to pull on his seatbelt. She drove back to the Outside Inn and parked along the street.

Hunter opened the door and nodded toward the ramshackle old inn. "Does this place have a secret, too? Or is it just the Mariposa buildings?"

"There are a lot of secrets in Bliss Cove." Aria experienced a brief misgiving about showing him the Outside Inn secret. It wasn't a good idea to let him in any further or to pretend like there wasn't a huge obstacle between them.

But maybe if he actually knew more about her and Bliss Cove, he'd understand why she was so opposed to the Imperial plan. Maybe he'd even back off a little.

"Follow me." She hopped out of the van. "I'll show you this secret."

She crossed to the front of the inn. A sagging picket fence lined the perimeter of the front yard, and an old wooden sign hung beside the mailbox.

Aria paused at the border of the lawn and pointed to a section of the sidewalk, where several sets of initials were carved.

"A.A.P." Hunter squinted at the letters. "Is that you?"

"My sister Rory and I, and a few other friends, snuck out here years ago when they were pouring new concrete." She shook her head with a smile. "Carving our initials ended up being stupid since it didn't take people long to figure out who'd done it. The concrete company told Mrs. Higgins they'd redo it, but she wanted to keep it. She said it told people that Bliss Cove was the kind of town where no one minded if kids carved their initials into wet concrete. So they've been here ever since."

"What does the A stand for?" He straightened, resting his hands loosely on his hips.

"Anne."

"Ariadne Anne Prescott." He said her name as if he were tasting it. "I like it."

"My father was a scholar of Greek and Roman history and languages," Aria explained. "He wanted to name me and my sisters after classical heroines. Calista, Ariadne, and Aurora, except Rory never liked her name, so that's why she's Rory. My mother is a big fan of nineteenth-century literature, so our middle names are from the Bronte sisters. Calista Charlotte, Aurora Emily, Ariadne Anne."

"How did they manage to name you that without knowing they'd have three girls?"

"My mother had a whole list of other options," Aria explained. "But my father said he just always knew he'd have three girls, like King Lear."

Hunter chuckled, and the deep vibration sank into Aria's veins. "Good thing he didn't want to name you after King Lear's daughters."

"Right? We've counted our blessings, believe me."

"So your sister Callie didn't participate in the concrete art?" He indicated the initials.

"Oh, no. She was way too good for sneaking out at night and vandalizing a square of sidewalk. She was probably at home studying."

"She's a brain, huh?" He turned as they walked back to the van. "I got that vibe from her."

"She's had that vibe since she was born." Though guilt and frustration nudged her at the thought of Callie, Aria couldn't help smiling faintly. For her entire life, her sister had been so unwaveringly constant.

"My father called us Rock, Paper, and Scissors," she said. "Callie, of course, was the rock. I was paper, which according to him meant light, flexible, always ready for a story or adventure. Rory was scissors, razor-sharp and with the ability to both shred things apart and shape them to fit perfectly."

"Your father sounds like a wise man."

"He was. We miss him a lot."

The back of Hunter's hand brushed against hers. A pleasurable tingle spread clear up her arm. She paused by the van and tilted her head to look up at him. Dusky shadows cut across his strong features, and the overhead street light shone on his hair.

"Destiny said you told her about our cat rescue encounter." He edged closer, his eyes darkening. "She also said it was *no coincidence* that we both happened to be there at the same time."

"She believes we're meant to be wherever we end up." Her heart began a low, heavy thumping in her blood.

"Then we're meant to be right here."

Tension threaded the air. She flicked her tongue out to lick her dry lips. The warning signal flashed in the back of her mind, but it was fainter now, almost distant. Despite his grumpiness when they'd first met, she'd sensed Hunter was a good guy the instant he helped her with her cat. She'd suppressed that instinctive knowledge after discovering he was with Imperial because it was easier to think of him as the enemy.

She didn't want to think of him that way anymore. She'd made her decision about the contract. He knew it. Nothing he said or did would change her mind.

So there was really no need to keep quarreling about it.

She gave him a shaky smile. "Thanks again for your help with the cats."

"Hmm." He furrowed his brow. "Last time you thanked me, you prefaced it with a very hot kiss."

Heat rushed to Aria's cheeks. "Well, that was…er, you kissed me first."

"Yes, I did." A husky note infused his voice.

The distance between them had shrunk. Her back came up

against the side of the van. He towered over her, his gaze trapping her, his body crowding her in. Shivers ran over her skin.

"And..." He planted one hand on the van behind her and slipped his gaze to her mouth. "I'm going to kiss you again."

Her breath shortened, every nerve coming to life at his mention of their kiss. *Kisses.* She wanted it too—their lips and bodies pressing together, his hands cupping her neck, his heart beating against hers. A light had turned on inside her the night they'd met, and despite the obstacles between them, she didn't want it to go out.

Not yet.

She gave him the slightest nod. His eyes filled with heat. He lowered his head. A thousand fireworks exploded inside her at the touch of his warm lips against hers. She lifted her hand to his muscular chest. His heartbeat pounded beneath her palm, a strong steady pulse that echoed in her blood.

He muttered a noise low in his throat, tilting her head back and increasing the pressure of the kiss. Pleasure twined through Aria's body, intensifying her simmering arousal. Then their mouths were locked together, hot and deep, and her whole body arched toward him in surrender. She drove her hand into his hair as their tongues danced and lips caressed.

Hunter planted his other hand on the van behind her, caging her in the secure circle of his arms. A striking sense of safety descended over her, as if her instincts had known all along that while they were in opposition, she had nothing to fear from him. He would use his strength to protect, not to threaten or provoke fear.

She unclenched her fingers from his thick hair and slid her palm down to his neck, where his pulse beat heavily. He eased his lips from hers and trailed a kiss over her cheek to her ear. She closed her eyes. He grasped her hips, edging his knee between her legs.

When had she last felt like this? So hot and hungry, her body already alive with sensation from one kiss. His stubble scraped her neck deliciously as he pressed his lips to her collarbone. He was so warm, as if he'd absorbed the heat of the afternoon sun, his skin smelling like salt and the faint aroma of citrus soap. Aria let out a soft moan of pleasure, the growing ache in her core tempting her to writhe against his thigh in a search for release.

He tightened his hold on her hips and lifted his head. He tracked his smoldering gaze over her face, her lips and heated cheeks, down to the arch of her neck and lower. His eyes lingered on her breasts, which rose and fell with the force of her breath.

Aria was seized with the urge to unbutton her dress and feel his hot gaze on her naked skin. Then she wanted to take off his shirt and touch all the sculpted muscles of his body that—

Abruptly, Hunter pushed away from her. His hands fisted. Frustration extinguished the lust burning in his expression.

Aria pressed her palm to her racing heart and tried to collect her composure. If she didn't know quite well that *fairness* was not part of life, she'd have railed against the irony of being so attracted to a man she could never actually have.

"Aria." He faced her, his voice rough. "I wasn't supposed to be here."

She blinked. "Where?"

"Here." Spreading his arms out, he stepped back onto the sidewalk. "The night you lost your cat. I was supposed to be in San Francisco for a meeting with one of the Oceanview investors. But his flight from Seattle was delayed, and he texted me to reschedule. So I drove down here a day early. Mrs. Higgins didn't have an upstairs room ready, so she asked if I'd stay in the Rosebud Room for one night. There are *five* rooms and a guest cottage at the Outside Inn."

"What does that have to do with anything?"

"There was a one in six chance that she'd put me in that room." He strode a few paces, his hands clenching and unclenching. "Given everything else that had to happen, I don't even know what the chances were of me being here on the night that your cat escaped. Much less the chances of Porkchop taking cover right under my window. Or of me even hearing you because I was going to take a shower and decided to answer an email first, which was the only reason I was sitting at the desk, which just happens to be next to the window. If I'd been in the shower, I wouldn't have heard you."

Not a coincidence.

"Hunter."

He stopped and looked at her, his eyes dark. "I don't believe in fate."

"You don't have to."

"Or in luck or destiny or any of that crap." A glower descended over his face. "I believe in hard work and rational thinking."

"So do I."

"Then how do you explain *this*?" He gestured abruptly between them, his glower deepening.

"I also believe that not everything can be explained." Aria approached him, her breathing shallow. "And that everything you just said means you *were* supposed to be in the Rosebud Room at the exact moment that Porkchop and I showed up. If you hadn't been, I never would have caught him. I wouldn't have climbed through the window of your room. You wouldn't have kissed me. Ever."

"And you wouldn't have thrown off my plans," he retorted. "I plan for everything in life. When I was a kid, I wanted a life that was the exact opposite of the shithole I lived in, so I planned my entire future. I have schedules, timelines, spreadsheets. I have strategies for all possible outcomes. But none of my strategies...*none*...could have prepared me for you."

Aria swallowed hard, her throat suddenly tight. "Is that a good thing?"

"I've always told myself the unexpected is not a good thing." He studied her. "That's why I plan."

"But sometimes you have to change your plans, right?" She felt as if they were poised on the edge of a cliff, primed to leap without knowing what lay at the bottom. "Life doesn't always go the way we expect it to. Coincidences, fate, serendipity...all of those things affect what we *think* is going to happen or what we expect to happen."

Hunter reached out to curl a lock of her hair around his finger. He tucked it behind her ear and dropped his hand back to his side.

"I sure as hell didn't expect you." He stepped away from her. "Ever. And I have no idea what to do with you now."

His expression closed off. He turned and walked back to the inn.

CHAPTER 13

*A*ria sat in the darkened van, her gaze on the lighted windows perforating the Outside Inn. She pushed the key into the ignition, then stopped. Before she could talk herself out of it, she jumped out of the van and hurried around the side of the inn.

Maneuvering through the boxwood shrubs and hydrangeas, she reached the window of the Rosebud Room and tapped on the glass.

The curtains shot aside. Hunter pushed up the window with a frown. "What are you doing here?"

"Avoiding Mrs. Higgins." She hitched herself onto the sill, muttering a curse when her foot couldn't find purchase on the wall and her skirt snagged on a rough section of brick.

"We seem to do that a lot." Grasping her waist, Hunter pulled her up through the open window and steadied her with one hand. "Not that I'm complaining."

Aria pushed her dress back down over her legs. "There's a singing fish on the wall of the Mousehole Tavern."

He blinked. "Okay."

"Rory hates it."

"Given what you've told me about her, I can understand that." He closed the window and pulled the curtains shut.

"She hates it because it's ugly and annoying, but mostly because it's useless. A singing fish has no purpose in Rory's life. She doesn't know what anyone would *do* with it."

A shadow darkened Hunter's eyes. He crossed his arms, his feet apart in his solid, tycoon stance. "Your point?"

"I am not a singing fish." Aria fisted her hands. Her heartrate kicked up. "If you don't know what to *do* with me, then you have seriously misjudged what's been happening here. Let me fill you in."

She spread her arms out. "Even though we are on opposing sides of a major negotiation, and I wanted nothing to do with you when I found out you're with Imperial, and even though I won't tell you the Mariposa Street secret, I just told you a great many of mine. I have a hundred reasons to distrust wealthy, successful men, and I have even more reasons to distrust my feelings about such men.

"But despite all of that, I've told you about my family, my father, my cat, and why I'm so determined to keep my property. I've let you kiss me, and I've kissed you back with profound enthusiasm. Honestly, Hunter, if you haven't figured out what to *do with me* by now, then you must need an instruction book because I have a very good idea what to do with you."

His mouth compressed. "I don't need you to rescue me."

"Please. I'm still working on rescuing *myself*. But we agreed to a truce. And you can't kiss me one minute and walk away from me the next. I will not let you treat me like a girl who's turning your life upside down just because we're attracted to each other and I'm standing my ground. If we..." she paused for a breath and gestured between them, "...if we can stick to talking and olive branches, it might be possible for us to maintain some civility."

He stalked to the other side of the room, putting the bed between them. His back muscles bunched with tension under his shirt.

"And remember." She flexed her fingers. "You kissed me first."

He studied her, his eyebrows snapping together. "I'm leaving in less than three weeks."

"I know."

"I live across the country."

"I *know*. We're not going to have a relationship." An odd pressure tightened her heart. Turning away from him, she picked up a sugar cookie from the plate resting on a table. "I'm talking about...well, maybe it's possible that we could be something resembling friends."

She bit into the cookie and risked a glance at him. He dragged a hand down his face and sighed.

"I work a lot." Deep lines appeared on either side of his mouth.

"I figured."

"I don't..." He cleared his throat. "I don't have a lot of friends. I never have."

Her heart constricted further. "I figured that too. You can be a little scary."

"You're not scared of me."

"Well, I'm apparently the only one who knows that big bad Hunter Armstrong can *purr*." Aria set the plate in the middle of the bed. She kicked off her sandals and settled against the pillows, indicating the cookies. "Want one?"

"I don't eat sugar."

"Big surprise." She bit into another cookie and put the plate on the nightstand. "Where's the TV remote? We can watch a movie."

"The TV is broken." He sat on the other side of the bed.

"Does Mrs. Higgins know that?"

"Yeah." He swung his legs onto the bed and adjusted the pillows behind his back. "She offered to bring in another one, but I don't watch TV."

"Too busy working?"

"Something like that."

Aria brushed crumbs from her fingers and shifted to face him. "So, what do you do for fun?"

He grunted. "I don't have fun."

"Come on." She poked him in the side. "Chasing Porkchop was fun."

"I don't have intentional fun."

Aria laughed. "You missed your calling. You should've been a Victorian butler, all stoic and serious."

Amusement flickered in his eyes. "You didn't miss your calling, Crazy Cat Lady."

"I almost did." She fluffed one of the pillows under her head. "Unlike you, I never had a plan for life. I drifted a lot, going from one great idea to the next, without ever getting anything done. Part of the problem was that my parents and sisters were always there as a safety net."

"Why was that a problem?"

"Because sometimes you have to fall. Or at least, I did. I had to pick myself up, and I realized I also had to learn how to be independent. To trust that I could actually make a plan and carry it through."

She tucked her hands underneath the pillow and studied the austere lines of his profile, which were softened by his beautifully shaped mouth and thick eyelashes.

"Why don't you know where your family is?" she asked quietly.

He let out his breath in a long rush, his gaze fixed on the opposite wall. "It doesn't matter."

"It does to me."

"Why?" He slanted her a narrow glance. "It has nothing to do with...anything."

"It's your story."

"Not anymore."

"Your story doesn't just leave you." She pushed herself to one elbow. "Neither does your history. It's part of you, even if sometimes you wish it wasn't."

"You're trying to figure out why I am the way I am?" Hunter shook his head with an abrupt laugh. "It's pretty straightforward. My mother died when I was eleven. I was sent to live with my uncle. It was a shitty situation, but I didn't have a choice. Getting into college meant I could leave all that behind."

"What about your father?"

He shrugged as if it were irrelevant, but the lines of his body tensed. "He was a deadbeat. Only worked when we ran out of money, which was often. Before my mother died, we moved around a lot because they never paid rent. My father took off after leaving me with my uncle. Never saw him again."

Aria sat up, her insides twisting. "You haven't seen your father since you were eleven?"

"I didn't want to. Even if I had, I didn't know where he was."

"What about your uncle?"

Muttering under his breath, he rubbed a hand across his face. "Why all the questions?"

"Guess what? This is what friends do. Talk about stuff. Even the hard stuff."

"Yesterday you hated me. Now we're friends?"

"I never hated you. I know what it feels like to hate someone, and this..." She waved her hand to indicate her heart, "...isn't it. I don't like what you want to do, but I understand that it's your job. And I didn't say we *are* friends. I said we could be *something resembling friends*."

"Where does kissing fit into the definition of that?" His eyes gleamed.

A flush rose to Aria's cheeks. "No changing the subject. Do you have any brothers or sisters?"

"No." He leaned back against the headboard and folded his arms. "For a long time, it was just me and my uncle. He was a veteran. Unfortunately, he was addicted to painkillers from an old injury. No benefits because of the kind of discharge he received. Tough guy to live with."

"Why?"

"He had a lot of mental health issues and couldn't get the right treatment." A frown carved brackets at the corners of his mouth. "He became an alcoholic and was often violent. The TV thing…I can't stand the noise because he had it on all the time, full-blast. He died when I was seventeen. I was able to get legally emancipated since the courts couldn't find my father."

Though he spoke in a monotone, as if he were just relaying the facts, an undercurrent of roughness threaded his voice.

"Did your father ever contact you again?"

Hunter shook his head. "I didn't care. I just focused on getting out of my basement apartment in that shit neighborhood and going to college. No way was I going to end up like my parents or uncle. I wanted a totally different life than the one I'd been living.

"I knew the only way I'd get it was by working hard. So after I got my MBA, I started climbing the corporate ladder. And that…" he reached out to tug on a lock of her hair, "…is how I ended up where I am today, Nosey. Aw, hell. Don't look like that."

"Sorry." She looked down to hide her distress, trying to school her expression into one of composure. He neither wanted nor needed her sympathy.

"Come here." Wrapping his arm around her, he hauled her across the bed to him.

Her breath caught. She hesitated for an instant, not certain if he really intended for her to settle against him, but he pulled her right up to his side. The light inside her burned brighter. She slipped her arm around his waist and rested her head on his chest. Her tension eased.

If she had any misgivings about the sheer strangeness of snuggling up to Hunter Armstrong, Imperial Properties VP, the thought dissolved into the warm strength of his body and the way he tightened his arm to pull her even closer.

CHAPTER 14

*S*unlight hit Hunter's closed eyelids. Reluctantly, he dragged himself from a tangle of hot, sweet dreams about a young woman whose body drove him crazy and whose heart seemed to have no boundaries. No closed spaces.

Sunlight?

Shoving to his elbow, he peered at the clock. *Nine.* When was the last time he'd slept past five? And why was he still wearing his shorts and T-shirt?

He turned. The space beside him was empty, but Aria's summer tropical scent lingered in the air. A note resting on the pillow had a doodle of a smiling cat.

He let out his breath slowly. She'd been real.

Still. *Nine?*

Swinging his feet to the floor, he stalked to the bathroom. Must be the sea air. Something about this small town was throwing him off.

Or *someone.*

He'd told Aria things last night that he'd never told anyone. The realization should have shocked the hell out of him, but it didn't. He hadn't been acting like himself since he saw her standing outside his room at the inn.

But he hadn't lost sight of his goal.

After splashing cold water on his face, he stared himself down in the mirror. His *get to know your opponent* strategy was either failing miserably or succeeding beyond what he'd ever thought possible. But not even in the coldest, most rational part of his brain could he convince himself that his deep attraction to Aria had anything to do with business.

It did, however, have everything to do with *her*. He'd known a lot of smart, driven women in his life, but he'd never known a woman whose fire came so intensely from her heart.

Though his instincts had rarely proven wrong, he should—technically—wonder if she was trying to play him. But he couldn't even bring himself to consider the thought. Aria was stubborn, but she wasn't manipulative.

She was too good for deception, too transparent for subterfuge. The way she'd looked at him after he'd told her about his past had almost broken his heart. He'd even had the unwelcome thought that he'd do anything to prevent that distress from shadowing her pretty eyes ever again.

Well. He clearly needed to start focusing on his job again.

He used the bathroom and took a quick shower. As he was taking clean clothes from his suitcase, a knock sounded.

Aria?

Without thinking, he strode to yank open the door. When he found himself face-to-face with Mrs. Higgins, he remembered he was only wearing boxer briefs.

The innkeeper's eyes widened. She gaped and stared at his chest as if he were buck naked.

He attempted a smile. "Good morning, Mrs. Higgins."

"Oh, Mr. Armstrong, I do apologize for interrupting you. I didn't see you leave for your morning run earlier, so I thought you might still be here."

"Yes, I…uh, overslept."

"Well, that's good. Sleep is so important. So is breakfast." She indicated the food-laden tray she was holding. "But since you refuse to join us in the dining room, it appears I need to bring breakfast to you."

"Thank you, but I—"

"I'll just put it on the table." With a cheerful smile, she entered the room. "Caramel cinnamon rolls, hot cocoa, stuffed French toast with boysenberry syrup, and a fruit bowl. Would you like anything else?"

"No, thank you. You're very kind."

"I like to keep my guests happy. Hank always said that our guests come first. He used to keep a spreadsheet of our regulars...you know, people who came to stay with us every year...and it would list all their likes and dislikes. If he knew a family liked a certain chocolate or candy, he'd have a supply of it waiting for them in their room."

She gave a wistful little sigh.

"That was nice of him." Hunter scratched his head. "If you'll excuse me, I need to get ready for work."

"Of course. Leave the tray outside the door, and we'll pick it up later." She left the room, casting a quick glance downward as she passed him.

Hunter closed the door and thunked his head against it. Small towns were not for him. He needed the anonymity and distance only a city could offer. As soon as his work was done in Bliss Cove, he'd be back in Manhattan, immersed in a world of twenty-year-old scotch and six-million-square-foot developments.

No little old lady innkeepers bearing stuffed French toast and boysenberry syrup. No artichoke festivals or streets with secrets. No falling asleep with Aria's soft body nestled against him as if she were made for—

Shutting off the direction of his thoughts, he finished getting dressed. As he was fastening on his watch, his phone buzzed with a call from Bruce Sinclair.

"How many commitments do you have so far?" the CEO asked. "I told you I want verbal agreements from all the association members before they go in for their vote."

"I know what I'm doing."

"What about that girl who owns a café...what's it called? Something to do with cats. Ariadne Prescott."

Cold snaked down Hunter's spine. "What about her?"

"She emailed saying she wasn't going to sign. You change her mind yet?"

"I'm working on it."

"That means you're not getting it *done*," his boss snapped.

"You want to come do this yourself?" Hunter gripped the phone tighter. "Not my first time locking down a deal. In case you forgot."

Bruce barked out a laugh. "Yeah, I know. Just not the kind of procedure we're accustomed to, you know? The investors are pumped about Oceanview, so I want to make sure nothing happens to fuck it up."

Hunter ended the call, smothering his unease. He didn't want Bruce knowing the first damned thing about Aria. He wasn't accustomed to his boss interfering. Imperial Properties always went full-force when launching a buyout strategy—or any other plan—but Bruce always left Hunter alone to do his job.

So why was his boss checking up on him now, especially for a relatively small project? Bruce knew he'd get the job done, regardless of the *procedure*. Hunter smothered the urge to call Juliette and dig for more information.

Close the deal. Get the promotion.

Whatever else was going on, he'd handle it when he was in charge of all of Imperial's West Coast properties.

He checked his laptop, which was open to the documents he

was compiling about the Mariposa business owners. Over the past two weeks, he'd learned a lot about them simply by asking casual questions. Small-town folk were chatty by nature, and his presence as a property developer hadn't stopped them from telling him their life stories.

He skimmed the pages, rereading everything he'd recorded about Nico Calozzi, the owner of the pizza restaurant whose father had started a restaurant in Sarconi, Italy, before immigrating to the States.

Nico's pizza recipe, handed down from his grandmother, was a delicious, thick, chewy crust that he topped with only basic ingredients of sauce, cheese, and meat. People went to Nico's for an authentic pizza, not one topped with arugula or salmon.

Hunter clicked on another document. Lois and Ray Howell had owned The Bloom Room for years. Without telling his wife, Ray had bought the shop before they were married. After the wedding, he'd brought her to the building and unveiled the Bloom Room sign as a present.

He'd told her she was his eternal flower and their love would never wither. *"Not only did it not wither,"* Lois had told Hunter, *"it grows stronger and more beautiful every year."*

It was a nice story—*cute*, even—but Hunter wouldn't let it soften his resolve.

The Howells were ready to retire, and Nico was amenable to the idea of reopening closer to the college. Gus and Martha Mortimer, the proprietors of the Vitaphone movie theater for forty years, were still on the fence. Annie, the owner of the thrift shop, wanted to get out of retail altogether so she could travel. Gary, who had inherited the Corner Store from his father, would consider opening closer to downtown.

Hunter closed the laptop, ignoring a pang from his conscience that he was making records of people's stories.

Business. That's all it is.

He never felt guilty about doing his job. He'd told Aria the truth that he didn't play dirty. He also didn't get emotion involved—least of all guilt.

Taking his briefcase, he headed out to his car. The sun had already dissolved the gray marine layer covering the sky, and the downtown streets bustled with locals and tourists.

Much as he wanted to see Aria again, he put work first. He stopped at the town hall and spent the morning checking the revised Oceanview plans against the city codes and zoning ordinances.

Close to lunchtime, he drove to Mariposa, parked, and walked toward Meow and Then. The street had a few customers—two college-aged girls sat drinking coffee in the window of the Cat Lounge, an older couple was coming out of the Corner Store, and a mother was leading a little boy toward the beach.

"Not *longing* so much anymore, are you?" Destiny's voice came from behind Hunter. "In fact, you seem rather satisfied at the moment."

He turned. As usual, Destiny was standing in the doorway of her shop with a beverage, her black hair pulled into a knot on the top of her head, and her silver jewelry glittering.

"If you sign the contract, I'll throw in some custom-made patio furniture for the front of your new store," he offered.

She gave a throaty laugh. "Duly noted. You look good."

"So do you, but rumor has it that not even flirting will get you to tell me the alleged Mariposa Street secret."

"Secret?" Her eyebrows shot up. "Mariposa Street has a secret?"

"So I've heard." Hunter glanced to where Nico was sweeping the front sidewalk of the pizza parlor. "Hey, Nico, what's the Mariposa Street secret?"

"Don't know what you're talking about, boy." Nico huffed and waved his hand dismissively.

"Guess you're out of luck." Destiny raked her approving gaze over Hunter's jeans and T-shirt. "At least in terms of so-called Mariposa secrets. Based on your energy at the moment, you might have some secrets of your own."

"Don't we all?"

"I hope so." She smiled. "Live in the light, honey."

Though Hunter had no idea what that actually meant, he said, "You too."

He crossed the street to Meow and Then. The two girls were coming down the porch steps, both of them carrying bags filled with cat-themed purchases.

Good.

The word popped into his head. Though his competitive side told him he shouldn't be glad that Aria had sold a considerable amount of merchandise—the last thing he wanted was for her café to increase in popularity—he couldn't help a surge of pride in her.

She'd started this café through hard work and determination, much the same way he'd started his career. Even if he took his intense attraction to her out of the equation, he'd admire her tenacity.

He entered the café, and the cat-shaped wind chimes above the door jingled. Aria was in the Cat Lounge, wiping down the tables and straightening the chairs.

Hunter's pulse increased. Just the sight of her flooded his veins with heat. Under her apron, she wore a cotton skirt and a loose shirt with the sleeves rolled up past her elbows. Her hair was pulled into a ponytail that swung behind her with every step, and she paused every now and then to pet one of the cats. He could almost hear her low, crooning voice.

He curled his fingers into his palm. He wanted to grasp her ponytail and tilt her head back so he could kiss her deeply until they both had to come up for air.

She looked up, her gaze colliding with his through the window separating the two rooms. Hunter's spine tensed. They'd come to more than just a *truce* last night, but he knew well that the cold light of day could change everything. And he had no idea if she—

A smile crossed her face. Though brief, it had the strangest effect of lifting his heart.

She crossed to open the Cat Lounge door. "Come in, quickly. After Porkchop's escape, I'm extra cautious with doors."

He stepped inside, breathing in her scent as he passed. A couple of the cats glanced his way, but most of them were too busy licking their paws or lazing in patches of sunlight to bother with him.

Hunter set his briefcase down. "I see you had some customers."

"Yes, they were students over at Skyline." Aria ran her hands over the front of her apron. "Taking a study break. Can I get you some coffee?"

He shook his head. She brushed a lock of hair away from her temple. The crystal stud in her nose shone in the afternoon light.

"I...I didn't mean to fall asleep in your room last night." Her mouth twisted as two spots of color appeared on her cheeks. "But really, you're a far more effective sleep aid than warm milk or even Ambien."

"That was the best night's sleep I've had in a while too, my *something resembling a friend*."

"I'm glad to know that." Pleasure flashed over her face. "So, what are you doing here?"

"I wanted to see you." The truth came out before he could think better of it. *I couldn't wait to see you.*

Though her smile shone briefly again, she turned away to continue wiping down the tables.

"Hey." He closed the distance between them in three strides and curled his hand around her slender wrist. The knot in his chest loosened. Wariness mingled with warmth brewed in her blue eyes. He could lose himself in her eyes. In *her*.

"I want…" He cleared his throat, rubbing his fingers against the soft skin of her inner wrist. "I want you to know I'm not a player. I'm not trying to change your mind by…uh, *this*. And even if I were, I'm not stupid enough to think it would work. I'm—"

"Hunter." She hesitated and bit down on her bottom lip. "I know."

Relief filled his chest, but before he could speak, a set of claws snagged on his jeans.

"Oh, dear." Aria clucked her tongue and bent to pick up Jumbo, who'd been about to use Hunter's leg as a scratching post. "He's either hungry or possessive."

"So am I." He glowered at the cat, whom he swore was grinning wickedly.

"Why don't you two get to know each other?" Aria plunked Jumbo into his arms. "I'll be right back."

Jumbo pierced him with a cold stare. The instant Aria closed the door behind her, the cat leapt to the floor, dragging his claws over Hunter's arm on the way down.

Infernal creatures.

He sat on the sofa, eyeing all the other cats who were lolling around in various states of swishing and stretching. They had it damned good here with plenty of food, toys, and a south-facing window that captured a lot of sunlight.

Not to mention…they had Aria. If Hunter were a cat, he couldn't imagine a better life.

He caught sight of Fang huddled behind an upholstered chair. The old cat peered at him with his single eye, his torn ear twitching. His posture was guarded and defensive, as if he were expecting a blow. Hunter knew the feeling.

"Hey." He leaned forward to get a better look at the cat. "You want to come out of there?"

The fur on Fang's back quivered.

"There's a good patch of sunlight over here." He pointed to the warm, bright square on the weathered floorboards. "That other cat...I think he's Buster...needed a drink, so you might want to grab the sun while you can."

Though he was surprised to find himself talking to a cat, Hunter was damned near shocked by the fact that he almost expected Fang to respond.

The cat blinked his eye. Hunter shifted cautiously closer to the chair. Fang stiffened at the movement, hunching farther into himself. Though Hunter didn't know the first thing about feline behavior, he figured it had to be a good sign if the animal didn't run away from him.

Not unlike human behavior.

"Here's a turkey and cheese sandwich." Aria came back in with a glass of iced tea and a plate. She pushed the door shut with her foot and set the food on the table in front of him.

"Thanks, but you didn't have to—"

"I have a dozen sandwiches on hand." She cut off his words with a wave of her hand. "I'm still trying to figure out how much food to order. At the end of the day, I donate what hasn't sold to a food pantry, but I still haven't regulated costs as much as I need to."

Hunter barely stopped himself from offering to help calculate her expenses. He turned his attention to the sandwich, though he was no longer hungry.

Aria leaned forward, resting her elbows on her knees as she studied him.

"Where do you go when you travel for pleasure?" she asked.

He blinked at the unexpected question. "I don't vacation much."

"No fun, right. But when you do," she persisted, "where do you go and what do you see?"

He scratched his jaw. "I went to India a couple of years ago and saw all the sites. Taj Mahal, the Red Fort, Varanasi."

"And what have you seen in Bliss Cove?"

"I'm not here on vacation. I'm here to work."

"Still, you said yourself that Imperial Properties intends to be a presence here if the vote goes in your favor, right?"

"What does that have to do with anything?" He took a bite of the sandwich.

"Shouldn't you get to know the town where you want to be a *presence?*" Aria sat back as one of the cats nudged his way onto her lap. "The proposal has a whole section about revising and finalizing the plans with input from the community. How can you do that if you don't even know the community?"

"We do a great deal of research before even starting the proposals. I've studied all the statistics for Bliss Cove."

"Like what?"

"Population, median income, occupations, climate."

"Oh, lord." With a sigh, Aria shook her head and scratched the cat's ears. "You do realize there's more to this town than statistics."

"The statistics were very specific." He put the sandwich down and creased his forehead in thought. "In my breakdown of the Bliss Cove population, I discovered there's only one sexy, cat-chasing blonde who smells like summertime and rocks my world with her kisses."

Aria stared at him, an appealing blush coloring her cheeks. "Oh, well...er, that's not what I meant."

"Rumor has it she's the Pied Piper of the feline world."

She laughed, and the sound was exactly what he remembered —a silver bell. Much as he liked her fire and spark when she was angry, he much preferred making her laugh.

He leaned closer to her, everything inside him wishing he had the right to pull her into his arms and kiss her again.

"In answer to your question." He took hold of a tendril of her hair and rubbed it between his fingers. "I haven't seen much of Bliss Cove. But what I have seen, I like a hell of a lot."

Her blush deepened. "Okay, then. Let me show you the rest of my town. I guarantee you'll like it even more."

Hunter didn't doubt it. For the first time in his life, *certainty* scared him.

CHAPTER 15

For the rest of the day, Aria found herself glancing at the clock often. Hunter was coming back at five for their date...er, *outing*, and she was increasingly jittery with anticipation.

A few customers stopped by, and after lunch, an older woman came into the Cat Lounge with an application to adopt Buster.

"I've decided he's the one," Edith announced, waving the paper.

"I'm so glad to hear that. Buster is a wonderful cat." Aria reviewed the application as Edith cooed at Buster as if they were already the best of friends. "I'll call you as soon as Sue processes your application. It usually takes her about twenty-four hours."

"Thank you so much." Edith slipped her purse over her shoulder, giving Buster another pat. "I'm so excited. It's been a bit lonely at home since Ed passed away. I've been thinking about adopting a cat for ages, but haven't found the right one until now."

"Buster has been looking for a forever home for a while, so it sounds like he might have been waiting for you." Aria handed her a sheet of paper. "Here's the supply list, and of course, don't hesitate to call me if you have questions. My cell number is there at the top of the page."

"Thank you so much, my dear." Edith cast Buster a loving look and headed out into the late-afternoon sunlight.

Aria returned to the Cat Lounge, pausing to stroke Buster's black-and-gray back. Though she was always thrilled when someone wanted to adopt one of the cats, she couldn't help feeling a touch of sorrow that the animal would soon leave her care.

As the cat leapt onto the window ledge, Aria saw her sister Rory striding down Mariposa, her boots clomping on the cobblestones and her long black hair loose around her shoulders. She went to open the front door.

"Coming to adopt a cat?" she called. "Oh, wait. You're the one who can't keep a houseplant alive."

"And you're the one who'd take in a rat if you thought it needed a home." Rory smirked and strode up the porch steps. "How's business?"

"Not bad. I just got an adoption application for Buster." Aria went around the counter and poured a cup of coffee. "Are you working at Mom's today?"

"Tomorrow morning." Rory hitched herself onto a stool at the counter and pulled the mug toward her. "I have some coding to finish up tonight, but I wanted to bring you this."

She pushed a large brown envelope across the counter. Aria eyed it warily. The last time she'd received one of those, the contents had been nothing good.

"What is it?" she asked.

"The stuff I found on Hunter Armstrong." Rory took a swallow of coffee.

Aria rubbed her hands on her apron. "What did you find?"

"Oh, no." Rory shook her head. "You want the intel, you need to read it yourself."

"But is it bad?"

"How would you feel if it were?" Rory studied her for a moment. "Vindicated? Or disappointed?"

Aria huffed out a breath of annoyance. "What difference does it make?"

"Because if you feel vindicated, then you'll be happy to have something to use against him." Rory leaned over and grabbed a takeout cup, then poured her coffee into it. "But if you're disappointed, then you'll realize that deep inside, you didn't think he really was a bad guy. And you'll be upset that you might have been wrong, which will tell you how you feel about him."

"God." Aria slumped and rested her head in her hands. "You are such a bitch."

Rory chuckled and slid off the stool. "Even if you and he hadn't been totally transparent at the bakery the other day, it would have been obvious that you're into him. So how much do you want to know?"

Aria grabbed the folder and weighed it in her hand. It couldn't have been more than a few pages at most, which hopefully meant Hunter didn't have a lengthy criminal history or a file with the CIA.

Although if he did, she'd have significant leverage in this negotiation. The question was—would she use it?

"Mousehole Friday?" Rory started toward the door.

"Maybe. I'll text you."

After her sister left, she turned the envelope around, fiddled with the sealed flap, and tested the weight again. Finally, she went upstairs and pushed the envelope into a drawer in her desk.

She slammed the drawer shut and went back downstairs. Though she'd come to know a lot about Hunter over the past few days, she didn't know nearly everything about him. And there was no question that she would be deeply, irrevocably disappointed if the report contained evidence of wrongdoing.

The problem was—she'd be far more disappointed in *herself*

rather than him. She'd never forgive herself if she were so wrong about a man again.

But she wasn't wrong about Hunter. The truth was a little glow right in the center of her being. Her trust in him had taken shape the moment she'd climbed through the window into his room. Both the first and second times. God knew falling asleep in his arms had solidified everything she'd believed about him.

She locked the front door, flipped the sign to *Closed*, and started cleaning up the café. As she finished feeding the cats, a knock sounded on the window. From the sidewalk, Hunter lifted a hand to her, his beautiful mouth curved with a smile and his dark hair flopping over his forehead.

Pleasure swirled through her. She didn't fully understand all her motivations behind wanting to show him around Bliss Cove —though she acknowledged a tiny dream that he would fall in love with the town and ease up on his plan to buy Mariposa Street.

However, she no longer lived in a world of dreams, and not for an instant did she think Hunter would back away from his goal. In some way, she might even be a little disappointed if he did. She'd been drawn to him partly because of his steadfast resolve, and she was proud of herself for holding her ground against such determination.

Not a coincidence.

It was crazy, yes, but what if Destiny had been right? What if this was meant to be a step on Aria's path back to trusting herself? Even before Steve, she'd been on shaky ground in that department, owing to all her stops-and-starts and her failures. Steve had just chipped away at what little faith in herself she'd had left.

But in some strange twist of fate, Hunter—of all people—had unknowingly bolstered her confidence. She'd trusted her instincts about him, stood up to him, let herself indulge in her attraction to him.

She'd launched a petition and fundraising drive to counter his proposal, and she was managing not to be intimidated by his money and power. She would work her ass off to get ready for their debate—and on some level, she suspected that he wanted her to do well. He wanted to win, of course, but he liked a good challenge.

As it turned out, so did she.

She unfastened her apron and tossed it into the laundry bin before hurrying to the front door.

"Hi." She stepped aside, taking an unnecessarily deep breath as he entered the café, just so that she could inhale his delicious scent.

"Hi." He held up a covered plate of sugar cookies. "Mrs. Higgins insisted I take these back to my room after teatime. She needs to rename her place the Sugar Rush Inn."

Aria smiled and took the plate, setting it on the counter. "Let's save them for later, so we can make the most of the light."

She picked up her bag and keys, ensuring all the doors were locked before they walked back out to Mariposa. The old street-lamps began to glow, and reddish light shone on the building façades.

"I heard that Gus over at the Vitaphone has a few cats of his own." Hunter nodded toward the movie theater.

"Yes, he's had a number of cats over the years, all from the Rescue House." Aria gazed at the old marquee. "He always goes onstage to introduce the movies himself, whether it's a classic or a new blockbuster. After telling the audience about the movie, he opens a can of cat food at the microphone. At the sound, his three cats come running down the aisle to the stage. One of them, Daisy, actually balances on the stair railing. It wouldn't be movie night at the Vitaphone if Gus's cats didn't put on a dinner show first."

"I might need to see that."

"I'd like for you to see it." She glanced at him. "You asked me last night why I opened the café here on Mariposa Street."

"You didn't answer."

"Because of things like that," Aria explained. "And because of what this district has stood for throughout history. The Hotel Casa Grande was the first hotel in all of Bliss Cove. The grocery store was built in the 1920s by a man whose father started the Bliss Cove Fishing Company."

She waved a hand to the opposite row of shops. "The thrift store is on a plot of land that once belonged to a woman named Nellie Paxton-Smith, who owned acres of orchard fields farther inland. After her husband died and left her the Mariposa plot, she constructed that building for commercial space and used it as a fruit stand to sell the oranges and pomegranates she grew."

"I've never denied the history of the district," Hunter said. "But the town could have worked to preserve it years ago."

"I know." Aria folded her arms around her waist. "Now it would be much more expensive to renovate. That's why everyone has chosen to forget about it, for the most part."

She felt his gaze on her. "Except for you."

"I'm not a crusader." Shame bubbled in Aria's chest. "I hadn't even thought about Mariposa in ages until the Sterling House came up for sale. Then I started remembering what it used to be like. It wasn't in great shape even when I was a kid, but my father used to love it here. Whenever we went to the beach, he'd make a point of detouring through Mariposa just so he could tell us about the history and the architecture. Of course, I was bored silly, but eventually I learned to appreciate his love for the area. Now I love it too. I think I always have. I just didn't know it at the time."

He was silent. She felt his regard like the graze of his hand against hers. Like the first time he'd touched her.

"Come on." She started toward her van parked in the alley. "I still won't tell you the Mariposa Street secret, but Bliss Cove has a few other secrets I can share."

"What about you?" His low, quiet question rubbed against her skin.

Tightening her hands on her keys, she turned to find him watching her with a pensive, shuttered expression. "I already told you my secrets."

"Not all of them." He moved closer, his dark eyes sliding from her face to her chest.

Her heart fluttered. He reached out and lifted the pendant around her neck. The brush of his fingers on her skin shocked her with heat.

"What kind of stone is this?" He rubbed his thumb over the crystal.

"Red amethyst. Destiny gave it to me." She gazed at the raw amethyst nestled in his big palm. "She believes crystals have healing powers."

"Why do you need healing?"

She shrugged, tugging the pendant gently out of his grip. "Buildings require regular maintenance, right? They get weather-beaten and need fixing up the older they get. People are the same way. If you have a strong foundation and are solidly built, and if you're lucky, then maybe you'll need less repair work than others. But as time goes on, we all need a bit of restoration."

A smile tugged at his mouth. "I've never heard anyone compare houses with people."

"Places are important." Aria opened the van door and climbed into the driver's seat. "My building is more than just stones and mortar. It was a home to my ancestor and her family and to other people through the years. Now it's mine, and it's where orphaned cats can find security and love before moving to their forever home."

"Your plan worked."

"For the first time." She pulled the van on to Starfish Avenue. "What about your plan? How far along are you now?"

"Not far enough." He turned his head to look out the window. "And maybe too far."

CHAPTER 16

*H*unter had never spent much time at the beach. He knew plenty of people who vacationed in Florida and the Caribbean, but the idea of lazing around at an oceanfront resort didn't appeal to him, and he'd never had much interest in a bunch of sand and water.

But *this*. The red glow over the Pacific horizon illuminated the rough, rocky coastline edged with sea-plants and cypress trees. Waves splashed against the outcroppings, birds soared, and a cluster of sea lions lolled on a large rock not far from the shore. The Bliss Cove lighthouse, which he hadn't yet visited, stood like a soldier guarding the bay.

"Have you been to the boardwalk?" The silver bracelets on Aria's arm jingled as she pointed to the boardwalk that ran parallel to the ocean.

"Not yet." He peered through the front window. The place was in full-swing on a Saturday evening, lights blazing and the Ferris wheel spinning in a multicolored circle. "Was that your local hangout when you were a kid?"

"Oh, definitely. We'd take in a movie at the Vitaphone…that was when it was the only theater anywhere nearby, but now

Rainsville has a multiplex that's taken away a lot of the Mortimers' business…and then come to the boardwalk for ice cream or funnel cakes. We also spent a lot of time at the Mousehole and Ruby's Kitchen or just wandering Starfish Avenue. Then in our teen years, it was all about sneaking around underneath the pier or going up to Lighthouse Point to make out."

"Wish I'd known you back then."

She shot him an amused look. "Somehow I don't see you as the type to sneak around under a pier. Even as a teenager."

"I wasn't." He gazed out the side window. The coastal hills melted into denser forests packed with redwood trees. "I didn't have much of a social life in high school. I was laser-focused on my grades and the extracurriculars that would get me into Harvard."

"Do you ever regret it? The path you took, I mean."

"No. I made the path."

"Still. It doesn't sound like much fun."

"I didn't do it for fun." He squinted at the rugged mountains. "Must be some good camping and hiking up there."

"Tons of it, on the public land, at least. Some of it is private." She guided the van around a curve hugging the coastline. "The redwoods have inspired a lot of fantastic stories about Bigfoot, fog spirits, Dark Watchers, even a rumored elf maiden. But the forest doesn't give up its secrets easily." She tossed him a smile. "Kind of like someone I know."

"Maybe it just takes the right person to discover the secrets." Hunter turned his attention to an outcropping of rocks jutting into the ocean. "This must have been a great place to grow up."

"Yes, but like many things, I didn't really appreciate it until later." Aria pulled on to a narrow dirt road, and the van rattled to a stop in front of an old wooden house. "But I guess it's better to figure something out late rather than not at all."

She hopped out of the driver's seat. Hunter followed, casting a glance over the weathered front porch and salt-encrusted windows. An Open sign was displayed in the window.

As Aria pushed open the door, a bell jingled to announce their arrival. The smells of salt and redwood filled the air. The gift shop held glass cases of jewelry, a rack of T-shirts, and several shelves of books and beach-related knick-knacks—sea animal statuettes, lamps, and snow globes.

"Aria." A man in his mid-fifties with graying hair shuffled toward them, peering over the tops of his glasses. "It's about time you stopped by. Lucifur has been wondering where you are."

He indicated the gray cat lounging in an old chair, whiskers twitching and ears perked. Aria smiled and stroked her hand over the cat's back.

"He looks great. Bert adopted Lucifur...that's F-U-R...from the café last month," she told Hunter. "Bert, this is my friend Hunter."

Friend. Though she seemed to say the word without even thinking, it sounded almost foreign. A flush colored her cheeks, as if she'd just realized what she said.

"Good to meet you." Hunter stepped forward to shake the older man's hand. "Nice place you've got here."

"Take your time looking around, and feel free to head into the museum." Bert pointed to a curtained doorway leading to another room. "I need to check on something in the oven, but I'll be right back to show you around."

He disappeared through another door, and Hunter shot Aria a quizzical look. "Museum?"

"The Sea Glass Museum."

"Sea glass?"

"Glass that's been polished by the ocean." Gesturing for him to follow her, she walked to the back room and pushed the curtain aside. "Say a hundred years ago, someone drinking a bottle of soda on the boardwalk carelessly threw the empty bottle in the ocean. The glass would break, and the waves would toss and tumble all those jagged pieces, smoothing out the edges and giving them a frosted patina. That's sea glass. Discarded bottles and containers that the ocean has turned into something new."

Though Hunter's immediate reaction was to wonder how someone could create a museum out of trash, he followed Aria into the room. Display cases held hundreds of pieces of silky, frosted glass, all arranged by color, as well as whole bottles and jars with barnacles still clinging to the surface. There was a display of marbles that had been found in the sea, each one smooth and clouded.

Bert returned to give them a tour, and Hunter learned more about sea glass than he even knew existed, from the value of different colors to its increasing rarity.

"Red glass is extremely rare." Bert paused beside a case displaying several red pieces. "Usually it comes from car taillights or perfume bottles." He opened a case and took out a piece of glass. "This is fire glass, which was melted before the sea took it over. That's why it has all those different colors."

Hunter lifted the piece to the light. Dark green curled through a fusion of red and clear, cloudy glass. If he were a poetic type, he'd make some correlation about how an ordinary piece of glass could become something both colorful and extraordinary after being consumed by fire and then endlessly tossed around by the ocean waves.

"Pretty." He handed the glass back to Bert.

They looked around for another hour before Aria told Bert she had a few more Bliss Cove secrets to show Hunter. After they got back into her van, she drove to a sprawling Victorian mansion with multiple stories and towers. A wooden sign in the front yard stated *Bliss Cove Library*.

"Bliss Cove has a long history extending back to Native American settlements," she explained. "But during the Gold Rush, it was officially founded as a shipping and fishing port by John Marcus, a sea captain from Maine. He built this place..." she gestured to the mansion, "...after he got married and lived here until he died in 1899. The property was sold several times, but the new owners always left shortly after moving in because they claimed it was haunted. They heard music coming from the conservatory even though no one was there, footsteps on the stairs, and a strange singing that sounded like a man singing old sea shanties. No one wanted to live here, so eventually, the town bought it and turned it into the library."

"Is it still haunted?" Hunter peered through the front windshield at the mansion with its wide front porch and arched pediment.

"Of course." Aria shifted into reverse and backed out of the parking space. "We'll go in one day when it's open. People often report seeing the figure of a man pass in front of the window on the third floor, even when the library is closed and no one is there."

Any other time, Hunter would have scoffed at the idea of a haunted library. But if there were such things as ghosts, and if Captain Marcus was one of them, then the hulking old mansion would be a perfect place for him to hang out and scare people.

"The library has a haunted house every Halloween." Aria turned down Starfish Avenue, where all the trees and lampposts were illuminated with white lights. "Interestingly, no one has reported seeing or hearing Captain Marcus on Halloween. I guess he considers it his day off."

She grinned. Her eyes sparkled. An odd tightness gripped Hunter's chest.

Aria pulled into a parking spot and cut off the engine. He followed her out to the sidewalk. He was beginning to think he'd follow her anywhere. And that he'd *like* it.

Shaking the thought out of his head, he fell into step at her side.

"Have you been to the Mousehole Tavern yet?" She slipped

her purse over her shoulder. "Home of Bliss Cove's famous arti-choke soup."

"No. That guy Grant doesn't think much of me," Hunter said. "I did want to try the soup, though. At the Artichoke Festival, I tried fried artichokes, artichoke ice cream, artichoke cupcakes, artichoke burritos, and artichoke hummus. Strangely enough, I couldn't find a booth to try any artichoke soup."

Aria laughed. "That's because Grant only serves the soup at the tavern. He bought the Mousehole a few years ago, and he inherited the secret recipe. He claims it has to be cooked in the same pot, on the same burner on his stove, and then served right away or it loses its flavor. So the tavern is the only place in town where you can have a bowl of artichoke soup."

She walked off the main street to a cluster of four ramshackle wooden buildings with steep roofs and ivy-covered walls. Light glowed through the windows, and music drifted on the air.

"Welcome to the Mousehole." Aria pulled open the door of the main building and stepped inside. "This used to be a stagecoach stop until about 1865, I think. Then it changed owners over the years until Grant bought it and moved into the house in the back. There's also a cottage. This is the restaurant and bar, and that fourth building is kind of a free-for-all space that's been used for everything from ballet classes to birthday parties."

She led him through the maze of tables. "Oh, there's the singing fish I told you about. I think Grant keeps it around partly to annoy Rory."

She indicated the mounted plastic fish behind the bar, where Grant was helping customers. Aria waved and gestured to a table by the window. "Can you bring us a couple of soups please, Grant?"

He nodded, slanting a narrow glance at Hunter. The scattered wooden tables were covered in red-and-white checked cloths and each held a single glowing lantern. The chairs and barstools were filled with locals drinking and talking. Weathered wooden rafters crossed the high roof, and a massive stone fireplace dominated one end of the room.

Despite Grant's wariness of him, Hunter knew businesses. Though he'd reviewed the Oceanview plans a hundred times over, he suspected that no matter what kind of high-end bar or restaurant opened up there, it would never replace this local hangout.

Aria left for a moment and returned with a couple of beers and a basket of hot sourdough bread. "I worked here for a summer when I was in college."

Setting the basket between them, she took her seat again. "A tourist from LA offered me five hundred dollars for the artichoke soup recipe."

"Were you tempted?"

"No, but even if I was, I couldn't have gotten it for him." She tilted her head toward the bar, causing her hair to slide over her shoulder. "Everyone who's owned this bar over the years claims the recipe isn't written down anywhere. It's passed in secret from owner to owner. Now Grant is the only one who knows it, and he keeps it locked in the vault of his brain. The only thing anyone knows for sure is that it contains artichokes."

Her mouth curved with a smile, and her blue eyes shone in the light from the glowing lantern. Tearing his gaze from hers, Hunter took a piece of bread. The tightness in his chest intensified, as if he were trying to contain something that wanted to get out.

Know your opponent.

The strategy was supposed to make it easier to win the battle. But the more he learned about Aria, the less he wanted to negotiate. He just wanted to know even *more* about her. It was like slowly uncovering a treasure—you couldn't wait to see the whole thing.

"Here you go." Grant appeared with two wooden bowls filled

with soup, which he plunked in front of them before narrowing his eyes at Hunter again. "Anything else?"

"This is great, thanks, Grant," Aria said.

He nodded and slouched back to the bar.

"You think he spit in my soup?" Hunter eyed the creamy, green soup warily.

"No." Aria smiled and draped her napkin in her lap. "He's not that type. But he was the first person to sign my petition. Sorry." She twisted her mouth with a grimace. "I didn't mean to bring up the *thing*."

Hunter shrugged and picked up his spoon. The *thing* seemed increasingly less relevant. "We have a truce, so it doesn't matter. We'll hash it all out at the debate."

She spooned up a bite of soup and blew on it. Her lips pursed, drawing his attention to the rosebud of her mouth. His shoulders tensed with the urge to kiss her again.

"You were on your high school debate team, weren't you?" she asked.

"How'd you know?"

"Easy guess. Ivy Leagues look favorably on forensics, from what I understand." She rolled her eyes slightly. "Not that I ever thought about the Ivy Leagues. That was Callie's domain."

"What was your college major?"

"English literature." She ate another bite of soup and darted her tongue out to lick her bottom lip. "Because I like to read, not because I thought I could make a career out of it. I didn't want to be a teacher...again, Callie's domain...and I couldn't figure out what else to major in. Then a friend told me about a non-profit animal organization that was looking for help up near Seattle, so I dropped out and moved up there. Not my greatest decision."

"You wouldn't have known that if you hadn't gone, though."

"Sadly, it was one of many bad decisions." She blew her breath upward, stirring a tendril of hair at her temple. "I also once joined an adventure travel company that folded six months later.

I went broke on a spur-of-the-moment road trip. I've put my savings into countless business ventures—a wildlife rescue program, an online macramé art store, a mail-order soap business—but I could never get anything off the ground. Or I couldn't stick with it long enough. Anyway, I have a terrible track record of going the distance with anything. How's the soup?"

Hunter blinked. He'd been too preoccupied listening to her and staring at her. He ate a spoonful of soup and nodded. "Really good."

She tapped the menu at the side of the table. "Grant's soup always gets the starring role here, but the supporting cast is excellent. When we're done, we'll split a piece of olallieberry pie. It's my sister Rory's favorite. It'll ruin you for all other olallieberry pies."

He didn't bother telling her he'd never heard of or had an olallieberry pie in his life. As they shared the sweet, tart pie and homemade vanilla ice cream, and as he grew increasingly captivated by her murmurs of pleasure, the way she closed her lips around the spoon, the flash of her smile...he began to suspect he was being ruined in more ways than one.

Smothering his unease, he set down his fork and indicated that she should finish the pie. After they were done and he paid for their dinner, Aria drove him back to the Outside Inn and parked beside the front gate.

"There's still more to see, and I can even tell you a few things about pirates, believe it or not." She pulled up the parking brake, her bracelets jingling. "But I hope that was a good start."

"It was a great start." He put his hand on the door handle, barely stopping himself from saying that he'd show her the secrets of New York when she came to visit him in Manhattan.

This was totally out of hand. He needed to get a grip.

"Well, thank you." She shifted, sliding her hand over the steering wheel. "We can do this again sometime, if you'd like to."

Say no. You're busy. Work to do. Thanks but no thanks.

"I'd like to," he said.

"Good." Her eyes creased with a smile. "So would I."

He started to get out of the van. His heart began a low, heavy beat. Before he could think, before he could talk himself out of it, he grabbed her shoulders and hauled her against him.

Aria gasped, her eyes widening right before he brought his mouth crashing down on hers. Lust and light exploded through him. He kissed her with a complete lack of finesse, aching only to claim her in the rawest way possible.

She stiffened in shock for an instant before a moan emerged from her throat, and she wrapped her arms around his shoulders. Her breasts pressed against his chest.

Fuck, yeah.

He was already hard, and they hadn't even done anything. Yet.

In one movement, he grabbed her waist and hauled her over the console so she was straddling his lap. Breaking her mouth from his, she lifted her head and stared at him, her eyes dazed in the dim light.

"God, Hunter." She pulled in a breath and shifted against his groin, her thighs hugging his hips. "What are we…"

He didn't know. He didn't care. All he wanted was her.

Sliding his hand to the back of her neck, he brought her lips back to his. She tasted like berries and cream. Her skin was hot, as if she'd soaked up the ocean sun. The bright orange scent of her filled his head, sank into his blood. She'd warm even the coldest New York winter, bringing an endless summer into his life.

He drove his fingers into her hair, slanting her mouth more firmly against his. Her breath heated his lips. She rocked against him.

He groaned, his whole body tensing with a painful combination of lust and a useless attempt at self-control. She grasped his shoulders, twisting her fingers into his T-shirt as she swept her tongue into his mouth and set his blood aflame.

Keeping his mouth locked to hers, he ran his hand over her smooth bare leg and underneath her skirt. He curved his fingers against her inner thigh. She twitched in reaction, then lifted her body upward slightly to give him better access. Hunter clenched his jaw, not sure how much longer he could hold off with her so ripe and ready.

Aria pressed her forehead against his, her grip on him tightening. "This is insane."

"That's one word for it." He could think of another one, too. Like *incredible*.

He slipped his fingers underneath the elastic of her underwear and found her hot core.

"Hunter." Her whole body tensed. She arched her hips toward him, her breathing fast.

"Come on." He pressed his lips to the curve of her throat and over her collarbone.

She responded to his touch with the effortlessness of a leaf curving into the wind. He rubbed and stroked her folds, and she rocked against his hand and panted. Right when he sensed her body begin to tighten with arousal, he latched his arm around her waist and kissed her. She cried out against his mouth, her body trembling with release.

Though Hunter had known many pleasures in life, the sensation of Aria coming in his arms left all the others far behind. She sank against him, her chest heaving and her body limp. He ran his hands down her back to her ass. He could have just sat there for the next hour or eight with her all warm and loose against him.

She lifted her head, pushing her hair away from her flushed face. Her eyes were dark with both satisfaction and a touch of uncertainty. She brushed her fingers over the bulge in his jeans. "Do you want…"

"No." He cupped his hand against the side of her face. "You're beautiful. That was for you. And that's all this is. Neither one of us is going to overthink anything."

"Agreed." She studied him, her sooty lashes creating shadows on her cheekbones. She rubbed her thumb over his mouth and eased off him to climb back into the driver's seat. "But I don't think we qualify anymore as *something resembling friends*. I'm pretty sure we're actual friends now."

"No. We're more than friends." He winked at her, glad when she smiled in response, and turned to open the van door. "Thanks again for tonight. Get a good night's sleep."

"You too."

He felt her watching him as he unlocked the inn's gate and headed up the steps of the front porch. He let himself into the foyer, where the front desk had a *Closed – Text For Service* sign followed by Mrs. Higgins' cell number.

Digging the key from his pocket, he started toward his room. Halfway there, he stopped. Female voices rose from nearby.

His spine tensed. He strode to the dining room.

Mrs. Higgins waved at him from where she stood speaking to another woman. "Oh, Mr. Armstrong, I thought I heard you come in. I believe you two know each other?"

"Of course." Juliette Sinclair turned and smiled. "Hello, Hunter."

CHAPTER 17

"*Say Catnip.*" Aria clicked a photo of a smiling Edith and Buster and lowered her phone. She uploaded the photo to the front page of the café website and added a congratulatory message: *Hooray! Buster found his forever home with Edith!*

"I'll take exceptional care of him." Edith hugged the cat before putting him into the crate.

"He'll take good care of you, too." Aria picked up the gift basket filled with toys, cat food, and treats that she gave to all the cats' new adoptive parents. "If you don't mind, I'd love to come and visit after he's settled in."

"Of course, my dear." Edith picked up the crate and started out to her car. "He'll be thrilled to see you. We both will. I'd love the company, too."

Aria followed her outside and set the gift basket in the backseat. She helped Edith arrange the crate in the front. She bent to peek into the crate at Buster. Her heart constricted a little.

"Be good, okay?" She stuck her finger through the grate and touched his paw. "I'll miss you."

He twitched his whiskers. She backed away and closed the car door, turning to hug Edith.

"I'll give you a call next week." Edith embraced her and started around to the driver's seat. "And I'll email you tonight to let you know how he's doing."

Aria nodded, waving as Edith and Buster pulled away and headed home. She returned to the Cat Lounge, where the other cats were roaming more than usual—as they always did when one of their own moved out. She sat down to both soothe the cats and to take comfort of her own in petting their silky fur.

Truth be told, it was more than just Buster being gone that had her restless and anxious. As if she hadn't been preoccupied enough with Hunter over the past couple of weeks, after their impromptu slumber party, then the town "date" and hot encounter two nights ago, she really couldn't stop thinking of him.

The uplifting movie trailer in her head had changed to *The Hunter Show, Starring Hunter Armstrong*. All Hunter, all the time.

Hunter when she was eating breakfast, Hunter in the shower —most definitely *Hunter in the shower*—Hunter when she was picking up her bakery order, making coffee, feeding the cats. Hunter when she was cleaning the litter boxes, for lord's sake.

She'd been so wrong about thinking he was cut from the same cloth as Steve had been. Hunter was rational and able to compartmentalize his life, but he didn't shut down his emotions. Even when he'd visibly tried to distance himself from her, she'd sensed his feelings and restraint simmering just underneath the surface.

She scratched Porkchop's ears and looked out the window at Mariposa Street. Afternoon sunlight glowed off the cobblestone street, and a couple sat at a table outside Nico's. Two young women walked toward The Bloom Room.

Hunter had texted her several times, apologizing for not being able to stop by since the other night, which had been both more fun and hotter than she'd anticipated. Just thinking about his intimate touch elicited a warm, swirling sensation in her belly...and the secret longing to learn the full extent of his expertise.

It had been a long time since she'd fully enjoyed sex. Any kind of intimacy with Steve had been trying on an emotional level because she'd been forced to keep her wants and needs to herself. She'd been voiceless in all areas of their relationship.

She certainly hadn't been that way with Hunter—from ordering him out of her café to refusing to sign the contract, to challenging him to a debate. She'd added another brick to her wall of self-confidence with every resolution. And even though they were on opposite sides, Hunter liked her fire. His appreciation shone in every quick smile and spark of admiration.

Setting the cat aside, she walked to the window and peered down the street at the Rags to Riches Thrift Shop. Hunter stood on the sidewalk, his tablet in his hand as he spoke to the owner, Annie.

Though he was no doubt trying to talk Annie into his plans, Aria would have normally experienced an intense burst of pleasure at the sight of him.

Except...another woman stood at his side. Elegantly dressed in a red suit and heels, she had sleek hair and a posture that commanded attention. Sunglasses covered her eyes, and she carried a slim leather briefcase. She appeared to have everything that Aria didn't—big city sophistication, wealth, elegance, and an innate poise.

Given the way she slipped her arm through Hunter's as they continued walking, she also had him. Or thought she did.

Jealousy snaked through Aria's gut. She didn't have a right to be jealous—it wasn't as if she and Hunter were even dating, after all—but she suddenly wished she had the right to touch him with the same casual ease.

She wished she was sophisticated and knew how to dress elegantly with everything coordinated—including her shoes. Instead she wore ragtag dresses, jeans with holes in them, and old sandals that displayed her toe-ring. The other woman's hair was styled to perfection with not a strand out of place.

Aria pushed a lock of her messy hair behind her ear and wondered when she'd last gotten it cut, much less styled.

Her heart crashed against her ribs. Hunter and the woman were walking toward the café. He shook his head, pointing toward the movie theater. Releasing his arm, the woman shrugged and started up the front porch steps.

Shit.

Aria hastily untied her stained apron and attempted to smooth out the wrinkles on her cotton tunic. She pulled a hairband off her wrist and managed to fasten a quick ponytail the instant before the woman strode inside.

Aria hurried to the front room, closing the Cat Lounge door behind her. She forced a smile as Hunter entered, his mouth tight.

"Welcome to Meow and Then." Her voice sounded high and thin. "Can I get you something?"

"Aria, this is my colleague, Juliette." Hunter stepped forward, locking his gaze to hers. "She arrived unexpectedly a couple of days ago."

Juliette took off her sunglasses, revealing striking blue eyes enhanced with artfully applied cosmetics. Her red lipstick was the exact shade of her suit. She smiled and extended a hand to Aria.

"Juliette Sinclair," she said. "A pleasure to meet you, Miss Prescott."

"You too." She shook the other woman's hand.

Sinclair. Not Bruce Sinclair's wife. Aria had seen photos of the older, dark-haired Mrs. Sinclair, and since Juliette resembled her...

"Are you Bruce Sinclair's daughter?"

"I am." Juliette swept her cool gaze around the café. "This is a nice place. I can understand why you would hesitate to sell it."

"We're not here to discuss the contract." Hunter put his brief-case on the counter and edged slightly between Juliette and Aria.

"Actually, I'm not *hesitating*." Aria stiffened her spine and eyed the other woman. "I've already made my decision. I'm not selling my café."

"That's what Hunter said." Juliette picked up a mouse-shaped catnip toy. Her mouth twisted. "Has he told you that we have verbal commitments from eight owners already?"

Aria swallowed her shock. "That's not a majority."

"Four more is all we need." Juliette gave her an arch smile.

"Juliette." Hunter's voice held a distinct warning.

"You need votes, not verbal commitments." Aria dug her fingernails into her palms. "And you may think you have this locked down, but no one knows what will happen until all the ballots are in."

"I'm quite confident people appreciate the attractiveness of our offer." Juliette peered through the window looking into the Cat Lounge. "I don't mean this to be rude, but why in the love of god would you stay *here*? I'm not a cat person, but some people lose their shit when they get within ten feet of a feline. With enough foot traffic, you could get rid of all these cats in less than a week."

Anger swept through Aria. "I don't want to get rid of them. I want to find them good homes."

"Of course." Juliette's voice was a verbal eye-roll.

"We're leaving." Hunter took hold of Juliette's arm and turned her toward the door. "Aria, I apologize."

"I didn't offend you, did I?" Tugging her arm from Hunter's grip, Juliette lifted her eyebrows at Aria. "I want women-owned businesses, including yours, to succeed. But the fact is that you need to be in a much better location or you're going to be forced to shut down. Then what will happen to your cats?"

Tension shot down Aria's spine. She couldn't formulate a response because she had none.

"I know that's not what you want to hear, but it's the truth." Juliette walked to the door, her heels clicking sharply. "Take it for what it's worth. For the record, it's worth quite a bit."

As soon as she stepped outside, Hunter closed the door behind her and turned to Aria. Irritation and regret glittered in his eyes.

"I see now why you haven't stopped by." She tried to keep her voice from wavering.

"I'm sorry." He approached, lifting one hand to touch her before dropping it back to his side. "I didn't know she was coming, and I didn't want to bring her here. But—"

Aria shook her head to stop his words. "It's part of the job. I know. It's okay."

She glanced past him to where Juliette stood on the porch, a phone at her ear. She stood like a model, one hand on her hip and her back straight as a metal plate. *Confidence* radiated from every pore.

"You should go." Aria went behind the counter to put a physical barrier between her and Hunter. "I'm sure you have work to do."

His jaw clenched. "We need to talk."

"I'm not interested in talking right now." Outside, Juliette had ended the call and was swiping the screen of her phone. "Hunter, please go."

For a moment, he stood there, immovable as a boulder. She walked to the door and opened it, pointing a finger to the sidewalk. His jaw clenched.

"I'll be back tonight." He grabbed his briefcase and stalked out the door, walking away so fast that Juliette had to hurry to catch up with him.

As Aria watched them continue down the street, she thought about Hunter's longstanding plan for his future. Deep inside, she suspected that his plan included a woman exactly like Juliette Sinclair.

CHAPTER 18

"*I*t's all very cute and quaint." Juliette slipped her sunglasses back into her purse as she and Hunter walked up the front steps of the Outside Inn. "Unfortunately, that doesn't translate to revenue unless you're doing the right marketing. My guess is that this town doesn't even have a tourism department."

"They rely on tourism during the summer." Hunter pulled open the door and stepped aside to let her enter. "But it's word of mouth, not because of marketing or advertising."

"That's their problem, then. Things will change when Imperial moves in. Let's go over the open space proposal again. Do you have the blueprints with you?"

"Yes, and they're also on my laptop."

"Good." She strode into the foyer, her nostrils twitching. "What is that smell?"

"Tea. Earl Gray, from what I can tell."

"Hello, Miss Sinclair, Mr. Armstrong." Mrs. Higgins came flitting out of the dining room with a flowered teapot in her hand. "You're just in time for tea and cookies."

Juliette gave her a thin-lipped smile. "I'm afraid we have work to do."

"Oh." The older woman's face fell.

Hunter stepped forward to take the teapot from her. "But we can spare fifteen minutes for a cup of tea and one of your delicious scones."

"Wonderful." Her eyes lit up, and she gestured for them to follow her into the dining room.

Juliette slanted him a disapproving look as they sat at the chintz-covered table while Mrs. Higgins bustled around pouring fragrant tea and loading up their plates with enough sugary treats for a party of elves. She chattered on about her garden and taking reservations for the summer, and wasn't it lucky that she had a room available for Juliette?

"I do not know how you've been able to tolerate living here for almost three weeks," Juliette muttered to Hunter after they'd each had two cups of tea and Hunter had eaten almost a dozen cookies to make up for Juliette's outright refusal to eat even one.

"It's not so bad." He unlocked the door of the Rosebud Room. "If you can get past the sugar rush."

"What have you done for fun?" Juliette dropped her purse on the bed and walked to the narrow desk covered with papers and plans. "Not that you're here for *fun*."

"No, but I went to the town Artichoke Festival." Hunter's blood warmed at the memory of the festival where he and Aria had established their truce. He picked up a roll of blueprints. "They have a local theater, and there are always events going on over at the college. The Vitaphone holds classic movie double features every Wednesday night. Not to mention, there's plenty to do outdoors. Hiking, swimming, boating, whatever."

"Well, bring out the Tourism Board." Juliette lifted her eyebrows. "Sounds like you should write their brochure."

"It's a nice town." Hunter rolled out the blueprint of Ocean-view Plaza. "Isn't that the reason Imperial wants to establish a presence here? Allocating space for a tourism office in Ocean-view isn't a bad idea."

"No, it's not." Juliette came to stand beside him, tapping her manicured fingernail on the blueprint. "I like the way the architect created a direct path to the beach between the buildings. We'll need to ensure private access for the condo owners as well."

Hunter studied the plan, pinpointing the spot where Meow and Then was right now. After Oceanview was built, a row of retail shops would take its place. The surrounding trees would give way to a multilevel parking structure, and Destiny's Moonbeams would become part of the open space plaza, where vertical programmable water jets would shoot out of the concrete-and-brick pavement.

Though the design was precise and well thought-out, the computerized fountains would be nothing compared to what visitors could see if they just drove a couple of miles along the coastal road parallel to Bliss Cove.

Ocean waves rolling and crashing against the rocky outcroppings—maybe even polishing bits of glass under their depths. Birds soaring over the coarse sand beaches, otters swimming on their backs, sea lions lazing about on huge stones.

He took a breath to ease the sudden tightness in his chest. Juliette's arm brushed against his.

He stepped away and rolled up the blueprints. "We should take these out to the foyer. More room there."

"Hunter."

Wary, he turned to face her. She stood with her hands on her hips, her shoulders back and lips slightly pursed.

"I won't prevaricate," she said. "Have you given any thought to my offer?"

He pulled a hand through his hair. Her *offer* could have led to the completion of another piece of his puzzle. Everything would have been neat and tidy, all parts fitting into place like a smooth-running engine.

Exactly what he'd wanted for his future. No surprises. No failures. Just hard work, acclaim, and enough success that he would never run the risk of sliding back to where he'd once been.

"I appreciate the offer." He met her gaze again. "But you and I getting involved personally could create professional complications that neither one of us will want to deal with."

A cool expression came down over her face. "I'll take that as a *no, thanks.*"

"It's not a good idea."

"You don't like to mix business and pleasure, hmm?" She reached out to straighten the collar of his button-down khaki shirt. She swept her gaze to his faded jeans and back up again. "This must be your Bliss Cove suit. You look great, but I prefer the Armani."

He took hold of her wrist and gently set her hand away from him. "Juliette, I couldn't have asked for a better colleague all these years. You're right…we could have had a great partnership, if things were different. But I still have to decline your offer."

Her mouth tightened. "It's that girl, isn't it? The one from the cat café."

Christ. He was that transparent?

"I was wondering why you've been going soft on her." She dropped her hand away from him with an abrupt laugh. "The Hunter Armstrong I know would have had that little girl's contract signed, sealed, and delivered in less than a day."

Tension ran through his shoulders. "She has nothing to do with this. I'm not interested, Juliette. I'm sorry if that's not what you want to hear, but it's the truth."

"Fine." She held up her hands and backed away, an invisible shield coming down over her. "But if you're losing your edge because she's batting her eyelashes at you and pouting about her poor abandoned cats, then you need to get your shit together fast. Have you forgotten that your promotion and quite possibly the CEO position is hinging on you locking down the Mariposa deal?"

"No, I haven't forgotten. How I handle this is none of your business."

Her eyes flashed. "It is my business if the Oceanview project goes to hell because you've got the hots for a small-town girl who was stupid enough to open a café in the worst district of Bliss Cove."

"Enough." He pointed to the door, his jaw clenching. "You need to leave. This is my project. I'll handle it my way."

"*Your way* better work." She spun on her heel and grabbed her briefcase. As she started toward the door, she swept her gaze over the room. She stopped at the chair in the corner, where Aria's torn dress and pink flowered bra and underwear were still folded. His insides clenched.

Juliette gingerly lifted the bra between her thumb and forefinger. "She has nothing to do with this, huh?"

"You need to go."

"Watch out, Hunter." Dropping the bra, Juliette drew her shoulders back and eyed him coldly. "That girl may look all sweet and innocent, but she'll play you like a grand piano if you're not careful."

"Leave now, Juliette."

With a toss of her hair, she strode out, slamming the door behind her.

Hunter dragged his hands over his face. Though he regretted hurting her, he wouldn't apologize for kicking her out.

He sank onto the edge of the bed and rested his head in his hands. His stay here was supposed to be straightforward. Simple. Get the lay of the land. Convince the Mariposa owners that signing the contract was in their best interest. Make sure the residents knew Imperial Properties was on their side. *We're all in this together, folks.*

But now? His thoughts—his stupid *feelings*—were increasingly knotted. He couldn't give Aria what she wanted—and she knew it —but he liked her more with every second he spent with her, every little thing he learned about her.

She had both fire and steel, two qualities he hadn't even known he liked in a woman. He'd always sought out women who were sedate and sophisticated—the ones who would potentially fit into his vision of the future.

Aria never would. It would be more than just "round peg, square hole." She was like a piece of glass tumbled by the sea, all multifaceted colors and smooth, soft edges. Even if she were cut to *fit* into his world, she'd lose all her natural appeal.

He stood abruptly and strode to the window. Why was he even linking her and his future in the same thought? His brain seemed to fire on the wrong synapses when it came to her. This was just a comparison, a reminder that his lifelong plan was still very much in place.

You're still a fucking idiot, Armstrong.

Grabbing his keys, he picked up Aria's clothes and headed out to his car.

CHAPTER 19

A knock came at the closed door of the café. Aria set the broom aside. Nerves tensed her belly as she went to let Hunter in. His hair was a disheveled mess, his jaw coated with stubble, and his features lined with tension.

Her heart constricted. She hadn't seen *this* Hunter before—not angry or charming or commanding or even grudgingly helpful. This Hunter was upset.

"Here." He set some clothing on the counter and jabbed his finger at it. "You left those in my room, and I forgot to give them to you the other night."

"I'd forgotten about them, too. Thanks." She waved toward the interior door. "Go into the lounge. I'll bring you some tea."

"I don't want any tea." He pulled a hand through his hair, his shoulders tightening. "I want to see you. I want to talk to you. I want..."

With a muttered curse, he closed the distance between them. Clamping a hand around her waist, he hauled her against him. His breath brushed her lips. His dark eyes seared into hers. A flame of hunger flickered in their brown depths.

"I want *you.*" He brought his mouth down on hers.

Aria stiffened for half a second before pleasure sparked through her. She curled her hands into the front of his shirt, aching to fall into his kiss. She wished their desire could banish all their conflicts and cross-purposes, ease the sharp edge of reality, and assure her that somehow, they could stay friends, become lovers, even—

She broke away and stumbled backward, her breath sticking in her throat. He lifted his head. His features tensed.

"We can't do this." She forced the words out. "I like you so much...and I *want* you so much, which is so completely crazy because even if we didn't have this contract sitting like a wall between us, I—"

"Forget the fucking contract." He strode toward her, his face darkening with frustration. "You're voting no. We'll discuss it at the meeting and deal with whatever happens. But it's not a goddamned wall between us. I don't want..." He paused, and his throat worked with a swallow. "I don't want there to be *anything* between us."

Aria pressed a hand to her racing heart. Tears stung her eyes suddenly.

"But how can there not be? Regardless of what happens, you're leaving Bliss Cove after the meeting, so...what? We have an affair for the next couple of weeks? Then you go back to New York, and I stay here, and we don't friend and follow each other on our nonexistent social media accounts? And maybe we exchange a few emails and phone calls...but then what?"

He cursed again and stalked back and forth from the Cat Lounge. "When I go back to New York, I'll be promoted to the vice-president of Imperial's West Coast operations. I'll be in control of all the company's properties from California to the Rockies. I'll relocate and work out of our Los Angeles office."

Aria wiped at a stray tear. Her insides were as tight as pulled yarn. She didn't dare ask about his future involvement with the Oceanview project. She still intended to fight and would go into the debate with all she had, but if Juliette was telling the truth and Imperial had *eight* votes already…

Ominous music filtered through the uplifting movie trailer in her head.

Aria had learned a thing or twenty during her relationship with Steve, not the least of which was that sometimes she had to face the hard facts. And the facts were still that Imperial Properties would always be more powerful, and that many Mariposa owners were happy about their contract.

The *fact* was that she might lose.

The debate.

The vote.

Her building.

Her café.

The cats.

Hunter.

With every fiber of her being, she didn't want to lose any of those things. She especially didn't want to lose Hunter.

"I will not let the contract or anything else come between us." He stopped in front of her, determination suddenly blazing from him. "I won't let it stop me from telling you that I'm falling for you. Hard. A goddamned freefall."

Aria's pulse cartwheeled wildly. "You…you are?"

"Yes." His features softening, he reached out to run his hand through her hair, combing the long strands back from her forehead. "This was in no way part of the plan, but it's the truth. The second I opened that window and saw you, I was done. I just didn't know it yet."

"Oh." A bubble of happiness formed beneath her heart, easing the painful ache of misgivings and insurmountable problems. "It was the same for me."

He stilled, his hand tightening in her hair. "It was?"

"You were bad-tempered and unpleasant, and totally captivating standing there with your sleeves rolled up and your hair all messy." A smile twitched the corners of her mouth. "In fact, you had me at *glower*."

"If I had you then…" He pulled her closer, tenderness flaring in the depths of his eyes. "There is no way I'm letting you go now."

He kissed her. Sparks flared in her veins. She wound her arms around his neck and threaded her fingers into his hair. All thought slipped away with the certain knowledge that she wanted this. She wanted *him* as much as he wanted her.

She lifted her head. Her breathing increased. Anticipation coiled through her along with a touch of nervousness. Twining her fingers with his, she led him up the narrow staircase to her room.

He cast a glance around at the plaster walls that she'd decorated with nature prints and photos, the old wooden bookshelf stuffed with books, the large bed covered with an Indian-print comforter.

"I saw you when I was out for a jog one morning." He indicated the window in the kitchen alcove. "Just the sight of you and my heart almost pounded out of my chest." He pressed a hand to his chest. "Like it's doing right now."

She smiled and slipped her arms around his waist, settling their lower bodies together. He cupped his hand under her chin, tilting her face up to his before kissing her gently.

A thousand songs broke open inside Aria because whatever happened in the future, she would always cherish the moment she stood in the strong circle of Hunter's arms and returned his kiss without reservation. She parted her lips under his, every nerve ending awakening as he swept his tongue into her mouth in a claim of possession.

Slowly he slid his hands down her sides to grasp her hips. She stepped backward toward the bed, keeping their lips locked together. When her legs hit the mattress, she grabbed his shirt-front and fell backward onto the bed, taking him with her.

Hunter caught himself and planted both hands on either side of her head as he gazed down at her. His breath brushed her lips. His eyes blazed.

"You're sure," he said.

"I'm sure." Yanking him closer, she pulled him down on top of her. "Are you sure?"

A hoarse laugh rumbled from his chest. "I've never been more sure of anything in my life."

"Kiss me."

He did. Desire flooded her. Winding her arms around his shoulders, she opened her mouth and wrapped one leg around his thighs. He muttered her name, pressing his lips across her cheek, down to her neck. Electric sparks shot to her core. With a few quick twists, he unfastened the buttons lining the front of her dress and parted the folds to reveal her blue bra and panties. Aria shifted to take off her bra, her heart racing.

"You're incredible." Hunter's breath escaped in a hard rush. He kissed the curves of her breasts and slid his hand down into her underwear.

Aria squirmed and gasped as he brought her to orgasm with an expert touch. Still quivering, she tugged at the front of his shirt. "Your turn."

He moved away to take off his shirt and jeans. Aria's mouth went dry at the sight of his sculpted abdomen with a trail of hair leading straight down to the impressive bulge in his boxer briefs. He hooked his fingers into his briefs and shoved them off before rejoining her on the bed and covering her.

Then there was nothing between them, not even air, as their bodies pressed and rubbed together. He kissed her everywhere, trailing his lips over her breasts, her belly, her thighs. She explored his body with both fascination and delight, stroking his chest and tracing all the slopes of his muscles.

A delicious spool of arousal coiled around her. Thought and time dissolved under the onslaught of pleasure. He eased away from her only long enough to put on a condom, and the brief separation felt like an eternity. When he edged between her legs, a hot, melting sensation spread through Aria's blood. Slowly he pushed inside her, his jaw set with self-restraint. She dug her fingers into his shoulders and hooked her legs around his thighs.

His easy, slick immersion into her was the sweetest torture, intensifying her urgency like silk pulled on a spindle. She let him set the pace of their union before she began arching up to meet his every thrust. Her whole body flexed and tensed. Their rhythm became harder and faster, driving them both toward the pinnacle.

A cry tore from her throat when bliss exploded over her nerves. She quivered and shook, tightening her hold on him. He lowered his mouth to hers and swept his tongue between her lips. Only when she calmed did he surge inside her with a rough groan, his own body shuddering with release.

Hunter collapsed on top of her, his chest heaving against her breasts. Aria wrapped her arms around him and pulled in a breath. Her blood hummed with lingering arousal.

He eased off her and flopped onto his back. He closed his eyes, his thick eyelashes softening the cut-glass angles of his jaw and cheekbones. A trickle of sweat ran down his temple.

Her heart constricted. She shifted to reach for her robe when he clamped his arm around her shoulders and hauled her against him.

God. Even in repose, his body flexed with strength and power.

His grip on her tightened. She rested her head on his shoulder and slipped her arm around his waist. He made a deep, contented noise low in his chest. The sound vibrated through Aria and settled inside her. She closed her eyes, soothed into sleep by his tiger rumble.

∼

Aria woke still pressed to his strong body. Warmth flowed through her. She listened to the sound of his heartbeat for a few minutes before lifting her head to find him watching her. His dark eyes gleamed in the light of the old streetlamps, the golden glow spilling through the windows.

"I can hear the ocean." He threaded his hand through her hair. "Must be nice to fall asleep and wake up to that sound every day."

"It is. I didn't think of it when I converted this place into an apartment." She ran her hand over his chest. "Then my first night here, I was so nervous and scared. I'd only been back in Bliss Cove for a few weeks, and I'd dropped all my money into an old building with the hopes of starting a business, even though I'd never been able to see one through before, and I was suddenly panicking and second-guessing every decision. Then I heard the waves, and I remembered walking along Mariposa Street with my father, and I felt like he'd sent the waves to comfort me. So I opened all the windows and stayed awake all night listening to them."

He was quiet for a moment. "What brought you back to Bliss Cove?"

"I needed to come home." Aria shifted to glance at the clock. "Oh, no."

"What's wrong?" He pushed to one elbow.

"The cats. I always feed them after closing, and I totally forgot." She reached for a pair of pajama pants near the bed and tugged them on, shooting him a mild glare. "I was a little distracted."

"I'll be happy to distract you again after we feed the cats." He winked at her and pulled on his jeans.

After slipping into a T-shirt, Aria led the way back downstairs to the Cat Lounge. The cats were restless and irritated, swarming toward the door as soon as she opened it.

"Sorry, sweeties." She bent to stroke her fingers through Garbo's fur. "You can blame Hunter for being irresistible."

"If being blamed gets me more of you, I'm entirely at fault." He patted her ass.

Aria couldn't stop a smile as she retrieved cans of cat food from the cabinet. Her whole body felt light and airy, like meringue. Even in her heart of hearts, there were no shadows, no pangs of worry or misgivings. Every part of her was *certain* about being with Hunter right now.

He refilled the water dishes and brought the food bowls over while she prepped their dinners. Hunter crouched to look under a chair where Fang was hunched, his eye slitted and his fanged tooth poking out of his mouth.

"He doesn't like eating with the other cats, so I usually bring his food to him," Aria said.

Hunter took a bowl of food from her and returned to Fang. He sat on the sofa and put the bowl at his feet.

"You'll have to come out to get it," he told the cat, then glanced at Aria. "What's his story?"

"He was found on the side of a road up near San Jose." Aria's heart tightened as she bent to look at Fang. "He was in really bad shape—malnourished, a lacerated paw, cuts and scrapes, plus his missing eye. He'd been abused, and then he either ran away or was just dumped off in the ditch. Thanks to Max, he recovered well physically, but obviously he still has emotional issues. Max thinks he was starved too because he's very protective of his food."

Hunter bent to study the cat again and pushed the food bowl toward him slightly. Fang's whiskers twitched.

To give him space, Aria returned to taking care of the other cats. After they'd all been fed, she took out the trash and cleaned up the counter space.

When she looked up again, Fang had emerged from under the chair and was hunched over his food bowl, eating noisily right next to Hunter.

"Wow. He rarely gets that close to people." Aria watched as

Hunter leaned forward and rested his elbows on his knees. Fang continued eating, unperturbed by the movement. Then the cat straightened and began washing his whiskers.

Hunter settled his hand on Fang's back. The cat stiffened, but didn't move away.

"Do you get the cats from all over the state?" he asked.

"Mostly from here to the San Jose area." Aria went to sit beside him. Jumbo leapt up to paw at her lap. "Sometimes Max gets a call from a pet rescue and transportation service that they need help with a particular animal, so if I'm able to foster them before they find a new home, I do."

"How many cats have you had adopted?"

"Seventeen since I opened. Buster just went off to his forever home yesterday. Sue is going to bring me another orphan tomorrow to join our little band of misfits."

She stroked Jumbo's head. Hunter straightened, lifting his hand away from Fang's back. The cat shook himself and stretched before returning to his crouched position under the chair.

"Are you thinking of adopting another cat yourself?" Hunter leaned back against the sofa cushions and stretched his long legs out in front of him. His bare, muscled shoulders gleamed in the light from the streetlamps.

"Maybe, but right now Jumbo is enough. He and I have been through a lot together." She nuzzled her nose against the cat's head.

"Was he with you when you moved away from Bliss Cove?"

Aria nodded. She'd never been able to tell anyone about Steve, but based on what Hunter had told her about his childhood, he was well-acquainted with hopelessness and pain. He knew what it felt like to blame yourself. He'd pulled himself out of a bad place by fixing on a goal and creating a plan for reaching it.

So had she.

"I lived in Denver for a while," she said. "I'd moved there not long after my father died. It's kind of a long story."

"I'm not going anywhere." His gaze was intent and penetrating, like he was trying to look inside her. Aria had the strange thought that he probably could.

"After my father died, we were all kind of a mess." She ran her fingers over the cat's back. "Well, except for Callie who launched into general-mode the second we got the phone call that Dad had been in an accident. Then she just took over everything—Mom's life, the bakery, the house, the arrangements, everything.

"We all let her because she's so good at that kind of stuff, but then we found out that Dad had left each of us equal amounts of money. Callie and Rory immediately put their shares into mutual funds or whatever, and I wanted to use some of mine to take a trip to Athens, which was Dad's favorite city. I'd never been there, and…I don't know. I guess I just wanted to see it.

"Well, Callie thought that was a total waste, especially since I didn't even have a job, and we got into a huge fight about it. She won, and I didn't go. But I was so mad that I refused to talk to her for about a week. I was also upset because I knew she was right.

"Then Rory got a contract job with a tech company, so in addition to helping at Sugar Joy she was working all the time, and of course, Callie was busy with teaching and all of Dad's paperwork. And Mom was focused on trying to get back to living her life again….

"I guess I felt alone and kind of adrift, except this time without them there to help me. With my safety net gone, I ended up in a bad place, though I did a good job of hiding it. I'd been dating Steve for a couple of weeks. He had it all…or I thought he did. Handsome, smart, successful. Somewhat ironically, he was an investment banker."

Though Hunter didn't move, the lines of his body tensed. "What happened?"

"I moved to Denver to live with him." She pulled Jumbo closer as he butted his head against her arm. "We were together for about eight months. It took me that long to figure out how to leave him."

"What did he do?"

"He was controlling. Very controlling. And I was perfect for him because he'd found me at my lowest, most vulnerable point. I didn't know how to stand up for myself. So I didn't."

"Was he—" Hunter's voice broke off. His hand curled into a fist.

"Physically abusive? He came close a few times. He liked to threaten me a lot and scare me by acting like he was about to hit me. He didn't cross that line, but I'm sure he would have if I'd stayed. As it was, he dictated almost everything I did—what I wore, what we ate, where I went. I went along with it because I didn't think I had a choice. I couldn't come back to Bliss Cove. I didn't even know how to access my inheritance because I'd let Rory invest it. Steve didn't like the idea of me having any friends, so I mostly stayed home by myself. Took care of the house, ran errands. Spent all my time with Jumbo."

She scratched the cat's ears. He rolled his eyes and blinked before jumping lightly off her lap and padding over to explore a hideaway.

"When did you leave him?" An undercurrent of anger roughened Hunter's voice.

"When he threatened Jumbo." She rubbed her hands over the goosebumps prickling her arms. "I should have seen it coming. He didn't like cats. Or animals in general. He tolerated Jumbo, but he had a short fuse about all things cat-related. He hated the smell of cat food, complained about cat fur, didn't want Jumbo on the furniture. I tried to keep Jumbo out of his sight for the most part, but of course that wasn't always possible."

She took a breath, her heartrate accelerating as her recollection of that night crowded into her mind. Hunter settled his hand on her knee, the weight of his grip a steadying force.

"One night Steve came home upset over a work deal that hadn't gone through, so he was in a bad mood to begin with. And I hadn't done something right...I can't even remember what. I probably bought the wrong bread or left a crumpled towel on the floor. Jumbo was upstairs and out of his way, but somehow he escaped and came into the kitchen. As he started toward his food dish, Steve kicked him."

She took a breath. "Of course, that made me angry, and for the first time, I shouted at him. Then he yelled back...which was scary because he didn't often raise his voice...and we started fighting. It was the first time I'd fought back, and he didn't like it. He started toward me...I *knew* he was going to hit me...and then Jumbo jumped onto the kitchen counter. That set Steve off even more. He grabbed Jumbo by the neck and shook...*strangled* him while threatening to kill him...and I was so scared he'd break Jumbo's neck. I knew he'd do it, that he was capable of it."

A cold shudder ran through her. Hunter tightened his grip on her knee.

"Then Steve's phone rang." A hollow laugh broke from her throat. "So Jumbo was saved by the bell. The instant Steve dropped him, I grabbed him and ran back upstairs to hide in the bedroom. Steve tried to get me to come out, banging on the door and shouting, and he only stopped when I threatened to call 911. The next day, after he left for work, Jumbo and I packed up and walked out. We caught the next bus back to California."

Hunter was silent for a long minute. "Did he come after you?"

"No. He called to hurl a bunch of insults at me and told me he was glad I was gone. I never heard from him again."

"Come here." His voice gruff, Hunter hauled her against his warm chest and wrapped his arms around her. "That's one of the bravest things I've ever heard. I'm only sorry that asshole didn't get what was coming to him."

"He will, at some point." Aria rubbed her cheek against his chest. "Karma is real, whether you believe in it or not."

He pressed his lips to the top of her head. "What I believe is that you deserve everything good. You are everything good."

"Thank you, but I've made plenty of mistakes and bad decisions." She shifted to kiss his chin. "The good news is that I've been making much better ones lately. Like hooking up with the guy who's supposed to be my arch-enemy...oh, wait a second..."

His eyes crinkled with a smile as he cupped her face and brought her mouth to his. After a warm, lovely kiss, he lifted his head.

"I don't think I'm falling for you." He brushed his thumb over her cheek. "I've already fallen."

CHAPTER 20

As falls went, it was the best one Hunter had ever experienced.

For the next few days, he reluctantly left Aria to her café work in the morning while he, even more reluctantly, finalized the Oceanview plans and continued his quest for signed contracts.

Juliette returned to Manhattan—and Hunter didn't know what she intended to tell her father about his progress. With eight votes locked down, he was doing his job as well as he ever had. He'd learned at a young age how to compartmentalize, so separating his work from his intense feelings for Aria wasn't difficult.

As long as he didn't think about it too much.

The second the clock hit five—or several minutes before—he was back at Meow and Then, impatiently waiting for her to turn the Closed sign and lock the door so he could pull her into his arms and kiss her deeply.

After he helped her take care of the cats—though his work mostly consisted of feeding and petting Fang—they went out so Aria could reveal more of Bliss Cove's secrets. She showed him the six historical murals scattered throughout town, the best rocky coves to explore tidepools, the ice-cream stand on the boardwalk where Ghost Pepper Chocolate was a secret menu item only attainable if you asked for it by name.

"It's delicious because it's sweet and spicy at the same time." Aria darted her tongue out to lick her cone, the action causing heat to rush to his lower body.

"Kind of like you." He kissed a drop of ice cream off the corner of her mouth.

"You sure you don't want one of your own?" She held up her cone to let him take a bite.

"I've got one of my own." He patted her ass, which he did as often as he could because first, he loved the sensation of her round, firm rear under his palm, and second, because she always flashed him a smile when he did.

After she finished her cone, they walked from the boardwalk to Pelican Beach. Aria pointed to a patch of sand near the pier. "Right about there was where you caught Porkchop. Oh, I meant to tell you, a family came in yesterday and filled out an application for him."

"Did you tell them he's a pain in the ass?"

"Hey." She swatted his arm. "If it wasn't for Porkchop, we wouldn't have met."

"That would have been a damned shame."

And *that* was an understatement. He couldn't even imagine how different things would have been if he'd walked into Meow and Then without having joined forces with Aria to catch an escaped cat. Without having kissed her. He didn't want to imagine it.

"So, what's Porkchop's story?" He pressed his hand to her lower back as they stepped onto the rocky pathway leading back to the inn.

"He belonged to an elderly woman who was a retired chef, and she cooked gourmet meals for him all the time. He got a bit hefty as a result, not to mention spoiled rotten. When she passed away, there was no one willing or able to adopt him, so he ended up at the Rescue House."

"I hope his adoption works out." Hunter started toward the front of the inn, when Aria stopped him with a hand on his arm. "What's wrong?"

She grimaced and indicated the windows. "I don't want Mrs. Higgins to see me going to your room."

He frowned, unexpectedly stung by the implication that she didn't want to be seen with *him*.

"Hunter, she's vice-president of the Ground Hogs…that's the gardening club run by Mrs. Bowers, the mayor, and she'll totally drop hints at the next meeting that Aria Prescott went to Hunter Armstrong's room at nine-thirty at night, and she's pretty sure they weren't going to discuss the stock market. Then because Sugar Joy provides all the pastries for the Ground Hogs meetings, Mrs. Bowers will casually mention to my mother that isn't it *interesting* how her daughter has hooked up with Hunter, of all people, and—"

"Okay, okay." He held up his hands in surrender and strode toward the window of his room. "We'll do this the old-fashioned way. Which I guess is also *our* way."

Glad that he'd left the window unlocked, he pushed it open and lifted Aria into the room before climbing in after her. He closed and locked it, as she went into the bathroom to check out the new bottles of lotion and shampoo left in the complimentary toiletries' basket.

He followed her, breathing in the fragrant air. "What kind is that?"

She dabbed lotion on her arms and studied the little bottle. "Orange flower and vanilla. Smell."

She thrust her arm under his nose. He sniffed appreciatively. "Nice. Did you know oranges are an aphrodisiac?"

"I suspect that for you, everything is an aphrodisiac." She

rolled her eyes and capped the bottle, leaning past him to return it to the basket.

"Everything about *you*, yes." He took hold of her hips and eased her forward against the counter. "Now that you smell like oranges more than usual, I'm revved up to full speed."

He pushed his groin against her rear so there was no mistaking his erection. She caught her breath, her eyes widening in the reflection in the mirror.

"That was quick," she remarked.

"But I'll go nice and slow." He pressed his lips against her warm neck. Heat spread through him. Grasping her skirt, he inched it over her bare legs to expose the thin scrap of cotton that she called underwear. "You might as well be wearing nothing under here."

"Maybe next time I won't." Though her tone was flip, her eyes darkened with arousal.

Though his own lust intensified, Hunter took his time stroking her bare thighs, edging his fingers under the elastic of her panties, and breathing her in.

He loved her scent, the warm smoothness of her skin, the sound of her breath catching in the back of her throat. He loved the silky glide of her hair, the way she opened herself without hesitation to his exploring fingers, the little trembles that made her body quiver. He loved—

Hunter blocked the direction of that thought. He went down on his knees, pulling her underwear off at the same time. Edging his hands between her legs, he opened her wider and leaned forward to pleasure her with both his mouth and his fingers.

Aria gasped and clutched the edge of the counter. "Oh my god, *Hunter…*"

He steadied her with one hand and worked her harder, feeling her body tense with readiness. When she came, his name escaping on another cry, one word burst into his head.

Mine.

Whatever happened, however it happened, he knew one thing for certain. She was his.

He rose to unfasten his jeans and took her up against the counter—slow and easy at first, like he'd promised. But the sight of her in the mirror, all flushed skin and desire-dark eyes, was too much to take.

Clamping his hands around her waist, he quickened his pace. He'd never get enough of her. He thrust into her until she shattered again, convulsing around him so tightly that his own urgency snapped, the explosion so powerful he felt it to his bones.

Chest heaving, he picked Aria up and carried her into the bedroom. He spread her out on the bed and stripped off her clothes, then did what he'd been aching to do since the night he first pictured her naked. He kissed her everywhere—starting with her lips and moving down to her collarbones, her shoulders, her breasts. He trailed his mouth across her belly, dipped his tongue into her navel, pressed kisses over her thighs and all the way down to her toes.

She squirmed, giggled, and breathed his name. And when he worked his way up her body to her lips again, she opened her arms as if to welcome him back.

As if to welcome him home.

He couldn't get enough of her. When he finally rolled away from her, every cell in his body wrung out, he pulled the flowered comforter over her and tugged her against him. She murmured in contentment, nestling against his side.

Though the inn's floral décor was over-the-top, he liked how Aria looked all snuggled against the rose-patterned sheets, her hair spilling like silk over the pillows. Like a little fairy in a flower garden.

An image of his Manhattan apartment appeared. Black leather and metal. Gray walls. Industrial appliances. Spare and austere.

Discomfort tightened his chest. He rubbed his hand down her smooth back.

He'd make this work. He had no choice. He wanted to be CEO of Imperial Properties, but he was starting to want Aria to keep her café even more.

Unfortunately, his quitting the job or leaving the company made it even less likely that she would keep Meow and Then. If Hunter left, Bruce would just put someone else—probably Juliette—in charge of Oceanview. And Juliette had no sympathy for Aria or her cats or anything else about Mariposa Street.

Hunter also still believed what he'd told Aria. Mariposa had been a drain on the town's economy for years. It was a prime piece of land that could be used to actually help rather than hurt Bliss Cove. Even if he did manage to kill the Oceanview project—which was unlikely—Mariposa, and by extension, the whole town, would still suffer.

No. He needed another plan.

He stayed awake long into the night as Aria slept soundly with her cheek pressed to his chest and her arm loose around his waist.

When sunlight filtered into the room, his phone buzzed with a text. Shifting away from Aria, he reached for his phone. She mumbled in her sleep and rolled over to hug a pillow.

Hunter pulled up the text from Bruce Sinclair. Cold slithered down his spine.

Mandatory NY meeting this week. Margaret will book your flight.

CHAPTER 21

After locking the door of Meow and Later, Aria drove to the Mousehole Tavern. She'd had to leave Hunter again early that morning to open the café, and she'd been unable to stop thinking about the fact that he'd be leaving tomorrow.

"Just for a day or two," he'd assured her, even though his jaw was tense and his eyes dark.

Though the Oceanview situation had never gone away, they'd both been able to separate it from what was happening between them. Not that Aria wanted to think too much about *them*. If she did, she was afraid she might come to some realizations that would only intensify the pain of their inevitable separation.

While she was able to suppress the fears swirling underneath her thoughts, her feelings, both emotional and physical, had a life of their own. Her body surged with awareness whenever he touched her, and just the sight of him made her heart go through a full cardio routine of hops, skips, and jumps. His kisses aroused her unbearably, and his smiles lit her up with happiness.

When they were apart during the day, she couldn't wait to see him again. And when she was with him, she didn't want to leave.

It was all wonderful, dangerous, and scary at the same time.

Which was exactly the reason she tried not to think about it in too much detail or to worry about what would happen in the future.

She pulled open the tavern door and walked to the bar, where Grant was serving drinks.

"How's the petition?" He tossed a dishtowel over his shoulder and started to make her a mojito.

"Three hundred signatures so far, which isn't bad considering I started it a week ago." She rested her elbows on the bar. "I'm trying to get Mayor Bowers to help fund the revival of the Historical Preservation Society. Unfortunately, she's not very enthused."

Setting the drink in front of her, Grant frowned. "Why not?"

"Oceanview Plaza, for one." Aria sipped the drink. "Everyone is convinced Imperial Properties will win the vote. Even if they don't, Mayor Bowers likes the idea of a Mariposa restoration, but she's worried that pulling resources from other city services will cause problems."

His frown deepened. "How did they fund the preservation society in the first place?"

"The town council subsidized it, but mostly it was funded with private donations and memberships. The society also partnered with a lot of corporations. The biggest sponsor was the Bliss Cove Fishing Company. When they closed, it started a domino effect, and membership declined because people were struggling financially. So that led to...well, where we are today."

"Have you tried the corporate route yet?"

"I've written letters, yes, and I've filled out some federal grant applications." Aria rubbed a spot on the counter, her mouth twisting. "Unfortunately, it's a very long process, and I don't have much time. The vote is in—"

Her heart stuttered. The vote was *next week*.

"All Imperial needs is a majority." She struggled against a feeling of defeat. "Even if I had enough money to counter their proposal, I don't have a solid, well-thought-out plan for how to make the Historical Preservation Society work in Bliss Cove. I'm making a plan, but it's just in the beginning stages. Imperial has the Oceanview plan, which is…well, you've seen it. It's like a masterpiece novel versus a board book."

"There's a lot to be said for board books." Grant slanted his gaze past her, his expression hardening.

Aria followed his line of sight to where Hunter was coming into the tavern. In a T-shirt, faded jeans, and a hoodie, his hair messy from the wind, he was the opposite of a corporate tycoon. He was warm, approachable, beautiful, and her heart ricocheted happily.

She climbed off the barstool and approached him. "Hi."

"Can I see you outside for a minute?" His expression inscrutable, he held open the door.

Wary, she stepped onto the front porch. The second the door closed behind them, Hunter crowded her up against the building and planted both hands on either side of her head. He bent to press a swift, hard kiss against her mouth.

"Hi," he murmured. "I missed you."

Breathless, she curled her fingers around his arms. "I missed you, too."

"Can we go somewhere private so I can ravish you?" He trailed his lips over her cheek, flicking his tongue out to caress her earlobe.

Aria shivered delightfully. "Later. I'm starving."

"Me too." He kissed her neck and slid his hand down to cup her breast. "I've been craving Aria pie all day."

She laughed and nudged his chest. "You'd better stop before someone sees us. Feed me some artichoke soup and chocolate mousse, and then you can take me home and ravish me to your heart's content."

"I guess I can wait." With a reluctant groan, he lifted his head away from her, pressing a lingering kiss to her lips.

As she preceded him back into the tavern, he rubbed his hand over her ass. She smiled to herself. She loved his surreptitious little caresses. Steve had used his physicality to intimidate and control her, not to assure her he was there and to show her how much he liked and appreciated her.

They crossed the dining room to an empty table. As Hunter pulled her chair out for her, Aria was acutely aware of Grant's suspicion, even from halfway across the room. To his credit, he brought her drink and took their orders without further comment.

"Did you get your flight straightened out?" She pushed the basket of sourdough bread toward Hunter.

He nodded. "The meeting is Wednesday at ten, so I'll take the seven a.m. flight from SJC tomorrow morning." The glow of the table lantern carved his face into planes of shadows and light. "Gives me a day to get some work done."

"Do you know what the meeting is about?"

"Oceanview, probably." His mouth compressing, he reached for his water glass. "I wish I didn't have to go."

She shrugged. Though she wished the same thing desperately, there was no use pretending that one day soon he wouldn't have to *go* for good.

"Aria?" Callie's cool voice broke through the air.

Oh, shit. Aria's heart plummeted. Fixing a smile on her face, she looked up at her older sister. "Hey, Callie. What are you doing here?"

"Rory and I were just grabbing a bite." Callie's gaze slanted to Hunter, her eyes frosting over.

"Hello, Callie." He stood and extended his hand. "Good to see you again."

She didn't respond, but shook his hand in return. Rory approached from the bar. In an almost identical manner, she shifted her eyes from Aria to Hunter.

"Rory." He held out his hand to her. "Hunter Armstrong."

"Yeah, I know." She grasped his hand briefly. "Didn't expect to see you two breaking bread together."

Aria frowned. Last week, Rory had picked up on her and Hunter's attraction, but she hadn't seemed to think it was a bad thing. But now, her sister both looked and sounded wary.

"We're just talking." Aria sipped her drink, schooling her expression into one of casual indifference.

She and Hunter had established that phrase as their "code" for what to say in the likely event that they ran into someone Aria knew. She hadn't considered it might be both of her sisters at the same time.

Not for a second did she think they didn't see through her flimsy comment. Or her. She'd never been able to hide from her sisters. If she hadn't moved to Denver with Steve, they'd have known immediately that something was wrong in her relationship with him.

Was it possible they'd also recognize that her feelings for Hunter felt *right*?

"Did you get my text?" Rory fixed her sharp blue eyes on Aria.

"Yes. Sorry I haven't responded. I was…" *Too busy thinking about Hunter. Too busy being with Hunter.* "Busy."

"We need to talk."

"Fine. I'll call you later."

"How about now?" Rory put her hands on her hips.

Irritation prickled Aria's skin. The last thing she wanted or needed was a lecture from her big sisters about what a bad idea it was to be romantically involved with Hunter. Rory and Callie could probably tell just by looking at her exactly how many times she'd slept with him. They probably knew she had his whisker burn on her breasts and a love bite on her shoulder.

"As you can see, I'm busy now." She gripped her napkin. "I said I'd call you later."

"Soon." Rory's features hardened.

"*Fine.*"

Grant, bless his heart, chose that moment to arrive with their food. As if sensing the tension in the air, he glanced at Rory, who met his gaze with a slight shake of her head. He deposited their food on the table and returned to the bar.

Tugging Rory's arm, Callie stepped back. "Enjoy your food."

Hunter remained standing as the two women said goodbye and left. Aria let out her breath slowly.

"You okay?" Hunter sat back down, his forehead creasing. "Maybe coming here again wasn't a great idea."

"No, I'm glad we did." She picked up her spoon, resolve straightening her spine. "It's none of their business who I choose to have dinner with."

"They seem very protective of you."

"They also always expect me to fail." She stirred her soup a little too vigorously. "Well, Callie does. With good reason. It might be easier to deal with if she didn't succeed at everything. You can guess what a lot of fun that was growing up. God. I'm sorry."

She groaned and reached for her glass. "I don't mean to whine. Callie is great. She dealt with everything after Dad died, and then Mom had a health scare a couple of months ago—she's fine now, but Callie took charge again and got us all through it. She's a control freak, but she's smart, committed, hard-working, organized, loyal. It's just hard to measure up to her."

"Maybe you shouldn't try."

Aria lifted her gaze to his. The way he was looking at her with such tender warmth caused an ache to constrict her heart. If he'd already fallen for her, then she'd tumbled down right along with him. Holding his hand.

"I've been around, Aria." A line appeared between his eyebrows. "I've dealt with a lot of different kinds of people. Some of them do what they're good at or have a talent for. Others work because they stumbled into the job or they inherited a parents' business. Some people tried to pursue certain careers, but either didn't succeed or got sidetracked. A select few are doing what they love."

He leaned closer, the lantern flame flickering in his eyes. "I realize this sounds ridiculous coming from a guy who worked nonstop for success and money, but my corporate ladder climbing came with a few lessons. Maybe the biggest lesson is that the luckiest people are the ones who have figured out how to use their hearts. And I've never met a person who puts as much of her heart into her work...into her *life*...as you do. You don't need to measure up to anyone. The rest of the world needs to measure up to you."

Aria stared into his candle-flame eyes, her heart thumping. She hadn't just fallen. She was spinning wildly, plunging headfirst into a kaleidoscope of colors and light. She was whirling like a star. She was descending as slowly as a green leaf carried on a breeze.

"Any dessert?" Grant's voice broke through the tense, lovely haze.

"Chocolate mousse." Hunter sat back but didn't take his gaze off her. "To go."

Fifteen minutes later, they were in her room above the café, pulling at each other's clothes with fevered impatience. When Aria's dress pooled around her ankles, Hunter lifted her to the bed, his eyes burning and his body corded with self-restraint.

He stripped her of her bra and panties before kissing her as if he wanted to devour her. His stubble scraped her skin, his hands gripped and squeezed her breasts, her rear, her hips. She stroked the ridges of his abdomen, nuzzled his throat, closed her fingers around his thick erection.

Along with the heat crackling through her like a wildfire, an astonishing sense of freedom filled Aria. With him, any lingering inhibitions or shyness slipped away, leaving room for nothing but passion and raw lust.

She asked for what she wanted in both words and sighs—*kiss me, lick me, oh yes please*—and he both heard her spoken desires and read her unspoken wishes. He taught her how to pleasure him and introduced her to new acts that had her arching off the bed and crying out in ecstasy.

She touched him without hesitation, pushing him to lie on his back while she kissed his chest and explored the landscape of his body, the slopes and ridges she could have mapped for hours.

When he took her from behind, his hands clutching her waist and his strong thighs pressing against hers, Aria buried her face in a pillow and squeezed her eyes shut. Endless pleasure streamed through her before it broke like stars shooting through her blood. His hold on her tightened, his rough shout followed by his own powerful release.

They fell back onto the bed together, breathing heavily.

"Chocolate mousse," Aria gasped.

"Left it downstairs." He kissed her bare shoulder. "I'll go get it."

"Cats."

"I'll take care of them."

"No, they're my responsibility." Reluctantly, she pulled herself upright and reached for her cotton robe. "But I'll share the mousse if you give me a hand."

"Done."

He tugged on his jeans, and they went down the worn stone stairway to the café. Aria's phone, also on the counter, blinked with notifications.

As Hunter went into the Cat Lounge, she checked her messages. Two texts from Rory, instructing her to call, a text from Edith with a photo of a very content Buster lounging in his new bed, and an email from Nico.

She scanned his message. Her heart dropped.

Clutching her phone, she went into the lounge. Hunter was slouched on the sofa, rolling balls of yarn across the floor for the cats to jump at. Fang sat near him—not close, but not hunched out of sight either. Every so often, Hunter reached out to give the old cat a quick, gentle pat on the back. Fang twitched his tail.

One week ago today they'd first stepped over the line together. Aria had no regrets and would do it a thousand times over. But the line was still there.

As she approached the sofa, Fang edged closer to Hunter before leaping off and heading for one of the hideaways.

Hunter gave her a lazy grin. Light shone in from the outdoor streetlamps, burnishing his chest golden-brown in the light. His dark hair was tousled from the grip of her fingers. "Where's the chocolate mousse?"

She extended the phone to him. A frown creased his forehead. After scanning the message, he let out his breath.

"Well, shit."

"We knew it was coming." She studied the agenda for the Mariposa Business Association meeting, which included one major action item. Her and Hunter's debate, followed by the vote that would determine whether or not the shop owners would sell their properties.

He dragged his hands down his face. "I fucking hate this."

"So do I." Aria set her phone aside and edged closer to him. He wrapped his arm around her and pulled her against his chest.

"There has to be something I can do." He spoke almost under his breath, as if he were talking to himself. "Quitting won't work because Imperial owns the contracts. They'd just send someone else in. But—"

"Hunter." Resting her hand on his chest, she lifted herself up to look at him. Tenderness flooded her at the distress in his eyes. "I wish…"

She swallowed past a sudden lump in her throat. "I wish things could be different, but they're not. They *can't* be. As much as I love you for wanting to find another angle, I can't let you do anything that might jeopardize your career or…"

Her voice trailed off. He was staring at her with dawning

shock. Only then did Aria realize what she'd just said. What she'd confessed.

"I mean…" She managed to smile weakly. "We have a plan, right? We're going to stick to the plan. There's no miraculous revelation where we find some never-before-seen way we can both get what we want. There's no magic wand. No ruby slippers."

"Juliette was right." Deep grooves bracketed his mouth. "We have eight verbal commitments. Possibly nine."

"I know."

"I don't want you to lose this place."

"I don't either. But I also don't want to keep it because of the way we feel about each other." She put her hand over his. "It took me a long time to learn how to stand my ground. I'm proud of myself for doing it against a company as powerful as Imperial. And against a man like you. No."

She held up a hand when he opened his mouth to speak. "You're an opponent like no other. You didn't go easy on me, even after what happened the first night we met. It's not in you to back down from a challenge. And I don't want to win this because you make a concession that you never would have made if we weren't sleeping together."

His face darkened with a glare. "We're doing more than just sleeping together."

"If you wouldn't make the exact same concession to Gary or Lois or Annie, then I don't want it either."

With a mutter of frustration, he pushed to his feet. "I meant what I said. This isn't a wall between us. Whatever happens, we'll figure it out."

"You said Imperial Properties intends to be a presence in Bliss Cove for years to come." She suppressed a surge of anxiety at the thought. "What does that mean for you?"

"I'd direct the construction of Oceanview and open a new Imperial office in LA." He stopped at the window and folded his arms over his chest, his profile rigid. "I could make trips up here when needed. But I'd come more often just to see you."

Where will I be?

"Aria, I'm telling you we can work this out." He rubbed his jaw, his eyes dark. "We *will*. We just need a plan."

Aria stroked her hand through Jumbo's fur. As much as she appreciated Hunter's certainty, the only way anything could be worked out was if Imperial lost the vote. Otherwise, she'd be forced to sell her property and move...and she didn't think she could be with Hunter while he oversaw the destruction of Mariposa Street and the building of Oceanview Plaza.

She couldn't imagine what that would look like—sleeping with him and cuddling up to him at night, having breakfast together in the morning...and then watching him go off to order one of the construction men to smash a wrecking ball into Meow and Then, Moonbeams, Nico's...

She tightened her fingers in the cat's fur. He bounded to the floor and walked away, tail swishing.

What if by some miracle, Hunter and Imperial lost the vote and she got to keep her building? Then he wouldn't get his promotion, and he might even lose his shot at the CEO position...which meant he'd return to New York and probably go build a complex in Hong Kong.

Would she ever see him again? And what *would* happen to Mariposa Street? Her little fundraiser would fix a few windows and maybe pay for some graffiti clean-up, but they needed a great deal more money to make viable, substantial changes.

If she couldn't convince Mayor Bowers and the town council to support a new Historical Preservation Society and if she couldn't get both private and corporate funding, then Mariposa might just limp along until another developer swooped in.

Winning would come at a price that she didn't know how she —or any of the other owners—would pay. Some of them would be upset with her for ruining what they considered to be a great deal. Lois and Ray might not be able to go on their cruise.

Had she been wrong all this time?

No. She'd known from the start what she was up against. She'd known her chances of winning were slim, but she'd chosen to fight the battle. She'd see it through to the end.

Aria rose to her feet and approached Hunter. She slid her arms around his waist, spreading her hands over his warm, ridged abdomen. She leaned her forehead between his shoulder blades.

"Of course." She swallowed past the lump in her throat. "We'll work this out."

CHAPTER 22

*A*ria set a box of Chaos Cookies onto the stack holding her daily café order. Hunter had left Bliss Cove three hours ago to drive to San Jose for his flight back to New York. Though he'd return in a few days, the town already felt different without him. *She* felt different without him.

"Did you get everything, honey?" Eleanor pulled a tin of hot muffins from the baker's rack and started putting them in a basket. "I made some cat cookies for you too."

"Thanks, Mom." Aria checked her order form. "Does Rory have a shift today?"

"No, she's working from home." Eleanor straightened and wiped her hands on her apron. "I hope all the contract jobs she's been taking lead to a full-time position. I've loved having her here, but she's too smart to stay working at Sugar Joy and doing remote work. She needs a job that's worthy of her."

"If she wants one, she'll get one." Of that Aria had no doubt.

Callie had always colored inside the lines, working steadily to advance her career within the rigid structure of academia. But Rory, the messy finger-painter, had thrown herself into the Wild West of the tech industry when she was a freshman in college.

She'd been hired at different companies over people with twenty more years of experience. She'd created her own positions, demanded better offers, started her own projects. She was a *force*.

It was a little strange that she'd stayed in Bliss Cove for a year and a half, but they'd all dealt with Dad's death in their own ways. Maybe Rory just needed to be *home* longer than she'd expected.

After saying goodbye to her mother, Aria brought the boxes to her van. Since she had a couple of hours before opening—and dealing with Rory alone was easier than confronting both her sisters—she drove to Rory's apartment building. The curtains of her sister's apartment were closed, but a flickering light shone behind them and Jimi Hendrix music thumped against the door.

When Aria's knock went unanswered, she texted *Open the door.*

A second later, Rory pulled open the door, her long hair loose and tangled, and her slender figure clad in torn sweats and a T-shirt reading *Coders Don't Byte*. "What're you doing here?"

"Nice to see you, too." Aria pushed past her sister into the near-empty apartment.

A mattress lay on the floor, and clothes were strewn around, but the only actual "furniture" was a huge desk topped with a shiny, state-of-the-art computer, a monitor the size of a TV screen, and high-level speakers.

"This is me finally responding to your multiple texts." Aria sat down in the plush office chair. "You told Mom you have a sofa."

"I told her I was *getting* a sofa. Haven't gotten around to it yet." Rory folded her arms, eyeing Aria shrewdly. "Where's your boyfriend?"

Tension shot down her spine. "He's not my boyfriend, but he had to go back to New York for a couple of days. If you're going to lecture me about him, I'm leaving."

"No lectures. I need to show you something, but be warned that you're not going to like it."

Aria frowned. "What?"

"When I was doing the search on Armstrong, I found a bunch of stuff about his Imperial Properties projects." Rory crossed to the computer and pulled the keyboard closer. Her fingers whisked over the keys. "Pretty straightforward. But then I started digging a little deeper. Bruce Sinclair has had some issues in the past, mostly questionable compliance with zoning, cutting corners, promising one thing, like affordable housing, and failing to deliver. Then I hacked...I mean, *found* some correspondence from Sinclair that indicates Imperial Properties might not be on the straight and narrow about Mariposa."

"What does that mean?"

"That they don't intend to stop with Oceanview." Rory punched another key, and a bunch of email messages popped onto the screen.

Aria scanned the messages. The correspondence was between Bruce Sinclair and several company lawyers about a "Venture project" in Bliss Cove slated to begin next summer.

Massive moneymaker...pristine coastline...exclusive access to private beaches...privatizing sections of the redwood forests...keep out the rabble.

Talk up as "eco-friendly." Town officials will be easily bribed...have them run interference for getting around zoning and enviro laws. After Marp. St. is finalized, we'll have them by the balls.

Aria's blood turned to ice.

Rory closed the screen, regret tightening her mouth. "I knew you wouldn't *not* want to see these."

"Was..." She swallowed past the constriction in her throat. "Was Hunter part of the email chain?"

"Not this one."

"Did you hack his account?"

Rory shook her head. That meant she hadn't tried. If she'd wanted to get into Hunter's account, she would have.

"Why not?"

"I told you it was obvious early on that you were into each

other." Rory sighed and brushed a strand of hair away from Aria's forehead. "Honestly, I'm on your side about Mariposa because you're my sister, but other than that, I don't have a dog in this race. So I never thought Armstrong was a bad guy. And you've been all lit up and glowing for days, which I was pretty sure had something to do with him. In that past few weeks, you've been more like yourself than you have in a while. Like you're finally letting go of whatever bad shit happened to you when you left Bliss Cove."

Aria's heart squeezed into a ball so tight she almost couldn't breathe. "How did you know?"

"I know *you*." Rory settled her hand on the back of Aria's neck, tugging her closer. "Remember, I've been through a lot of shit with scumbag men in the tech world. I've learned a thing or two. My instincts about Armstrong aside, I didn't *want* to find out a guy who's obviously good for you is involved in dirty dealings."

A strange relief nudged through Aria's growing despair. Had it been the same with Callie and her mother? Had they seen it on her, sensed it in her? Had they known she'd distanced herself from them, avoided their texts and calls, because she hadn't wanted them to know how weak she'd been? Had they been giving her the space to find herself again?

She rested her forehead against Rory's side. "What about the envelope you gave me after you did the search on Hunter?"

"Open it. But what's that old saying…two wrongs don't make a right or something about good deeds not going unpunished? I have no idea how much he's involved in this Venture project thing. There are probably countless deleted emails about it."

"I feel sick." Aria wrapped her arms around her stomach. "I'd wondered why a company as big as Imperial Properties was interested in Mariposa Street. It didn't seem like a very important project compared to the stuff they've built in Tokyo and Manhattan. But they were using it as a foothold into Bliss Cove so they could construct whatever the *Venture project* is. God."

She hated the anguish rising to the surface, threatening to overwhelm her. She couldn't believe Hunter would spearhead a project that Imperial was keeping a secret from Bliss Cove residents. A "massive moneymaker" involving attempted bribery.

But Mariposa Street was Hunter's deal to make. He was slated to direct Oceanview. He'd be president of Imperial Properties holdings on the West Coast. Bliss Cove was in his domain. And when he became CEO…

She shook the thought out of her head. She'd have to worry about Hunter later. The immediate issue was that she'd been right in her suspicions.

"I have to tell the other Mariposa owners." Pulling back, she looked up at her sister. "They'll never vote to sell their properties and make way for Oceanview if they know what else Imperial is planning. I'll just tell them about this Venture project…hell, I'll tell the town council, Mayor Bowers, and anyone else who'll listen. No one will be in favor of Oceanview after hearing about this."

"But we don't even know what *this* is," Rory pointed out.

Aria groaned and pinched the bridge of her nose. She couldn't just give the Mariposa owners some vague accusations against Imperial and expect them to rally around her cause. She needed concrete evidence of their actual plan.

"Thanks, Rory." Picking up her bag, she pushed to her feet and headed to the door. "I'm sorry I didn't listen to you sooner."

"Wait." Concern laced Rory's voice. "What are you going to do?"

"I don't know yet."

She hurried back to her car before her razor-sharp sister realized she was lying. Because Aria knew exactly what she was going to do.

CHAPTER 23

Though his twenty-eighth-story New York office was silent, Hunter could almost hear the noise of traffic on the streets below. Two days since he'd left Bliss Cove, and he still wasn't accustomed to the shift from ocean waves to cars honking.

He checked his phone for the thousandth time. Aria hadn't responded to his texts or phone calls since yesterday morning. There was no one he could call to find out if she was okay.

Unless...

He pulled up a website and dialed the number for Moonbeams. "Destiny? Hunter Armstrong."

"Oh, hello, darling. How's the Big Apple?"

"Big. Listen, have you seen Aria? I've been trying to reach her, but she's not responding."

"Sure, I saw her yesterday. She said she was going away somewhere, and she asked me to take care of the cats for a couple of days."

Hunter's heart slammed against his ribs. "She went away? Where?"

"Hopefully for some energy cleansing. Her aura has been rather stressed recently."

He pushed his chair back and strode to the windows. Forcing his voice to stay even, he thanked Destiny and ended the call. He called Meow and Then, but the phone went to voicemail.

He took a breath and told himself to calm the fuck down. Aria wasn't under any obligation to tell him where she was going or why. Maybe she was taking advantage of his absence to visit an old friend. God knew he'd been greedily occupying as much of her time as he could. She probably needed *space* or whatever.

Before the vote.

He turned away from the window and studied his computer screen, where the financial information for Oceanview Plaza was displayed in a spreadsheet.

He'd always loved starting a new project. Finalizing the plans, breaking ground, getting underway after months of prep work. *Starting* always meant that the paperwork was done and the physical work was about to begin. The building was the part he enjoyed the most.

Under normal circumstances, he'd be anticipating closing the deal that meant he could start phase two. Not to mention gain a substantial promotion and eventually a virtual lock on the CEO position. A huge piece of his plan, right within his grasp.

He'd always done everything he could to keep his plans from going wrong. To keep things on track. It was his own shit luck he hadn't realized that because plans didn't go as…well, *planned*, that didn't mean they went wrong.

Just the opposite, in fact—plans that went awry could sometimes lead to the best place ever.

Too bad for him that he couldn't figure out how to stay there.

The complications buzzed like wasps in his brain.

Kill Oceanview. Come up with a new negotiation. A new design, a new plan. Undercut Bruce Sinclair and tell Mariposa owners to vote no.

Close the deal and change everything when he was president of West Coast operations.

None of that would work. There was always a snag that would either hurt Aria unbearably or leave Mariposa Street to fester and die. Even if he turned over his hefty personal savings and investments to her renovation fund, it wouldn't be enough to sustain the street's revival. And the town council wasn't in favor of holding on to Mariposa either.

Quit his job and convince Aria to run away with him to a secret island where they could laze naked in the sun, eat sweet, juicy mangoes, and make love under waterfalls.

That was the best option of all.

He typed an address into his computer and brought up Meow and Then's website. A little message flashed at the top of the screen. *Eighteen cats adopted since we opened! Congratulations, Porkchop, on finding your forever home with the Bennetts.*

The message was accompanied by a photo of a smiling family —two parents, a boy of about ten, and a girl of five or six. The little girl was holding Porkchop, who was so large he overflowed her arms. The cat peered into the camera, his expression appearing both smug and happy at the same time.

"Good luck, old friend," Hunter murmured. "Thanks for running away and ending up outside my window."

"I'm sorry, did you say something, sir?" His assistant Margaret paused in the doorway with a sheaf of papers.

"No, just thinking out loud." Hunter swiveled to face her.

"I wanted to remind you the meeting starts in fifteen minutes."

"Thanks."

"Here's the agenda and the revised blueprints for the plaza." Margaret approached and placed the papers on his desk. "Oh, what an adorable cat." Her eyes widened as her gaze shifted past him to the computer screen. "Is that an adoption site? Are you getting a cat?"

"Perish the thought." Hunter set the screen back to the search engine.

"I have a mixed breed named Misty," Margaret remarked. "She's the sweetest thing. I don't know what I'd do without her. I only wish I had room for more animals. If I didn't live in the city, I'd have a menagerie. You should think about adopting a cat. They're wonderful pets."

"So I've heard." He pushed back his cuff to check his watch. "I'd better get up to the conference room."

He shrugged into his suit jacket before picking up his briefcase filled with Oceanview paperwork. He took the silent, mirrored elevator up to the top floor.

As he stepped into the plush lobby, he pushed all thoughts of Aria and cats out of his mind. Time to focus on work.

Bruce, Juliette, three of the company lawyers, and another VP were already seated around the massive oval table. An aerial photo of Bliss Cove was displayed on the presentation screen. After greeting everyone, Hunter took a seat across from Juliette.

"Welcome back." She met his gaze levelly, one arched eyebrow lifting. "How is your progress on the Mariposa deal?"

"I have ten verbal commitments now. Two more will give us a majority."

"Hmm." She pursed her lips. "Who's holding out?"

"Must be that little bitch from the cat café." Bruce huffed out his annoyance. "She emailed me…what, one or two days after she got the contract? She probably doesn't know the first thing about real estate."

"Her name is Ariadne Prescott," Hunter said coldly. "She's not going to change her mind."

One of the lawyers, Mark, shrugged. "We can put pressure on her."

"No." Tension gripped Hunter's shoulders. "No one contacts her."

"We might not need her vote." Juliette tucked a lock of hair behind her ear. "Who else is undecided, Hunter?"

"A woman who owns a new-age shop. She's leaning toward a yes vote." He narrowed his eyes on the projection screen. "You didn't call this meeting to ask me about my progress on Mariposa."

"Of course not." Bruce stretched his lips into a smile. His phone lit up with a notification. "Just that our investors are getting a little anxious with the vote coming up."

He picked up the phone, his brow furrowing. "What the hell is she doing here?"

He pushed the phone toward Hunter. The notification screen displayed a text from Bruce's assistant. *Sorry, but urgent! Woman here—Aria Prescott—says she needs to see you, wants to come up to the mtg. Security?*

Aria? Here?

"No idea." His voice level, he handed the phone back to his boss.

"Let her come up," Juliette suggested, her attention on Hunter. "Maybe she wants to tell us she's finally ready to make a deal."

With a shrug, Bruce responded to the text. Hunter excused himself and went into the corridor. He strode toward the elevator, his heart racing.

Forget "aura cleansing." Aria had come to New York. But why—

The elevator doors opened. He struggled for a breath. He almost didn't recognize the polished, elegant woman walking toward him. She was dressed in a fitted navy suit, a crisp white shirt, and heels with her hair pulled back into a tight knot at the base of her neck. Little silver earrings dangled from her ears, and she was wearing makeup.

Though she was a vision of loveliness, she looked totally different from his tousled Aria with her flowing cotton dresses, jangling silver bracelets and loose, disheveled hair. As she neared, he saw that she'd even taken out the crystal stud in her nose.

What in the—

"Hello, Hunter." She smiled, and his tension eased for a second. But it wasn't the warm, private smile he'd gotten used to over the past couple of weeks, the smile he craved like a drug. The one inviting him to touch her. The one that said she was his.

Now she looked as if she were behind a pane of glass. Unreachable.

"Aria." Her name tasted like a mint. He swallowed hard. "What are you doing here?"

"You said the meeting was about Oceanview, and since I have a significant stake in what happens to Mariposa Street, I wanted to speak directly to your planning committee." She stopped in front of him, and he caught a whiff of perfume.

"Hunter." Juliette stood at the conference room door. "We're ready to get started. Hello, Miss Prescott. We weren't expecting you."

"I'm surprised you didn't invite a Bliss Cove representative in the first place." Squaring her shoulders, Aria walked to the conference room. "I won't take up too much of your time, I assure you."

Ignoring Juliette's penetrating stare, Hunter followed Aria into the room and pulled out the chair beside his.

"Thank you, but I'll stand." She extended a hand to Bruce. "Mr. Sinclair? Aria Prescott, owner of the Meow and Then cat café on Mariposa Street."

"I know who you are." He shook her hand, his eyes turning cold.

Hunter wanted to remain standing, but he couldn't risk visually aligning himself with Aria. He pushed his chair back and sat.

"Why don't you tell us what you're doing here, Miss Prescott?" A hard note edged Bruce's voice.

"Certainly. I'd like to remind you that I have no intention of selling you my property."

Another lawyer chuckled. "We know. Truth be told, we don't need you to agree. Once we have a majority vote, we'll be able to buy your property for far less than what it's worth. So by all means, vote no. We'd appreciate your help saving money."

Bruce laughed. Hunter fisted his hands.

"I'm sure you would." Aria gave the lawyer a sharp smile. "Just as I would appreciate you explaining what the Venture project is."

The lawyers stilled. A thick, ominous silence fell.

"How did you know about the Venture project?" A muscle ticked in Bruce's jaw.

"I'd suggest you explain it to me, or I'll just tell the other Mariposa Street owners that you have something else planned for Bliss Cove, but you refuse to be transparent. I know you think we're a bunch of small-town hicks, but remember what happened when your last *developer…*" she threw Hunter a pointed look, "…came to negotiate with the town council and the Mariposa owners? He leaked the plans for the project you wanted to build at the time, and everyone hated it. So he effectively killed the whole deal. I'm sure you don't want that to happen to Oceanview. Not at *this* stage in the game."

The silence lengthened. Hunter narrowed his gaze at Juliette, searching for a hint of what the hell Aria was talking about, but she looked as clueless as he felt.

Venture project?

Suspicion lanced through him, sharp and pointed. He suddenly knew his instincts had been right. He'd just been too fucking distracted to pay closer attention.

"Miss Prescott." A thin smile curved Mark's mouth. "I guarantee you don't want to threaten Imperial Properties."

"It's okay." Bruce held up a hand, his attention fixed on Aria. "I appreciate gumption. I'll tell you about the Venture project." He punched a key on his laptop, advancing the slide to an artistic rendering of a large resort spreading over the coastline bordering

Bliss Cove. "This, my dear girl, is the Venture project. Or rather, the all-inclusive Venture Resort and Spa."

Cold ran down Hunter's spine. "You didn't tell me anything about a *resort*."

"Or me." Juliette folded her arms, her expression pinched.

"Of course not." Bruce rose and approached the screen. "I wanted you both focused on your respective projects, and this would have been a distraction. But now that you're both finalizing the details, I can tell you that I haven't yet decided on who is going to direct the execution of the Venture Resort."

Juliette frowned. "Why wouldn't it be Hunter?"

"It might well be Hunter," Bruce said. "Or it could be you."

Her eyes widened. "Me?"

"The Venture Resort and Spa will be our biggest penetration into California—hell, the West Coast—to date," Bruce said. "I intend to turn the execution of the project over to the person I believe will make the most effective CEO of Imperial Properties."

What the—

Beside him, Hunter felt Aria stiffen with shock.

"You want me and Juliette to *compete* for CEO?" he asked.

"I want to ensure that I'm turning over my company to the right person." Bruce pursed his lips and squinted at the screen. "Remember when you told me Oceanview was a step down from your other projects? You were right. It's a nice little complex, but we need to think bigger for such a perfect location. Hence, our plans for a luxury resort right along the Bliss Cove coastline."

"Also known as a cash cow." Mark grinned.

"Why the hell didn't you tell us about this sooner?" Juliette snapped.

Bruce lifted a hand. "Because I wanted you to focus on your jobs. And, as Miss Prescott correctly pointed out, Hunter's predecessor fucked up the original negotiations by telling the town residents too much about our development plans. I couldn't risk that again."

"So you deliberately kept us out of the loop?" Anger flared in Hunter's gut.

"For your own good." Another lawyer, Len, arched his brow. "And for confidentiality reasons."

"After reviewing the architectural designs proposals for the Venture Resort, you will each prepare a presentation for the board of directors," Bruce explained. "You will assemble a team of designers and contractors, work up detailed blueprints, explain your plans for zoning and permits. Whichever one of you has the best proposal, the one most aligned with Imperial's goals, will be one step closer to CEO."

Hunter stood so fast his chair rolled backward. He approached the screen and narrowed his gaze on the sprawling resort located right on the coastline.

"This is one of many proposed designs." Bruce made a sweeping gesture and advanced to another set of slides. "Now that we've softened the residents up and proven we know how to play nice and follow the rules, we'll hurry and get Oceanview built. They'll learn how the increased crowds and tourism will benefit their community, and at the right time, we'll push forward with the Venture Resort and Spa, a luxury getaway resort covering approximately seven acres of land. Our guests will be afforded stunning views of the pristine coastline, exclusive access to private beaches, swimming pools, fine dining. The best part is, we'll *still* be the only player in town."

Hunter felt Aria's shock and dismay as if it were tangible. He didn't dare look at her, knowing he wouldn't be able to hide what he was feeling. And right now, he had to conceal every shred of emotion.

He pointed at the screen. "There's a hundred-year-old boardwalk here."

"That's a possible location for the spa," Bruce said. "We can tear down the boardwalk to give us more room for a promenade or perhaps rental cottages. Maybe an infinity pool. This is the kind of thing I want you and Juliette to discuss in your presentations. You'll also need to work out the details of the private beaches along this area here."

"The beaches are open to the public."

"Not when you're finished with them." Len tapped his pen on the polished table. "The plan is to privatize some of the redwood forest, too. Our guests will want exclusive hiking and camping sites. We'll want to advertise all the rejuvenation and wellness crap, as well as shopping a short distance walk at Oceanview Plaza."

Hunter folded his arms. The imagined hotel was a massive horseshoe with a long drive accessible from Starfish Avenue and a parking lot not far from Mariposa Street. There were multiple buildings, manicured gardens, swimming pools, and pathways to the "private" beaches. There were restaurants, tennis courts, staff accommodations, sports facilities, and a multi-stories spa with a fitness center.

Why the fuck did they need a fitness center? All anyone had to do was walk outside and breathe the ocean air to get the best exercise of their lives.

"Is that a golf course?" Juliette jutted her chin at the design scheme.

"A golf *links*," Mark corrected. "72 par, naturally."

"You expect to get all the right permits and approval for this?" Hunter asked.

"That's where you and Juliette have to do your work." Bruce regarded his daughter. "We anticipate pushback from environmental activists worried about the endangered field mice or whatever, but you should be able to deal with their protests easily enough. Once the residents know about things like projected revenue and job growth, they'll be salivating to give us their approval."

He advanced the slide again to a drawing of the resort alongside the completed Oceanview Plaza. "Our projected completion for Oceanview is spring of next year, which means you'll have plenty of time to charm the townsfolk into seeing the beauty of the Venture Resort. Talk it up as a rustic, eco-friendly resort that's going to bring a crap ton of employment and revenue to the town. You've already earned their trust with Oceanview, so this will be a piece of cake. Tell them you're all about what's best for the town."

"Funny thing is..." Hunter rested his hands on the table and leaned closer to Bruce. "I actually *am* about what's best for the town."

"Sure you are." Bruce smiled thinly. "I expect you to get Oceanview underway before the month is out."

"Excuse me." Aria's voice cut through the tension-thick air, soft but deadly. Her hands were fisted at her sides, and her eyes blazed. "I guarantee you that the Bliss Cove town council will never approve this kind of monstrosity. Have you forgotten that the Mariposa Business Association hasn't even voted yet? Do you seriously think they'll agree to sell their buildings to Imperial, knowing what you have planned?"

"Oh, I'm sorry." Bruce turned to face her, his brow furrowing with feigned surprise. "Are you under the delusion that you can actually tell anyone about this prior to the vote?"

Hunter stepped toward his boss, every muscle in his body tensing for a fight. Aria's throat worked with a swallow. Her gaze flitted to Hunter. The glint of fear in her expression almost snapped his self-control.

Almost.

"Miss Prescott, we've taken substantial measures to keep this confidential," Len remarked smoothly as he typed on his laptop. "No one outside of this room, including you, should have known about it. So if you would be good enough to tell us...how, exactly, did you learn of the Venture project?"

Her expression turned icy. "I don't believe that matters at all."

"On the contrary." Though Bruce still had a smile plastered

on his face, his voice took on a hard edge that Hunter recognized all too well. The one that warned his boss was about to attack.

Hunter put himself partway between Aria and Bruce. "What are you talking about?"

"After I received your email rejecting our offer, we did some research on you, Miss Prescott." Bruce stepped around Hunter to take his seat again. "We found out about your father…our condolences, by the way…and the rest of your family. Your sister Aurora…Rory, isn't it?…has quite a history with tech companies in the Bay Area. Given her projects and knowledge, we've little doubt that she knows all about cybersecurity."

Aria flinched. It was quick, a blink of the eye, but Hunter saw it. He gripped the back of a chair, using everything he had not to move.

"Were you aware that breaches of a company's cybersecurity is a crime?" Bruce continued. "An act like hacking into an email account can be a felony, or at the very least, leave one open to a civil lawsuit."

"To say nothing of more serious incidents," Len added. "Ransomware. Spear-phishing. Information and identify theft."

"My sister is not a cyber-criminal."

"We're not accusing her of anything." Bruce held up a hand. "But we have a team working on recent cyber intrusions at Imperial, and I assure you we won't hesitate to prosecute those we find responsible. Since you are in possession of confidential information, which you are threatening to make public, you're putting yourself in a very suspicious position. You don't appear to be the type who knows the first thing about cybersecurity—" the lawyers chuckled "—but your sister does. If it turns out that she's responsible…"

He let his voice trail off ominously and lifted his hands in a shrug.

"Your move, Miss Prescott." The lawyer looked at Aria over

the tops of his glasses. "Think very hard about what you intend to do next."

"And whether or not you really want to fuck with us." Bruce smiled.

"Enough." Barely managing to keep his tone even, Hunter forced his hands to unclench and strode around the table to Aria. His blood burned. "This negotiation is—"

"No." Aria held up a hand to stop him from getting closer. She leveled Bruce with a hard look, her mouth thinning. "You can threaten and bully me all you want, Mr. Sinclair, but you can't scare me. You're a fool if you think you'll ever find evidence that my sister instigated a cybercrime. And the fact is that you still don't control Mariposa Street. All you have are a few verbal commitments, and words are cheap. People are fickle. I don't need to tell anyone anything about your horrible hotel to get them to reject Imperial's offer."

Spinning on her heel, she stalked to the door.

"I won't lose, Miss Prescott," Bruce called after her.

"No, you won't, Bruce." She speared him with a glare. "You can't lose something you never had."

She strode out of the room, the door closing partway behind her. Hunter started after her, every cell aching with the urge to grab her up into his arms, haul her against him, promise her everything would work out. That he would fix this fucking mess.

Just before he reached for the door, the weight of stares hit him. His shoulders felt as if they were about to break. His heart was jackhammering so hard it echoed through his head.

Pulling a heavy breath into his tight lungs, he slammed the door shut and turned back to the meeting.

"Mariposa Street is ours." He walked back to his seat, shooting Juliette a cold glance. "I'm closing the deal. I know that town. The Venture Resort is mine."

She gave him a smile as sharp as a sickle. "Then let the games begin."

CHAPTER 24

*I*n the two days following the disastrous meeting at Imperial Properties, Aria expected her phone to flood with messages and calls from Hunter.

Instead, he sent her only one text with two words. *Trust me.*

Though the words burrowed into her heart, Aria deleted the message right after reading it. Before leaving for New York, she'd put a "Gone Fishing" sign on the café door and recruited Destiny to take care of the cats while she was gone, but she hadn't told anyone—not even Rory—where she was going.

Stroking Jumbo behind the ears, she set bowls of food down for the cats and ensured all the doors were locked. She felt tight, like a piece of paper crushed into a ball, her insides knotted with the pain of keeping secrets.

Despite her bold words to Bruce Sinclair, she didn't dare breathe a word about the Venture Resort, not with his threats hovering over her like toxic smoke. Though Rory was a cybersecurity expert who would never leave her fingerprints on anything, she still had done something illegal.

Aria had no idea what kind of security team Imperial employed, but given the size and reach of the company, she didn't want to find out firsthand. She would never knowingly put her sister in harm's way.

She wouldn't tell Rory about Sinclair's threats either. Her sister would either barge in and confront Sinclair herself or dare them to try and come after her.

No. Best to keep it all inside, festering and hot. Aria had learned how to lock up her dismay and confusion when she was with Steve. It was cold comfort to discover she still had the key.

Trust me.

Hunter had seemed as shocked about the Venture Resort as she had been. Juliette, too. Maybe Bruce really did intend to use the project as a "test" to determine his successor CEO.

If that was the case, then Hunter would win. He already had a foothold in Bliss Cove, and all signs pointed to him winning the Mariposa vote at the meeting tonight.

Aria was out of time. If she'd convinced any of her fellow business owners about the value of saving Mariposa Street, then they'd prove their support at the ballot box. If not—

Well. She wasn't out yet. She'd studied and prepared for her debate with Hunter as if she were about to take the most important test of her life. She would give it everything she had, keeping her focus sharp on the issue and not thinking about the worst possible outcome.

After a hot shower, she dressed in a simple, A-line tunic dress with an embroidered bodice. She took off most of her rings and bracelets so they wouldn't be a distraction and applied a light coating of makeup. The red amethyst Destiny had given her glowed at her neckline.

Picking up her notes, she walked downstairs and into the warm evening air. Crowds of people—more than they'd had in months—wandered Mariposa Street. Lights blazed from the Hotel Casa Grande.

"Aria!"

She turned, her heart jumping as her mother and Rory hurried toward her. "I didn't know you'd be here."

"Of course we wanted to be here." Eleanor embraced her. "You look lovely. I know you're going to do great."

"Thanks, Mom." Aria glanced hesitatingly at her sister. "Is Callie coming?"

A brief shadow crossed Rory's face. "I haven't heard from her, but I'm sure she'll be here."

"She wouldn't miss this." Eleanor brushed a piece of lint off Aria's shoulder, her smile touched with sorrow. "Your father would be so proud of you."

Aria's throat tightened. "I hope so, Mom. I'm going to head over to get ready. I'll see you both after the meeting, okay?"

"Best of luck, sweetie. We'll be rooting for you."

As Aria started toward the hotel, Rory caught up with her and grabbed her arm. "What's going on? I didn't want to worry Mom, but where have you been?"

"Just needed to get away." Aria kept walking. "I'm sorry, Rory, but I need to focus on the debate. We'll talk after the meeting, okay?"

Pulling away from her sister, she entered the old hotel with its plaster walls, warped floorboards, and old wooden desk. A platform stage had been set up against a wall, with folding chairs arranged in neat rows throughout the rest of the lobby. People were already beginning to fill the seats.

"Aria."

She turned and blinked. "Destiny? What in the…"

"Right?" Her friend twirled around to show off her tweed suit and low pumps. She wore the single-breasted blazer over a white shirt pinned at the neckline with a gold rose. The skirt fell in a straight line to her knees, and she was even wearing nylons.

"Um. Wow." Aria swept her gaze to Destiny's long, raven curls, which were scraped back from her face and fastened into a tight chignon at the back of her head. "Where did you get that?"

"Rags to Riches. Annie helped me pick it out." Destiny smoothed her skirt. "What do you think?"

"It's definitely a change."

"I'm hoping it's more in line with what Joe is used to." She nodded toward where the hardware store owner sat in the third row, studying the meeting agenda. "I'm going to accidentally run into him later and see if I can get him to talk to me."

"Make sure he recognizes you first." Aria hugged her friend. "You look beautiful."

"You too, honey." Destiny patted her cheek. "Good luck tonight."

Aria headed toward the stage and ducked into the small alcove behind the curtain. Her pulse accelerated the instant before she realized Hunter was standing there, his head bent as he checked his phone.

When he glanced up, their eyes met with a sudden jolt that ricocheted through Aria's entire body.

"Oh." She backed up a step, unable to stop herself from drinking in the magnificence of him in a navy suit and perfectly knotted striped tie, his dark hair brushed away from his forehead. "I didn't know you were here already."

"I got in a couple of hours ago." He slipped his phone into his pocket, tracking his gaze over her face. "Did you get my text?"

Her stomach twisted. "Yes."

"I couldn't..." He glanced behind him, his mouth tightening. He lowered his voice. "I couldn't risk calling you. But I need to—"

"Hunter." A woman's voice, smooth and cool as silk, came from behind Aria before Juliette Sinclair walked backstage. "Hello, Aria."

Managing to hide her surprise at the sight of the other woman, Aria nodded. "Juliette."

"I believe they're about to begin."

"We'll be right there." Hunter's tone indicated that she could leave.

Juliette gave a sharp nod and returned to the stage.

"Look." Hunter let out his breath and dragged a hand through his hair, rumpling its glossy perfection. "I'm sorry everything got so fucked up. I didn't know about the Venture project. Please believe me."

"I do." Aria swallowed past the constriction in her throat. "But that doesn't change anything, does it? It's not going to stop Imperial from going through with the resort, is it?"

His jaw clenched. "No."

"This whole time, everyone has been telling me how big and powerful Imperial is, that I couldn't possibly go up against the company's billions of dollars." Aria shook her head, suppressing an ache of longing. "Even you thought I couldn't win. And deep inside, I've always known it was an uphill battle. So as much as I *want* to believe you could never succeed with something like the Venture Resort, I know that wishing and reality are two different things.

"When you tell Bliss Cove residents everything Bruce Sinclair said, about employment and revenue and all the benefits to the town, people will find that hard to pass up. Some will be against it. Some won't. It will become a much bigger controversy than Mariposa Street ever was. It might even divide the town. And I... as much as I love what you and I have had, in some ways I wish you'd never come to Bliss Cove in the first place."

Pain darkened his eyes. "I didn't want to come here at first, but when—"

"I'd like to call the meeting to order!" Nico spoke into the microphone on the other side of the curtain.

"Aria." Urgency threaded Hunter's voice, and he curled his hand around her arm. "Trust me. Please."

His gaze burned into hers for an instant before he released her. He turned and walked to the front of the stage, the curtain falling behind him. Chatter and rustling noises came from the lobby as people settled into their seats.

Aria closed her eyes and took a deep breath. She touched the red amethyst pendant. She'd trusted Hunter from the moment he helped rescue her mischievous runaway cat. She'd trusted him with her heart and her body. And in trusting him, she'd learned how to trust herself.

She tightened her fingers around the amethyst, then let it go. She pushed the curtain aside and stepped onto the stage. Folding chairs had been set up on either side of the podium, and a whiteboard was set up beside a large screen.

To the left, at Hunter's side, sat Bruce and Juliette Sinclair, and three of the company lawyers. All five of them stared her down as she took her seat.

Aria schooled her expression into one of cool impassivity, even though anxiety clenched her nerves. Past the bright lights, she located her mother, Rory, and Destiny sitting in the third row. Brooke waved at her from the Press section, where she was the only reporter. All the seats were full, with several people standing in the back. Her nervousness intensified.

"Meeting called to order." Nico thumped a gavel onto the podium and set a pair of reading glasses on his nose. "We'll have a quick reading of minutes from the last meeting before getting to our main agenda item."

As they waited through the reading of the minutes, Aria glanced at Hunter. In his tailored suit, with his sculpted profile, he looked untouchable and almost otherworldly, as if he belonged in a magazine ad. He shifted his gaze to hers. A current sparked between them.

Nico leaned toward the mic. "You've all been given a summary of the debate topic involving Mr. Hunter Armstrong, vice-president of Imperial Properties, and Miss Aria Prescott, owner of the Meow and Then Cat Café."

He peered at his notes. "The debate format is as follows. Each party will present their opinion about the offer of sale issued by Imperial Properties and the proposal to build a multiuse complex known as Oceanview Plaza on the land currently occupied by the owners of Mariposa Street businesses. After each party speaks, they will have a chance to refute each other's arguments. Then we'll open the floor for questions before the Mariposa Business Association members place their votes."

He paused to glance at Aria and Hunter. "Mr. Armstrong has given Miss Prescott the choice of whether she'd like to speak first or second."

Aria blinked. She'd expected a coin toss. "I...I'll go first, thank you."

"The floor is yours, Miss Prescott." With a slight bow, Nico descended the stage to sit in his reserved front-row seat.

Letting out her breath slowly, Aria approached the podium and adjusted the mic.

"I'd like to thank you all for being here," she said. "As most of you know, Mariposa Street means a great deal to me, and it's to my everlasting regret that as a community, we've allowed it to deteriorate to the point that a property development company is advocating the destruction of the entire district. But it is not too late. With your help, we can still save our town's history and culture. To explain why this is so important, I'll begin by telling you about my father."

She opened her folder. Her chest tightened. Though her voice shook, she told the townspeople about the history lessons her father had taught her as they walked through Mariposa to the beach.

She talked about the indigenous settlements, the Spanish mission, the development of the fishing village and influx of people during the Gold Rush. She told them about the people who built and lived in the Mariposa buildings—Nellie Paxton-Smith, Christine Sterling, Robert Welford who'd turned the corner saloon into a grocery store, and the former printer's shop that was now Al's Bar.

"I recognize and appreciate Mr. Armstrong's belief in the

Oceanview project." Aria felt Hunter's gaze on her as if he were touching her. "And I concur that renovating Mariposa Street will take a great deal more effort and money than my petition and donation jar can provide.

"But I believe in this town. I believe we value our history more than we value revenue from chain retail stores and high-rise condos. I believe we need classic movie double-features, healing crystals, penny candy, purring cats, wildflower bouquets, slow-churned ice cream, and pizza made from a recipe handed down by Nico's grandmother. I believe that if we work together, we can not only save Mariposa Street from destruction, we can bring it back to magnificent life. Our collective past deserves no less."

She lifted her head. Silence fell over the room. She saw her mother wiping her eyes. Her own vision blurred.

Rory whistled, a sharp burst that split the quiet, and started clapping. Eleanor joined in, and within seconds a thunderous applause filled the room. Several people stood.

The tension gripping Aria's shoulders eased, and happiness lifted her heart. Picking up her notes, she turned to take her seat.

Both Juliette and Hunter were applauding politely, but Bruce and the lawyers sat stone-faced. Bruce muttered something to Hunter, who nodded.

After the applause died down, Nico introduced Hunter. As he approached the podium, Aria caught sight of Callie standing toward the back.

Callie met her gaze with a slight nod and an even slighter thumbs-up. Aria relaxed into a smile. She'd never seen her sister give an actual *thumbs-up.* Apparently anything was possible.

No surprise, Hunter was a wonderful, eloquent speaker. His deep voice rolled over the room as he spoke about Imperial Properties' projects across the nation that had revitalized small towns and brought in both employment and revenue.

He discussed environmental initiatives, planning cooperation, and the natural evolution of towns as living entities. He explained how Oceanview was designed to fit into the landscape and serve as both an extension of downtown and its own neighborhood.

"I also have a confession to make." He paused and cleared his throat. "I didn't want to be put in charge of Oceanview Plaza. I thought it was too small compared to Imperial's other properties. I wanted a project that was about the same size as my ego."

The crowd laughed. Bruce gave a satisfied grin, as if he sensed the tide shifting in his direction.

"But for several reasons, I agreed to come to Bliss Cove." Hunter scanned the townspeople, his hands tightening on the edges of the podium. "And though my intention was to get the job done as soon as possible, I quickly discovered it wouldn't be as easy as I'd thought.

"While all towns have a history, Bliss Cove has roots that run deeper than most. The decline of Mariposa Street speaks not to the townspeople's lack of interest, but to the fortitude of the residents who have kept the town alive by focusing on the areas that contribute most strongly to progress. The fact is that cities are living entities that change and evolve. So are people."

He took a breath. "Somewhat to my surprise, during my visit here, I discovered that I'm capable of change, too. Maybe even evolution, if that means I'd rather eat artichoke soup at the Mousehole than dine at a five-star restaurant in Manhattan. I'd rather take a sunset walk on Pelican Beach than spend an evening at the Met. I'd rather go to the Sea Glass Museum than visit the Louvre, and I'd rather be on Mariposa Street than…well, almost anywhere else."

Applause rose, but the approbation wasn't as loud as it had been for Aria.

"Because I've learned to appreciate everything about Bliss Cove, I want to assure you we have your best interests in mind," Hunter continued. "Imperial Properties intends to uphold Bliss

Cove's past while looking toward a future of growth and change."

He turned to the whiteboard and uncapped a dry-erase marker. Swiftly, he wrote a dollar sign.

"This…" he faced the audience and pointed to the board, "…is the future of Bliss Cove."

A few people in the front row glanced at each other.

"Profit." Hunter approached the podium again. "Revenue. Tourism. Oceanview Plaza will bring all of these things not only to Mariposa Street, but to the entire town. However, Imperial Properties won't stop there. Oceanview is only the beginning of what we consider a complete renovation of this town. We have *plans*, ladies and gentlemen. You're going to love them."

The crowd stirred, murmurs rising. Bruce skimmed his gaze over the audience, his expression warily hopeful.

"As I always say, the bigger the plans, the bigger the profit." Hunter clicked a remote control on the podium. "This is Imperial's biggest plan for the West Coast yet."

The audience's attention snapped to the screen, where a huge artistic rendering of the sprawling Venture Resort was displayed.

"We plan to build *this*, the luxury, full-service Venture Resort and Spa, on the coastline right near the boardwalk." Hunter extended his arm to the screen as if he were showing off a new car.

Aria's heart almost stopped. Bruce's eyes widened. The lawyers blanched. Juliette grabbed her father's arm.

"You'll be delighted to learn about the proposed golf course, the private beaches, the tennis courts and high-rise towers that will give guests incredible views of the coast." Hunter waited for a rustle of whispers to quiet. "Both Oceanview and the Venture Resort will provide Bliss Cove residents with many employment and partnership opportunities, which could lead to exclusive contracts and investment in new factories. That's just the start of our plans."

A smile stretched across Bruce's face. "All for the good of Bliss Cove, of course."

A few people in the front row frowned, looking at the screen and whispering to each other. Bruce's smile began to fade. Aria couldn't think past her shock.

"Mostly good," Hunter allowed. "We'll unfortunately be forced to increase taxes and establish fees for things that are currently free, like park and beach access. Likely we'll need to increase costs for municipal services and rezone the boundaries of the public open spaces as well, but I'm sure you'll agree that's a small price to pay for what the Venture Resort and Spa will bring to Bliss Cove."

"Wait a second." Nico stood, his face creased into a frown. "You never said anything about a *resort* being part of your plan."

"We were waiting for the right time," Hunter replied smoothly. "Oceanview is our litmus test, if you will. Once Bliss Cove residents see how much good a large development does for the town, you'll have no problem turning over the coastline to us. This is the perfect time for you to discover how a change of plans can change the future."

"Excuse me." Bruce rose, his smile gleaming. "I don't believe Mr. Armstrong is explaining this very well."

"On the contrary, it's quite accurate." Juliette folded her arms.

"It's only fair that you all know what Imperial is planning," Hunter informed the audience. "Yes, we'll make changes. I mean, who needs a hundred-year-old boardwalk anyway, and the lighthouse is just a blight on the landscape. But all of our changes will be in the name of profit and modernization. New roads to accommodate increased traffic. Zoning and infrastructure modifications. By turning Bliss Cove into a mecca on the Pacific Coast, the Venture Resort and Spa will make this..." he underlined the dollar sign on the whiteboard, "...our collective future."

Silence dropped. Aria gripped her shaking hands together.

She could practically feel Bruce Sinclair's anger from across the stage as he conversed in whispers with the lawyers.

Callie and Rory were speaking in low voices, their heads bent. Brooke scribbled furiously on her notepad. Nico was still standing, his frown deepening.

"I must say." Mayor Bowers stood, her flowered hat obscuring the people behind her. "I don't like the sound of this."

"Neither do I!" called a man from the back of the room.

Hunter held up a hand. "I assure you, we will explain everything in much greater detail soon."

"Imperial Properties is committed to the good of Bliss Cove." One of the lawyers smoothed down his jacket and swept the crowd with a smile. "We would never do anything without your consultation and approval. Though Mr. Armstrong's speech was a bit...er, uneven, there's no question that a well-planned development will do wonders for the town's economy."

"Mr. Armstrong, do you have anything further to say?" Nico approached the podium, casting Aria a quick glance. "Miss Prescott? If you can both keep it to the topic at hand, which is Oceanview, we can open the floor for questions."

"I'd like to place my vote." Destiny stood, straightening her blazer. "The Mariposa Association members have heard all the pros and cons about Oceanview...rather *ad nauseum*, if you want the truth. Since we're the ones making the decision about selling, we don't need to hear anything further."

"Agreed." Lois got to her feet, with Ray standing beside her.

"I'm ready to vote, too." Gary stepped out of the row of chairs to let Lois and Roy precede him to the folding table in front of the stage, which held a wooden box and stack of paper ballots.

"All right, then." Nico indicated that Hunter could sit back down. "Now it's up to the Mariposa property owners to decide if they want to collectively sell their buildings. It's a simple yes or no vote. Yes, you agree with the terms offered by Imperial Properties, and you agree to sell your building and land. No, you disagree with the terms and decline to sell your building. Should Mr. Armstrong obtain eighty percent or more of the association votes—that is twelve out of fifteen votes—the Oceanview Plaza project is approved. We'll tally the ballots immediately following the voting."

Though only fifteen members of the audience would be voting, the entire room fell silent. Aria's heart began a low, heavy thumping. She walked toward the stage steps. As she passed Hunter, he brushed his hand against hers.

Unable to bring herself to look at him or anyone else, she took her place in line beside the voting table. She closed her shaking fingers around a pen and marked her ballot. After slipping it into the box, she returned to her chair onstage.

"Here." Callie appeared at her side and extended a cold bottle of water. "You were amazing. You have a true gift for public speaking."

Aria managed a smile of thanks. "You didn't know that from all our arguing?"

Her sister chuckled and reached out to straighten Aria's hair bow. "Maybe if I'd known you were engaging in persuasive speech rather than arguing, I'd have gone easier on you." Her expression sobered. "For what it's worth, I am sorry. I should have been more supportive. Did you know about the resort?"

"Not until recently. But I thought it was strange that a company of Imperial's size would be fighting so hard for Mariposa Street. The resort was their endgame."

"If you'll take your seats again, I'll read the votes," Nico called.

Aria's stomach clenched. She had no idea what to expect. Hunter's speech had been calculating, but some people might want a luxury hotel on the coastline.

Callie rested a hand on her shoulder.

"One vote in favor of selling." Nico placed the unfolded ballot on the table and reached into the box again. "One vote against."

A smattering of applause filled the air. Aria tightened her

fingers around the water bottle. Her sister gripped her shoulder harder.

"One vote in favor of selling."

Hunter stood to the side, his arms folded and his expression implacable. Not a flicker of emotion shone in his eyes.

"One vote against selling." Nico unfolded another ballot.

More applause rose. Aria pulled a breath into her constricted lungs. Every nerve ending was on alert.

Nico dropped the ballot. The audience rustled with impatience.

He straightened and unfolded the paper. "One—"

"Just tally the votes!" a voice boomed from the middle of the room.

The crowd murmured in agreement.

"All right, all right." Nico held up his hands to quiet everyone down and quickly sorted through the remaining votes. The lines on his forehead eased.

He picked up the gavel and leaned toward the mic. "In a final vote of thirteen to two, the sale of Mariposa Street to Imperial Properties is rejected."

CHAPTER 25

*H*unter heard the deafening applause and cheers. Bruce's fury and the lawyers' frantic voices buzzed like wasps around him. But every cell in his body was focused on Aria.

She stood beside her sister, her eyes wide with both shock and the dawning recognition that she'd won. He wanted nothing more than to push through the crowd to reach her.

"You son of a bitch." A vein throbbing in his forehead, Bruce grabbed the front of Hunter's shirt. "How fucking dare you screw this up for us?"

"Watch it," a lawyer muttered, indicating a uniformed police officer eyeing them from beside the stage.

"I will ruin you," Bruce hissed at Hunter.

"No, you won't." Pulling away, Hunter put himself between Bruce and Aria in a warning to the other man not to get any ideas about confronting her.

"You're fired!"

"You can't fire me." A crushing weight rose from his chest, letting him breathe again. "I quit."

"Dad, let's get out of here." Juliette slipped her purse over her shoulder and took her father's elbow. "We'll re-strategize this. Without *him*."

Bruce's face was so red he looked as if he were about to explode. Juliette threw Hunter a cold glare and guided her father backstage.

Destiny, Nico, and the other Mariposa owners were converging on Aria with hugs and even a few tears. The audience swarmed toward the doors, their voices rising in excited conversation.

One of the lawyers, nostrils flaring, got into Hunter's face. "Do you have any idea what you just did?"

"I know exactly what I just did." Hunter shoved past the other man, bumping his shoulder deliberately as he made his way outside.

His heart raced. He loosened his tie and took a deep breath. Despite his relief over Aria's win, a sudden unease stabbed him.

He'd accomplished Mission One. Mission Two would be much more difficult. Just because Imperial had failed to buy Mariposa didn't mean everything was *fixed*.

He strode down the street, the old lamps casting a yellow glow on the cobblestones. Crystals glowed in the window of Moonbeams, and Jumbo twitched his tail from his perch on the back of a sofa in the Cat Lounge. The cat regarded him through the glass, his golden eyes penetrating and strangely wise.

"Hunter."

Her breathless voice spilled like sweet honey into his veins. Aria ran toward him, her hair billowing behind her and her face flushed. Everything inside him contracted and loosened at the same time, like a heartbeat. He clenched his fists to stop himself from reaching for her.

"I…." She stopped, searching his face, her teeth coming down on her lower lip. "I don't know what to say, except…thank you."

His jaw tightened. "Don't thank me. If I'd known about the Venture project before I came to Bliss Cove, I'd probably have backed it. Hell, I'd have fought to be the one directing its execution."

"Maybe that's what you *would have done*, but it's not what you did."

"Aria, I..." Something stuck in his throat. He turned away from her to the window, where Jumbo still sat looking at them. "I've fallen in love with this town. I've fallen in love with you. I love your strength, your determination, your goodness. You're everything I want to be, even if it took me too long to realize it."

"Hunter..." She put her hand on his arm.

"But it's not enough." He dragged in a heavy breath and closed his hand over hers. An ache tightened his chest. "Rejecting Imperial's contracts doesn't mean Mariposa Street is suddenly saved. It can't be saved without money and support."

"I know." Her eyes were luminous, her mouth so lush that it was all he could do not to kiss her and let everything else fall away. "Mayor Bowers just told me she's going to advocate for funds to restart the Historical Preservation Society so we can determine what needs to be done next. A bunch of other people have already asked how they can help support us."

Her hope was like a sunrise. Hunter desperately wanted to tell her how happy he was, that they'd work it out, that this was such a great start.

But he'd been in this business for much too long not to know that it wasn't enough. Mariposa needed more. Bliss Cove needed more. Aria needed more.

For most of his life, he'd lived by a plan. He'd worked hard to make one, to stick by it, to see it through. Now he no longer had one.

"I'm going back to New York." He stepped away from her, unable to shake the feeling that he was no good to her without a damned *plan*. "I have a lot of stuff to deal with. Tell Rory I hired a cybersecurity expert to make sure no one can trace her steps. Though I'm guessing she already knows."

"Is that why you only sent me one text?"

"I had to make sure you were safe. You should also tell Rory to check all the security on your networks and devices…though she probably already knows that, too."

"She's probably already done it."

Hunter expelled his breath in a long rush. "Good."

Aria studied him, a crease appearing between her eyebrows. She rested her hand on his chest. His heart sped up, thumping against her palm. The ground seemed to shift under his feet. How could he leave her? How could he not?

"Come with me." She reached for his hand, her fingers closing tightly around his. She led him to the florist shop. She stopped and peered up at the building façade. "See if you can find the butterfly."

"The what?"

"Every building on this street has a hidden butterfly somewhere on the exterior." She gave him a smile so gentle it almost broke his heart in two. "Mrs. Paxton-Smith started the tradition. Over the years, when new properties were built, the architect would add a butterfly somewhere. Owners of the older buildings added butterflies, too. Some are carved into the concrete, others are painted. A couple even used tile designs."

Hunter looked up at the old stone building. Hidden butterflies.

"It's the Mariposa Street secret," Aria said.

He searched the façade and pointed to a painted Monarch right beneath the awning. "Every building has one?"

"Every building." She squeezed his hand. "So you not only helped save Mariposa Street, you saved the butterflies."

"Where's the Meow and Then butterfly?"

"You'll have to find it yourself."

Hunter rubbed his chest. If he wanted to find the butterfly—and he did—that meant he *had* to come back. He had to figure it out, make a new plan. One that was much bigger than him, that encompassed so much more. One in which the most treasured spot was reserved for the woman who'd shown him how life was meant to be lived.

"I love you." He stroked his fingers against her soft cheek. "By the way, you were amazing in there. I was so proud of you."

She smiled again, her blue eyes shining with both warmth and tears. He curled his hand around the back of her neck and lowered his head. Heat and light exploded through him the instant her lips touched his. All of his unease and wariness solidified into the knowledge that he'd done the right thing—for himself, for the town, for Aria.

Now he had to ensure it stayed that way.

"I'm sorry for what a mess this all turned into." He lifted his head, letting his hand linger on her neck.

"I'm not." She curled her fingers around his wrist. "I take back what I said before the debate. If it weren't for this mess, we wouldn't have met."

A smile tugged at his mouth. "And you wouldn't have changed my life."

He took a few steps backward, loath to turn and walk away from her. He imprinted the picture of her in his mind—blond hair shining in the streetlights, her skin flushed pink, her face as lovely as a painting.

"When are you coming back?" she asked.

"When I can offer you something better."

"Hunter, all I want is you." She wiped at a stray tear. "That's the absolute best you can offer me."

He shook his head. Pressing a hand to his heart, he lifted his palm toward her and then turned and walked away.

CHAPTER 26

*F*or the next couple of days, Mariposa Street grew busier, but Aria's heart grew emptier. People who hadn't been to the neighborhood in ages came to see what was still there, while others strolled through on their way to the beach.

On Saturday afternoon, several people sat eating pizza outside Nico's, a crowd gathered at the door of the bar, and in the window of Moonbeams, Destiny was conducting palm readings for a group of young girls. It felt like the way Mariposa Street might have once been.

Several customers who'd come into the café congratulated Aria with cheerful remarks of, "You did it!", which always made her think, "*We* did it."

If Hunter hadn't revealed the Venture plans, he would certainly have won the vote. Though she was immensely relieved and happy about the outcome, Hunter had given up far more than she might ever know.

Mariposa. Oceanview. His promotion. The Venture Resort. Possibly the CEO position. Maybe even his job or his entire career. Bruce Sinclair would want revenge for Hunter's betrayal. There might even be legal repercussions.

She picked up two cups of iced tea and brought them into the Cat Lounge, where Callie and Rory were sitting at a table with a laptop, a thick, three-ringed binder, and an open bag of gummy worms. Rory had spent the past day double-checking firewalls and their network security to ensure no one had or could get into their personal data.

Aria was no longer worried that Bruce had his sights set on Rory. The Imperial Properties' CEO now had good reason to target much bigger quarry in Hunter.

"I've made a spreadsheet of all federal and state grant application deadlines for historical preservation." Callie turned the laptop screen toward Aria. "I'm sure the town hall has information on each individual building."

"I'll get going on a central Mariposa Street database." Rory chewed on a gummy worm. "All of the owners can have access to the files."

"Hey." Callie nudged Aria with her elbow. "What's wrong?"

"Nothing." Aria wiped her hands on her apron and sat at the table. "I mean, thank you both for all your help. I'm...I thought of this when I was asking people to sign the petition and donate to the renovation fund, but now that it's actually happened, I'm just wondering if I've screwed things up for the other building owners."

"They voted no," Callie reminded her. "They've all thanked you. Lois even sent you a bouquet of flowers."

Aria smiled faintly. Lois and Ray planned to close the florist shop while they went on their cruise and considered other sale options for the building. The flowers told Aria they had no hard feelings about her campaign.

"If you hadn't been the sole crusader against Imperial, they'd not only control this neighborhood, they'd be plotting like evil geniuses how to take over the entire town and coastline," Rory added. "The more they bought, the more power they'd have. We all thought they were going to stop at Oceanview, so to find out they were like...what's his name...Lex Luthor...well, you helped this town dodge a bullet. Everyone knows it."

"You could have caved," Callie added. "But you didn't. Not everyone can say that."

A lump formed in Aria's throat. She felt Rory's gaze.

"You did the right thing," her sister said softly. "For Mariposa Street and for you."

Aria fiddled with a wrinkled straw wrapper. Aside from her months with Steve, she'd never known life without her sisters. She'd compared herself to them so often, wishing she had Callie's intelligence and Rory's aptitude for data, and their constant, intense determination to get the job done.

She'd wished she had their drive, confidence, and sense of their place in the world. She'd wished so hard that she had something she was good at. She'd wanted to point to books, awards, diplomas, completed projects, prestigious jobs, and say, *That's me. I did that.*

But as Hunter had told her, she didn't need to compare herself to anyone. Not anymore. She already *was* everything she wanted to be. She was smart, caring, dedicated, loyal. She could sense instinctively what both animals and people needed. She'd learned how to stand her ground, even when the odds were against her. She liked herself.

Jumbo nudged at her leg. She picked up the cat and set him in her lap, then straightened to face her sisters. "I need to tell you both about Steve."

∼

"Margaret, there's no need to cry." Hunter put a lid on the last cardboard box and patted his assistant on the shoulder.

"I'm not crying." She sniffed and dabbed at her eyes. "It's just allergies. Are you *sure* you want to leave?"

"Never been more sure of anything in my life." Hunter shrugged into his suit jacket.

That wasn't entirely true. His love for Aria was *sure*. The most certain thing he'd ever felt. Not until her had he realized that his lifelong plan for himself wasn't a path, but a wall. An obstacle preventing him from seeing all the other directions he could take.

Aria had shattered that wall. She'd shown him that loyalty and friendship meant more than corporate ambition, and that having a place to call *home* was infinitely more important than building a billion-dollar complex.

Bliss Cove had proven the importance of afternoon teatime, bits of glass tossed endlessly by the sea, healing crystals, and refuges for lost cats. He no longer wanted to be multiple floors above ground level in the penthouse, the CEO's office, the private jet.

He wanted to walk barefoot on the beach with its icy ocean water and warm sand. He wanted to live beside the boardwalk, the redwoods, Mariposa Street. He wanted artichoke soup, cold beer, and chocolate ice cream spiked with ghost peppers. He wanted to make out with Aria underneath the pier. He wanted to fall asleep with her in his arms and the sound of the ocean drifting in through the open windows.

"You have my personal cell number, Margaret." He put his briefcase on top of a cardboard box. "I'm going to need to hire employees soon, so if you're ever in the mood to move to a small town on the Pacific Coast, give me a call."

She lifted her eyebrows. "You're serious?"

He frowned. "How long have you been my assistant?"

"Six years."

"Have you ever heard me crack a joke?"

"No." A smile twitched her mouth.

Hunter lifted the box into his arms. He walked to where a security guard stood waiting to escort him from the building.

"Bliss Cove is a great town," he told Margaret. "I'll be working at a place that rescues cats, if that helps *purr-suade* you to relocate."

He was almost to the elevator when he heard her laugh.

As he descended to the ground floor and crossed the lobby, Juliette entered the glass doors of the building, blade-like in a red sheath dress and matching coat. Her heels clicked sharply on the marble floor.

"Glad I caught you." She stopped in front of him, her lips pursing. "I wanted to tell you I convinced my father to call off his attack dogs. It took some work, but when I explained that taking you down wouldn't make us look good with our clients, who think you walk on water, he agreed to leave you alone."

"I'll consider that a favor, then."

"You should." She straightened her shoulders. "I intend to call in the favor when I'm CEO, which will be before the end of year. You know as well as I do that Mariposa Street needs more than a donation jar and a petition. Play your cards right, and Imperial Properties, under my command, could help you out."

"There will never be anything close to a luxury hotel in Bliss Cove," Hunter said.

"Of course not." She brushed a lock of hair away from her forehead. "That was a ridiculous and over-the-top plan, and frankly, my father is a bastard for thinking he could force us to compete. I've already proven my worth, and even if you hadn't done what you did at the meeting, I wouldn't have lowered myself to a competition."

"So what do you want?"

"I still think that town could be more than it is," Juliette said. "When your friend Aria went pit-bull on us, I did some research about both Mariposa and historic properties in general. There aren't a lot of development companies that have a staff dedicated to historic preservation. Not that Imperial is going to start crusading on behalf of Great-Aunt Mildred's father's horse stable, but there are a number of cases in which the modernization of historic buildings has helped change a city's landscape. So I can see the value of Bliss Cove wanting to bring Mariposa Street to life again."

"In return, Imperial Properties still gets a foothold in the town." Hunter narrowed his eyes. "You will never get approval to build a new development anywhere in Bliss Cove."

"Did you not hear what I just said?" Juliette retorted. "I'm not talking about new construction. Restoring old buildings might be a sound investment for Imperial Properties. Mariposa Street could help us build a reputation in the area of historic preservation. Look."

She held up a hand. "You and I have worked together for years. Yes, I've played my father's game, but I've also disagreed with him countless times and stopped him from doing things I considered unethical. Do you know why I want to be CEO? Because I want to run this company exactly the way it should be run. I want to make changes and try new things and create opportunities. If you won't give me the chance to prove that, then fine. I can go elsewhere. But I'm good at what I do. I keep my word. You know that."

She smirked. "And don't tell me you didn't consider my offer before that cat girl swept you off your feet."

Hunter almost smiled. Juliette was right. He knew how she worked and what her strengths were. They'd collaborated on several successful projects. Bringing her in to help with Mariposa Street wasn't a bad idea.

It might not be a great idea either, but he was learning to keep all options open.

"I'll give you a call before the end of summer," he said. "We can talk."

Juliette smiled. The effect was almost surprising, brightening her eyes and face. Hunter was all too familiar with her tight smiles and wicked-witch lip curves, but he'd rarely seen her smile with pleasure.

"Good luck, Juliette." He stepped toward the glass doors.

"You too. Stay in touch." With a toss of her hair, she strode toward the elevators.

Hunter walked outside into the glaring sunshine of Manhattan. Time to start his new lifelong plan.

CHAPTER 27

*R*ain splashed against the windows of Aria's room above the café. Metal-gray storm clouds billowed across the evening sky, and water streamed in rivulets over the cobblestone street. Jumbo lolled on the bed, tail twitching.

Almost two weeks had passed since Hunter had left Bliss Cove. They'd exchanged emails about general day-to-day things, but she'd sensed his need to keep his distance. For how long, she had no idea.

She sat at the narrow desk, giving her grant application one final review. She'd asked Callie to proofread it, and she'd gotten input from both Mayor Bowers and the town council. If approved, they'd get federal funds to invest in Mariposa Street renovation.

She hit the Submit button and waited for her old laptop to churn through the process. She printed out the receipt and opened the top desk drawer to fish out a pen.

Right beside the pen tray rested the envelope Rory had given her—the results of the "deep search" she'd done on Hunter.

The envelope Aria hadn't opened.

Her heart thumped. Would it matter what Hunter had or

hadn't done in his past? He'd already made a huge sacrifice for her. Was there anything she wouldn't forgive?

She ripped open the envelope and took out a few sheets of paper. Across the top, scribbled in Rory's messy handwriting, was *"Anonymous is H.A."* The other papers held copies of news articles about the anonymous funding of a veterans' center and charity fund in a struggling, low-income area of Chicago.

Aria sank back in her chair and read all the articles about how the center provided resources and help to any veteran who needed assistance. In addition, there were a number of "anonymous" donations to national veterans' charities and hospitals.

For years, Hunter had been giving a place to people who didn't have one. He'd been helping those who needed it.

No wonder her soul had fallen in love with him before her brain caught up. She'd known in that deep, mystical part of herself that despite all their surface differences, she and Hunter were, at heart, the same.

Clicking her fingers at Jumbo, she headed downstairs to feed the cats. The animals purred and twined around her legs as she prepared their dinner. Fang crouched under a chair, eyeing her warily. He hadn't eaten much for the past week.

"Here you go, old boy." Aria set a bowl in front of him and reached out to scratch his ears. He jerked away, tail swishing.

"Sorry." She held up her hands and backed away. Of all the orphaned cats, Fang had now been with her the longest. If she didn't find him the right home soon, he might end up becoming a lifelong member of the Lonely Hearts Club.

"We'll find you a forever home," Aria promised the old cat. "Everyone needs someone to love, and everyone deserves to be loved."

She started to prepare the other dishes. The cats swarmed around her feet.

As she took cans from the cupboard, a knock came at the window. She turned. Her breath caught in her throat. Hunter stood outside, rain drenching his hair and coat, his eyes fixed on her with a combination of wariness and hope.

Dropping a can of cat food, she hurried to the front door. Her hands shook as she unlocked the door and pulled it open. "What—"

He ran up the porch steps and hauled her against him. Words, questions, thoughts...everything dissolved into a burst of pure happiness and love. Aria threw her arms around his shoulders as he brought his mouth down on hers.

In that instant, caught in the strong circle of his arms, she knew he was really here, that her Hunter had come back. His coat was soaking wet, and the rainwater seeped through her thin cotton dress, but his body heat burned away the cold.

She drove her hands into his hair and parted her lips under his. He kissed her hungrily, as if he couldn't get enough of her, as if he wanted to devour her. Finally he lifted his head, his expression filled with warmth.

"I'm getting you all wet." He shed his raincoat, tossing it on to the coat-rack.

She drank in the sight of him. Lines of fatigue creased his face, but he looked as heartbreakingly beautiful as ever in worn jeans that hugged his long legs and a faded T-shirt stretching over his broad chest.

He pulled a piece of paper from the pocket of his coat and handed it to her. "First, I need to give you this."

Aria unfolded the paper. It was a hand-drawn map of Mariposa Street. Each building had one little star somewhere—on the roof, under an awning, beneath a window.

"What is this?" She lifted her eyes to his.

"I found all the butterflies."

A smile started from deep inside her. "You went on a butterfly search?"

"Before I left, yes. I wanted to know all of Mariposa Street's secrets." He shut the door with his foot, his gaze never leaving hers. "So that we can keep them together."

"Oh, Hunter." She pressed the paper to her heart. "I missed you."

"Not as much as I missed you." He kissed her again, sliding his hands down to clutch her hips. "You feel so damned good."

Heat flooded the space between them. Cupping her chin, he tilted her head back and slanted his mouth more firmly against hers. An upwelling of emotion filled Aria's heart.

Hunter muttered a sudden curse and broke away from her. At their feet, Jumbo let out a yowl, snagging his sharp claws on Hunter's jeans.

Aria laughed and bent to pick up the irritated cat. "That's his way of saying *welcome back*."

"I like your way better." He brushed his knuckles against her cheek.

But are you back to stay? What happened? Why didn't you call? What about your job?

The questions clogged her throat. She wasn't entirely sure she wanted to know what their relationship, what his sacrifice, had cost him.

"I need to finish feeding the cats." Still holding Jumbo, she led the way into the Cat Lounge. She tossed him a clean towel to dry his hair. "When did you get back?"

"Just now. I haven't even had a chance to see if Mrs. Higgins has a vacancy."

Aria suppressed the instinct to tell him he could stay with her. Everything had happened in such a tumultuous, crazy rush with them that she didn't want to make assumptions. She needed certainty.

"So what have you been doing?" Keeping her tone casual, she filled the rest of the cat bowls. "You didn't say much in your texts or emails."

"I'm sorry." His expression darkened. "I knew that if I talked to you, I wouldn't be able to stop myself from getting on the next plane. I've been desperate to come back to you, but I needed to close the door on my old life before I could ask you to start a new one with me."

A blossom right in the center of Aria's heart began to open and unfurl. He was looking at her with what seemed like a thousand emotions—tenderness, warmth, uncertainty, even fear.

"I quit Imperial right after the Mariposa Association meeting, but I couldn't tell you until I was sure there wouldn't be legal issues. There won't be," he added quickly when she started to speak. "Leaving the company ended up being pretty straightforward, but there was a ton of paperwork, and I had over ten years of clients to contact. Not to mention, a decade of living in New York to leave behind."

Her breath caught. "Leave behind?"

"I need…" He paused, his throat working with a swallow. "I needed to leave it behind because I want to start again with you. Here, in Bliss Cove. I've never felt at home anywhere in the world. I don't think I even knew what that meant…at least, not until I came here. Not until I found you. I know it's only been a month, but it feels like so much longer. As if everything I did before coming to Bliss Cove was just a rehearsal for my real life. The life that started the instant I opened the window and saw you."

He got all blurry behind her tears. Aria grabbed a tissue and wiped her eyes. She'd been working so hard to prove herself, to start a new chapter, to succeed. But she hadn't dared to hope that love would be a part of it.

She hadn't dared believe a man like Hunter would stand at her side, make sacrifices for her, and believe in her. Whether their first encounter had been due to cat spirits, coincidence, or just plain luck, the fact was that it had happened. They'd both been right where they were supposed to be.

Okay, universe. Maybe you weren't playing a cosmic joke on us after all.

"I love you, Hunter." She pressed her palm against his chest. "I think I tried *not* to love you, but you…you're kind of like Jumbo the way he eased right into my heart when I wasn't looking and then decided to stay."

"No wonder." He smiled, his beautiful eyes creasing at the corners. "Given that your heart is filled with so many warm patches of sunlight, he must have felt right at home there. I know I do."

He cupped her neck and kissed her again. Every curve and crevice of Aria's soul filled with happiness. When they came up for air, she brushed her fingers against his lips.

"What happens next?" she asked.

"We'll have to figure that out together." He tucked a lock of her hair behind her ear. "I have some plans, but I can't do anything without you. I want to live here with you and explore all the town's secrets and do something…I have no idea what… with Mariposa Street, and help take care of your cats… Oh, that reminds me."

He eased away from her to dig another crumpled piece of paper from his pocket. Smoothing it out, he handed it to her. As Aria scanned the paper, a fresh wave of love washed over her.

She looked up at him. "You're sure?"

He smiled again. "That old cat and I have a lot in common. It'll take some time for us to get used to each other, but I'm willing to adopt him, if he'll have me."

Aria laughed, wiping a stray tear from her cheek as she stood on tiptoe to kiss him. "Fang will have you, all right. I can't think of a better companion for him than Glowering Stranger."

He cupped her face in his hand, tender warmth filling his eyes. "And will you have me, Aria Prescott, love of my life?"

"I'll have you, Hunter Armstrong." She wrapped her arms around him, happiness lifting her heart like a bright, colorful butterfly. "Welcome to your forever home."

EPILOGUE

*A*ria locked the door of Meow and Then and slipped her keys into her bag. A ribbon of sunset light streaked over the horizon, and the breeze carried the ocean's scent. Across the street, Destiny stood outside Moonbeams, squinting up at the roof. A Metalworks Hardware truck was parked at the curb.

"What's going on?" Aria approached her friend, who had forgone her suit and was wearing a bright, Indian-print caftan and gold jewelry. "Did the understated look work on Joe?"

"I haven't had a chance to talk to him since the meeting, so I asked him to check on my roof." Destiny fiddled with the chain at her neckline. "Hunter hired him to assess the structural stability of all the buildings before the surveyors and inspectors come in. He didn't even seem to notice my sedate look. Joe, I mean. Not Hunter."

"Destiny, you'd be the first to tell me that your One True Love should adore you exactly the way you are."

Her friend arched a plucked eyebrow. "Who said anything about One True Love? I'm just hoping for a good boink."

Aria laughed. "It *is* possible to have both. Just saying."

"Speaking of One True Loves and boinking, I saw Callie the

other day." Destiny clucked her tongue and shook her head. "That girls needs help in both departments. I'll do a reading on her and see what the cards say."

"Good luck with that." Aria rolled her eyes in amusement. Though her relationship with Callie had smoothed out, her sister still viewed the whole Mariposa situation—and Aria and Hunter's relationship—with wary caution. Now that she no longer felt the need to prove herself, Aria was making an effort to accept her sister's protectiveness and practicality.

Taking the red amethyst necklace out of her pocket, she extended it to Destiny. "I wanted to return this. It gave me all the courage I needed."

"Oh, my little Dorothy." Destiny held up the stone, turning it to capture the light. "You always had the courage. The necklace just reminded you of that."

"Thanks, Glinda." Aria hugged her friend. "Good luck with your man behind the curtain."

With a wave, she headed to her van and drove to the Outside Inn, where Hunter had been staying for the past week until he found an apartment.

Both he and Aria had agreed that since things had happened so fast for them, it would be best if they didn't try and find a place together right away. He wasn't happy about her staying alone on Mariposa Street, but he was at the café and her apartment so often that he might as well have been living there.

After parking in the lot, she walked to the inn's gate. Dressed in cargo shorts and a T-shirt streaked with dirt, his hair rumpled and his jaw unshaven, Hunter was crouched beside the front walkway with a trowel and a plastic flat that held several blooming plants.

In neat rows on either side of the flagstone path, he'd planted at least twenty zinnias. The flowers were bright bursts of purple, red, yellow, pink, and orange. Alongside the zinnias, he'd planted pansies, daisies, and petunias, creating cheerful rivers of color all the way to the porch.

"Hey." He rose to his feet with a smile, his eyes sparking with appreciation at the sight of her.

"It's lovely." She indicated the flowers.

"Yes, it is." He kept his gaze on her.

Aria smiled and moved in for an embrace.

Hunter hesitated and gestured to his shirt. "I'm a mess."

"You're perfect." She wrapped her arms around his waist and stood on tiptoe to kiss him, breathing in his scent of sunshine and clean sweat. "Has Mrs. Higgins seen this yet?"

"Nope." He checked his watch. "She's supposed to be back in about ten minutes or so. She said she had a few errands to run."

"You did an incredible job." She eased back to admire the flowers again.

"Good to know considering I've never planted a flower in my life."

"First time for everything."

An old Cadillac pulled into the inn's driveway, and Mrs. Higgins got out of the driver's seat, a red handbag looped around her arm and a straw hat perched on her head.

"Oh, Aria, I'm glad you're here! What in the…" Her voice trailed off as she took in Hunter, the flowers, and the array of gardening equipment. Her eyes widened, and she pressed a hand to her chest. *"Zinnias."*

"Three dozen." Hunter proudly spread his hand toward the flower beds. "I know you said Hank used to line the front walk with zinnias for you, but I thought it would be nice to include flowers that represented all of the Outside Inn rooms. Except for roses because they seemed kind of complicated, but I'm going to do some research and find out where to plant—"

Mrs. Higgins flung her arms around him so hard that Hunter almost stumbled back a step.

"Thank you so much." Tears choked her words. "You have no idea what this means to me."

Aria couldn't stop smiling. Hunter hugged the older woman and grinned at Aria over the top of her head. Mrs. Higgins fumbled for a tissue in her handbag.

"This is the most wonderful surprise I've had in ages." She dabbed at her eyes. "I do hope you'll both join me for tea."

"We were just waiting for you to ask." Hunter bent to start collecting the gardening tools. "Did you make those seven-layer bars with the butterscotch and chocolate chips?"

Mrs. Higgins beamed. "A whole pan, just for you."

"Excellent." Hunter patted his flat stomach and rumbled a noise of appreciation.

"And I finally had this made for you, my dear." Mrs. Higgins dug into her bag again and extended a bright red ribbon to Aria. An old-fashioned key dangled from the loop at the end.

Aria took the key with faint bafflement. "What's this for?"

"I thought you might want your own key." Mrs. Higgins winked at Hunter. "So you can stop climbing in the window of the Rosebud Room."

Aria's face heated. She opened her mouth to respond, but nothing came out.

Hunter chuckled. "So much for subterfuge."

"Oh, Hank and I climbed through a few windows in our day, too." Eyes twinkling, Mrs. Higgins started toward the front door. "I'll go get the tea started. Come in whenever you're ready. And thank you, Hunter. Hank would have liked you a great deal."

Aria suspected the older woman couldn't have paid Hunter a greater compliment. She slipped the key around her neck and helped Hunter clean up the walkway before they joined Mrs. Higgins for tea. Hunter drank three cups of Earl Gray and ate about five seven-layer bars and a dozen cookies while Mrs. Higgins waxed rhapsodic about Hank's love for gingerbread.

After returning to Mariposa Street, they fed the cats and

cleaned up the lounge. Aria wrote out her Sugar Joy order for the following day while Hunter sprawled on the sofa with his laptop. Fang leapt up from underneath the table, prodding at Hunter's thigh before stretching out beside him.

Unlike the other cats, Fang wasn't a snuggler, but ten days after Hunter had officially adopted him, the old cat was increasingly less fearful and nervous. He was starting to eat with the others, and though he still preferred to crouch under the sofa, he always ventured out when Hunter was nearby.

His gaze on the screen, Hunter absently reached over to rub Fang's head. The cat half closed his single eye in pleasure.

"Does that work for you, too?" Aria ran her hand through Hunter's hair.

"Oh, yeah." He closed his eyes, his chest rumbling with the deep tiger purr that sank deep into Aria's blood.

She bent to kiss his forehead before settling on the other side of him. "How's the research going?"

"Not bad. The plan is underway."

"Uh oh."

He pinched her thigh gently before clicking to a lengthy spreadsheet.

"Even if we get denied federal funding, we've got commitments from several investors who want to support historical preservation," he said. "We also got a sizeable donation from the VP of the Intellix Corporation up in San Francisco. Juliette is sending in her proposal next week, and I have a meeting with a firm up in San Francisco called Studio Twenty-Five. They're a group of designers and architects who specialize in historic architecture."

"That's fantastic."

"It's a start." He leaned over to set his laptop on the table. "I used to have an idea of starting my own company one day, but when I started climbing the Imperial ladder, it got pushed into the background. Especially when the CEO position was within reach. I never thought I'd start a property development company that specializes in urban restoration and revitalization."

"First time for everything." Aria nudged him in the arm, her heart swelling with pride as it always did when Hunter talked about Monarch Properties.

Though still very much a fledgling company, Monarch had a strong foundation with support from Hunter's wide network of friends, colleagues and property developers—many of whom had offered him lucrative positions with their own teams after discovering that he'd left Imperial. Though he'd turned down all offers, his excellent reputation preceded him, and he'd been fielding frequent calls from colleagues wanting to work with him and support his company.

Mariposa Street would be his first project—a complete overhaul and restoration of the old district, starting with the basics of graffiti clean-up, inspections, assessments, and repairs. Hunter had been studying countless guidelines and standards for rehabilitating historic buildings, and he'd become a veritable encyclopedia about Mariposa's history and architecture. His goal with Monarch was to maintain the historical context of the district while also opening it up for appropriate modernizations and turning it into an asset for the entire town.

Aria nestled against Hunter's side—unlike Fang, she was most definitely a snuggler—and rubbed her cheek on his shoulder. He pressed his lips to the top of her head.

As Jumbo pounced gracefully onto her lap, Aria thought that maybe Destiny had been right about a few things. Like the wisdom of cat spirits. No coincidences. And that all events in her life had led Aria right to this moment with Hunter, the place where she was meant to be.

ABOUT THE AUTHOR

Nina Lindsey writes romances filled with heart, heat, and happy endings. She is delighted to introduce readers to Bliss Cove, California, a coastal town with an abundance of warm cookies, ocean breezes, and the ever-present possibility of love.

Nina loves all things spicy and sweet, with chili chocolates being at the top of the list. She is also a fan of glossy magazines, pop culture, Gilmore Girls, energy bites, Orangetheory, and the sound of silence.

She lives in Wisconsin with her meteorologist husband (yes, she asks him daily, "What's the weather forecast?"), their two children, an overly energetic dog, and a snail named Pipsqueak.

www.ninalindsey.com

Sign up for Nina's newsletter and receive a free exclusive Bliss Cove novel!

f facebook.com/ninalindseyauthor

⊙ instagram.com/ninalindseyauthor

g goodreads.com/ninalindsey

ALSO BY NINA LINDSEY

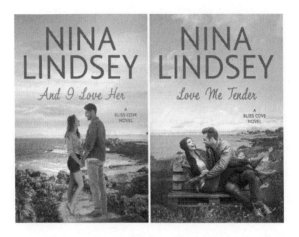

AND I LOVE HER
(Bliss Cove #2)

An expert on the hot, wild tales of mythology, Callie Prescott leads a tidy life. And that, thank you, is exactly how she wants it…until action hero Jake Ryan arrives in town and wants some close-up action with the brilliant, beautiful professor.

LOVE ME TENDER
(Bliss Cove #3)

Rory Prescott and tavern owner Grant Taylor make a deal — she'll be his date to his brother's wedding if he'll let her stay short-term in his cottage. But what happens when this fake relationship becomes passionately real?

Made in the USA
Columbia, SC
29 September 2019